ns IN THUNDER**

DUCKS IN THUNDER

Paul Puccioni

MINERVA PRESS
LONDON
MONTREUX LOS ANGELES SYDNEY

DUCKS IN THUNDER
Copyright © Paul Puccioni 1998

All Rights Reserved

No part of this book may be reproduced in any form,
by photocopying or by any electronic or mechanical means,
including information storage or retrieval systems,
without permission in writing from both the copyright owner
and the publisher of this book.

ISBN 1 86106 899 9

First Published 1998 by
MINERVA PRESS
195 Knightsbridge
London SW7 1RE

Printed in Great Britain for Minerva Press

for

A

Certain

Someone...

Acknowledgements

I would like to thank my family – my father Giancarlo, my sister Annette, my brother Robert – for the tremendous encouragement and patience they have always shown me. And especially, I would like to express my gratitude to my mother Wendy, for her generous and unstinting support for anything I have ever attempted in my life, from my first steps, to the publication of this book.

I would also like to convey my thanks to the following people without whom this novel would have been a dead duck. The inimitable Geoffrey Bailey, Dr Keith Gooding, Sophie Vincenzi, Jenny Chapman, Gilly Vincent, Beth MacDougall, Mike Kerrigan, Ian Hughes, Gill Henderson, Paul Maycock, Jon, James and Danielle Harris, and my dear friends around the world who have shown such interest in my writing; they know who they are and they know what they have done for me. Above all, I am forever indebted to my beautiful wife Jo for her inspiration, understanding, and love.

Prologue

Jim walked in pigeon steps to the window of his hotel room in Padstow and stared outside to try and distract his thoughts from the murder.

The sun hovered above the horizon out to sea. It had lost its earlier intensity and it burned tamely but deceptively, like a disc of red-hot metal that had been recently punched out of a greater sheet. It was now more friendly to the eye, and during those dying moments it seemed impossible that this gentle glow could be solely responsible for the life of the planet. Soon it had disappeared beneath the water and a wall of burning colour was left in its wake.

Twinkles of white were appearing on the hill across the bay. Tiers of houses rose steeply to a lookout point at the top and, as each one disappeared into the dusk, a light came on in its place.

The moving picture of life in the town had been replaced by an underexposed monochrome print of itself. Now anything could be out there; it was like staring at the glossy black surface of a deep lake at night and trying to imagine what unknown forms were hidden below. The longer he looked, the more he believed he could see the shapes of strange beings forming in the shadows. It was like staring at the broken-down West Pier back in Brighton. He had always wanted to have the courage to swim out to the rusty ladder that hung from its side, and tread down underwater to see how deep it went. He shuddered.

He could now see the beginnings of the storm Mrs Muurling had predicted. She had said that it was going to rain even before she had seen any clouds. Earlier, when she had told Jim that they ought to leave the beach because the tide was nearly in, and digging would be dangerous, he had noticed the first sign of her trepidation about what they might find. She had been so calm until then. But, as she turned back from the empty sky, she had swallowed nervously before suggesting that they return. They had both prepared themselves for finding the casket later rather than sooner. The contents had come from another time and it seemed right that they should have to struggle before its secrets were revealed to them. But standing in the hotel room now, Jim was starting to understand why Mrs Muurling had been shocked when his shovel had been stopped short by the hollow thud of metal on wood. She was feeling her illness and her age. Jim hoped desperately that the secret letters she and her husband had written so many years before on their honeymoon would cure, rather than kill her.

A strong wind attacked the town. A piece of newspaper flapped around under a street lamp. A flash of lightning signalled the imminence of the storm and the first rumble of thunder sounded in the distance. The trees stood with their bare limbs spread wide as if they too were in shock. There was a small pond to the right of the hotel. Three ducks stood motionless in the exposed shallows.

The incoming weather seemed a final curtain on what felt like the end of everything. In his heart Jim had always been sure that he would kill someone. From the first understanding of death as a small boy he had realised that murder was something far too momentous for him not to witness it at first hand.

Glenda was in the shower, washing away the salt of the sea, and of her tears. It was nearly over. So far they had survived with their liberty. Glenda now had nobody to fear. Bill was dead, and in order to go on as he had planned, Jim just had to believe that the police would not catch him, with the same certainty that he had known that Bill had to die.

Another flash of lightning lit up the sky and, for a moment, a silhouette of the world emerged from the darkness. The black streets shone silver and startled passers-by were frozen open-mouthed in the moment. A second later the light had gone, and another crack of thunder rattled the windows. It was so black now that the lights up on the hill were barely visible.

The shower had been turned off. Jim moved away from the window and flopped onto the bed. His mind went back six months to his first date with Glenda when all this had begun. He did not want to think about it and tried to draw his thoughts back to the safety of the present. He wanted Glenda to hurry and come and lie with him on the bed. Immediately he knew her face would remind him of Bill.

His body could only be forgotten by the death of the mind containing that memory. So could the constant worry of being caught and punished by the forces of law. He realised that he had given up his right to the most civilised of all freedoms: the freedom not to kill. He had succumbed to an instinct – so strong in him at the time that it did not seem possible it could be the result of some convenient post-rationalisation, like lack of parental attention, a broken home, or an unhappy school life. He blamed himself for not being stronger, for not having a greater will that could put a stop to these thoughts once they had begun. But all along, he supposed, it had been inevitable.

He imagined he had always thought a little differently to the way other people did. When he was seven years old Jim had followed his frail grandfather down the stairs of his house and had wanted to push him so that he could watch him fall and die. He had known he was old and would probably die soon anyway, but Jim had wanted it to happen there and then. Whatever *being dead* was would be in their house once his grandfather's neck was broken. He knew dead people were taken away somewhere, by something or someone; and he would be there to see what it was. But he did not push, because it was teatime and his mother would have been angry. And after, he had forgotten about his earlier impulse and had enjoyed playing hide-and-seek with the smiling old man.

Occasionally Jim told himself that everything had been determined before he even came to exist – that it was not really his fault and that the murder had become inevitable when his parents had first kissed and then married, and he had been born out of the selfish, sticky mess they had made together. But whatever had been fated, and however he had been moulded by his surroundings, he was the raw material he knew, and within him was the power of choice.

The room was warm. The electric bars of the fire glowed amiably. They looked soft, and Jim wanted to touch them and feel the comfort of the heat. He wanted to make love to Glenda; and afterwards they would go and see Mrs Muurling and revel in her happiness. That thought was nice and he pulled back forcefully from where he was being led. This fear was beginning to call on him frequently; he would have to learn to endure it – maybe eventually enjoy it. He was thinking about the electric fire again, imagining that his hands really were gripping onto the bars. By the time he felt the pain it would be too late. His skin would have melted, and the others would have seen the bare bones of his hands. They would certainly go without him. He would be alone, looking at ten clenched claws which would be naked and grey except for the blood left on them.

He walked back to the window. It was raining hard now and the streets were empty. The ducks in the pond were still motionless. They were passive, stupefied, waiting for the storm to pass.

Chapter One

Glenda looked around nervously and then rushed onto the Palace Pier. She kept her head down as she hurried along, gazing vacantly through the wooden boards at the choppy sea. She passed the Shellfish Bar, the American Do-nuts, the Indian palmistry stall, trying to lose herself among the smiling faces and the seagulls. Holiday chatter filled the air. For most people it was a nice day.

She thought she heard *him* again close by. Immediately she broke into a run and began to dodge through the mass of dawdling tourists. In her haste she tripped and fell. A circular space quickly appeared around her. People stared as they passed, giving this strange person a wide berth. She floundered on the ground like a young drunk. People chose to look away, or shake their heads and tut; but nobody helped. She got up quickly. Someone was laughing a loud gleeful chuckle. It *was* him. He was enjoying the spectacle. Glenda did not look to see where he was, but staggered off.

A cynical voice chased her. 'Nice one, Glenda. Very cool. Sheer poetry in fact.'

She did not look around but moved on past the hall of mirrors. She checked her watch. Fifty minutes until her parents would be back from their trip on the Brighton Tour Bus. She hurried past the rows of darts and archery stalls, towards the Racing Dolphins.

There was another shout, but this time it was an angry, violent call. She turned and scowled. The man was twenty yards away from her stuffing a hot dog into his mouth.

Glenda was standing by the crossbow stall. 'ONE POUND THREE SHOTS' said the yellow banner. She paid the girl and loaded the hard wooden bolt into its slot. She fired at one of the clumps of colourful balloons. She missed and the bolt clattered into the hardboard backing and then onto the floor. She reloaded. The bows were chained to the counter and she stepped back as far as she could. She shot again, this time bursting a green balloon. She drew the bowstring back a third time and loaded. She looked out of the corner of her eye. He was rubbing his jeans where he had dropped some tomato sauce.

She took aim at the target and then slowly turned ninety degrees towards him. She pointed the crossbow at his crotch. The man looked up. His eyes widened and for a second he dropped his grin. Glenda stroked the trigger. It felt good. It felt like she was touching the fire button of the doomsday bomb.

It was a rare happy moment, earned from years of misery. She wanted to smile but she was scared to put any expression on her face. She felt herself trembling and was sure she was about to collapse. The world was silent. People passed her by like soundless, projected images. They had no bearing on her life; they would neither touch her nor talk to her, just as she would not interfere with them. He was the only one who would overstep the boundary. She squeezed the trigger and imagined what it would be like to have him dead. To be free.

Suddenly the girl from the stall was shouting and Glenda was snapped back into reality. The girl leant across the counter and pulled the crossbow out of her hands. As she did the crossbow fired. Glenda looked up at him. He smiled as the bolt fired harmlessly into the floor a few yards to his side. The girl from the stall pushed Glenda away and swore at her. Glenda looked helplessly at the man. The mustard at the corners of his mouth exaggerated his new grin. He smiled and shook a finger of admonishment at her. Still forty-five minutes.

She moved away quickly. At the end of the pier she turned and scanned the faces of the day-trippers and clumps of sullen-looking teenage exchange students. She looked quickly behind her and could not see him. A little to her left she noticed there was no queue for the ghost train. She darted over and jumped into the front car. For an agonising thirty seconds a ratchet wound up, clicked and then clicked again before the car jolted into movement. It began to rattle slowly along its narrow tracks. Quickly it gained speed and a few moments later it had bumped through the heavy black entrance doors.

Glenda closed her eyes as the carriage crashed into the darkness. Soon she was hurtling around tight corners and speeding through the sickly black tunnel. She held on tightly and hunched her shoulders as if someone were about to hit her. Sudden explosions of light seared into her eyes like misdirected fireworks and she instinctively brought her hand up to guard her face. She screamed in anger at the thought of him waiting for her in the daylight by the exit, but her voice was lost in the cacophony of wails and screeches. She hated the ride but would rather it never ended if it meant not seeing him.

On a tight corner, the car suddenly slowed and a skeleton lit up. Glenda took her opportunity. She wrapped her bag around her arm and jumped out of the car. While the skeleton was still lit she rolled quickly away from the track and pressed herself up against a cold wall. The car sped off, leaving a procession of sounds and mechanical tricks in its wake. Soon it was quiet. She looked down at her watch and waited for her eyes to become accustomed to the darkness. After a few moments she made out the dim green of the luminous arms and digits. Thirty-nine minutes to go.

———— JJ ————

The man knows something is wrong when the empty car comes out of the ghost train. A family of four are just going through the black doors. Three minutes later they appear from the other set of doors squinting in the sudden sunlight.

The slag's in there, he thinks. He laughs and walks from his hiding place to the back of the ghost train. There is a door marked 'PRIVATE'. He opens it and steps inside. He is in no hurry, and searches quietly but thoroughly, following the track, darting to the side as the occasional car hurtles through, and then resuming his meticulous progress.

After no more than five minutes he has a huddled figure in his sight. He will have her again: he has no doubt about this. And what is more, even though she may not realise it, she needs him as much as he needs her.

———— JJ ————

A strong arm curled like a snake's tail around Glenda's neck and dragged her kicking and shouting along the wall. A moment later a hand gripped her mouth and she was being forced to swallow her screams.

'Shut the fuck up,' the man whispered in her ear. 'You know I don't want to hurt you, so just shut the fuck up. Pretty please,' he added. He loosened his grip but kept his hand over her mouth. 'Nod once if you promise to be a good girl and keep quiet. You might as well. It'll be easier for both of us, but especially you.'

Glenda wanted to fight him but she was impotent. There would be no divine intervention, she knew that. This was how it was: ghost trains were meant to be scary. She nearly began to cry as she nodded her consent to stay quiet.

The hand released.

The man stroked her hair and pulled her close to him. It was the first time he had touched her like that since they had been boyfriend and girlfriend in what seemed like another lifetime. Glenda had been to the police, but he was clever and that had come to nothing. Now all she knew was the fear of him. It was with her regardless of his presence, hidden from her parents and friends as though the fault were her own.

She was rigid and her mind was cold. The man touched the side of her face. She wanted him to squeeze or pinch so there would be proof that he had harmed her. He caressed the back of her neck. She bent her head back hoping that he would snap it and then the misery would be ended. She considered her parents and was sad that they would think she had been abducted by a stranger. And, if she lived, in whatever way she survived she could still never admit to them the indignity of having been this man's plaything for so long.

He pulled her closer and cupped her breast with his other hand. There was alcohol on his breath, and for a moment she hoped that he was drunk enough to do something foolish.

A train approached. He slid his hand onto her stomach but stopped when the stunning light of a skeleton jumped at them.

They were motionless for several moments, both holding their breath. When the train had passed he slid his hand further down her stomach and began to trace circles with his fingers.

This was the lowest point of Glenda's life. She wished she could detach her mind from her body, so that her body would be a trap in which he could ensnare himself.

'You know you want me,' he said. A trace of anger came into his voice. 'You think you have no choice, but you do. It can be the easy way or the hard way.' He slid his hand between her legs.

Glenda had already made her decision. In an instant she was thinking clearly. She knew she would rather be dead than let him touch her. But her thoughts were stronger than her body. She was petrified. She could not move her arms and legs to punch and kick him as her mind was telling her to do. It yelled at her to call for help, to swear at him and force him to leave, but the rising bile in her throat was choking her. She was limp and afraid. She closed her mind and tried to cease to exist.

A few seconds passed, and then suddenly he had let her go and was standing away from her, laughing. 'You think I'm stupid, don't you? I'm not going to give you the pleasure,' he sneered. 'Not here anyway. Not yet.'

She winced as the reality of her situation thrust its way back into her body.

'Can't bear to see me go, can you?' he said. 'Poor little Glenda. All alone on the floor. Well, sod you! That's where you belong.' He huffed and walked away.

She could not lift her head to watch him go.

'Be seeing you soon if...' His distant voice was drowned by a passing train. Soon there was silence again.

'Come back, you bastard!' she screamed. 'I'll kill you the first chance I get.'

She looked down. The floor looked like a bottomless pit which she was only just floating above. She tried to walk but her heavy feet were being pulled downwards. She bowed her head. She wanted it to be time to leave. The hands of her watch were blurred through her tears. It looked like there was still a long time to go.

———.//———

Glenda sat in the ghost train for the next half an hour. She had crawled into a darker spot and pulled her knees up to her chest and closed her eyes. She counted the seconds in her mind and checked off each minute on her watch.

She was becoming used to the sudden flashes of light. The wrenching noises exploded like the shrieks of a baby that was no concern of hers. Soon the passing cars clattered by unnoticed like distant night traffic. The mystery of this world was gradually disappearing as her eyes became accustomed to the dark. She saw wires and bulbs where there had been cobwebs and huge spiders. Gaping black mouths were suddenly speakers shouting their childish electrical noise. Fearful walls of death were no more than draped cloth that was disturbed by the slightest gust of air.

It seemed natural that she should be in this place at this time. She was a prisoner in a clandestine world of fear. It was natural that people passed quickly and excitedly by, unaware of her presence and her dread. Her parents would be sitting on the open-top deck of the tour bus, enjoying the views and the sea air, probably chatting away to another couple, knowing her dad. They would be excited about their day out. Wrapped up warm against the cutting sea breeze and armed with a thermos of hot soup, they would be immune to the cold and the drab commentary. Their lives were ordered and safe. They had earned their retirement after years of hard work. They were good and honest people. They did not understand evil. They had never seen Glenda sad, nor would she ever let them. They would never know that while they were marvelling at the reconstruction of the Brighton Pavilion, their daughter was so terrified about the thought of the short walk to the toilets beside the dodgems that she had been forced to urinate in a webby corner of a ghost train.

Glenda straightened her clothes and moved further down the track to find another spot. Fifteen minutes to go. She sat motionless, drained. She willed the time to pass. If she could make the choice to forego the passages of her life that would be spent in fear of him in the future, she would agree without a thought. If it meant dying a year or even ten years before her time, it would be worth it. Four long years had passed like this so far, and sometimes she found it hard to believe that she was not dead already.

———*JC*———

The man is hiding beside the Racing Dolphins stall, scanning the exits to the ghost train. He is pleased with the encounter. He just left her there. No messing around, no arguing. He simply disappeared and she called after him. Maybe this was the beginning of the turnaround? There was no mistaking her words. 'Come back.' The scent of her is on his clothes and it reminds him of when they were together. Two weeks of exploring her soft, responsive body. The sex they enjoyed fills his mind. The urges return as they often did. Just now he wanted to rip her clothes off and experience the release of his impatient body. But he knows there is no point unless she is willing. She has to desire him with the same passion that consumes his thoughts for days on end. Then, and only then, will his satisfaction come.

He is still certain that he can wait. He does not know that this is the last day of his life. A warmth comes over him and he looks out to sea and smiles at a pair of seagulls who are fighting in the air. The sky is cloudless and the kind of deep blue you only ever seem to see when you are happy. For a few moments he experiences tranquillity. There is time, and he has to admit that he enjoys the pursuit almost as much as the thought of the catch. He is pleased with the patience he has demonstrated. Of course things will be fine when they get back together.

But an instant later the sky no longer seems so blue. He shuffles on his feet and stares at the ghost train. First she has to pay for what she did to him. And he will make her pay. He knows he could ruin things so easily if he does not concentrate. His anger has, for once, been subdued and it feels good. The violence that took him away from her for that short time when he went to prison has remained hidden.

He watches couples walk around arm in arm and is disgusted. They only think they are in love. They do not understand what it is like to be involved with someone who occupies every waking thought of your life: they do not understand the intensity of emotion that an absolute desire to be with someone brings. They are all pretending; wishing they were like him and the girl, but knowing they are not.

Suddenly he has strolled out from behind the Racing Dolphins stall. He walks quickly and purposefully. He pays the man in the booth of the ghost train and steps into a car.

–––––––)(–––––––

Glenda clutched her ears and started to hum loudly when she heard the car bashing through the opening doors and a threatening 'yoo-hoo' being called at her from a distance. Immediately the voice called again, this time adding her name. She pulled her knees closer to her chest and screwed her eyes shut. She could picture his angular face smiling in the dark. He could not be happier than at that moment. She imagined his angry eyes burning brightly with pleasure. He was coming for her; very soon he would be upon her again. He was unstoppable. It was not just that she was a woman. She had seen him fight too often; she knew that she could have been a six foot ten commando and being afraid would still not cross his mind.

She tracked the progress of the rumbling car in her mind. The first siren blared like a warning at the beginning of a military raid. A second followed quickly. The car shuddered hard and shook the wooden floor as it swung round a tight corner then doubled back on itself. There was a brief silence and then the rumbling returned as the car gathered speed. A shrill whistling pierced the air and soon after came a shriek. The light of the skeleton raced through the tunnels.

'I'm coming to find you!' the voice called through the sounds.

Glenda wanted to run but knew she could not move.

She hummed louder and felt a tear of anger rolling down her cheek. She shuffled to her side and her hand bumped into something hard. She grasped at the object and lifted. It was a fist-sized rock. She gripped it tightly and lifted it above her head, ready to throw.

Soon she heard a snap and saw the flickering grin of a moving face coming towards her behind the blue flame of a lighter. She wanted to look away but could not stop herself from staring. The face was only a few feet away. It was no longer smiling. She dropped her arm and curled herself into a ball.

The flame disappeared as the car passed by. Glenda listened with relief as the next siren blew and the car sped around the corner. She sat up and checked her watch. Five minutes. A few feet to her left she heard another snap. She spun around and saw the bright red coal of a lit cigarette coming towards her.

Chapter Two

Glenda and Bill had met four years earlier in a club on the seafront. She had spotted Bill standing at the bar. He was smartly dressed, holding a pint of beer, not particularly good-looking, but even from a distance Glenda noticed that he had a powerful presence that obviously commanded the respect of his entourage. Very quickly he had seen her and had walked over to chat. They had talked and drunk and, by 2 a.m., they were walking hand in hand out of the club on their way to Bill's place. They kissed briefly in the cab and then were soon standing outside his flat without talking as he fumbled for his keys. It was like nothing Glenda had ever done before: in that moment, she did not consider that she needed to diet, nor that she was plain-looking. She was a woman, and an astonishing sexual warmth had suddenly saturated her body. For the first time in her life, she had no doubt that she was desirable.

She had been lured back to his flat night after night by the compelling remembrance of having been skewered to the centre of the earth by a force that usurped the mere act of sex. Yet, the more intense their passion had become, the more distant from each other they had grown. The silences increased, and soon what they had once done together had been transformed into nothing more than a sublime masturbatory experience. It was an addictive opiate nevertheless, and for some time it had helped mask the shattering differences that they had quickly discovered out of bed. When they talked it was clear that they were wholly different beings who just seemed to occupy proximate spaces and tolerate each other's presence.

Glenda had never imagined that this 'affair', as she regarded it, would ever actually come to an end, despite the fact that she had known that sooner or later it had to. Even years later, as she tried to distance herself from the intense pleasure of those evenings, a vivid memory of a need she had never known before remained with her. However hard she tried, even now she found it difficult to deny her very physical response to these thoughts.

She had subdued her misgivings about the dominant and potentially violent side she had begun to notice in Bill's character: the odd strange comment, the odd aggressive reaction to the most innocuous of situations were dismissed as side effects of fatigue or of alcohol. She continually reassured herself, calming her fears like a mother soothing a frightened child.

And then one day it *was* suddenly over. It was a cold Tuesday morning, and Glenda was lying alone in bed before work staring at her ceiling. She was in a mild state of shock, but conscious of the fact that something terrible had just come to an end. Her feelings for Bill had suddenly ceased to exist. It was as if she had been given a second chance to see him for the first time: this time she had no difficulty in recognising the evil in his eyes.

She felt sick as she remembered how things had ended. They had been drunk, kissing against the wall in the alley beside Bill's flat. When the policeman had appeared, and had shaken his head with his startled but appreciative smile, Glenda had felt an exhilaration that was exciting and unfeigned. She had seen the films and had heard the stories, but had never believed that she herself could be so beguiled by a man. She was happy that she had passed so close to the flame and had enjoyed the intensity of its heat, and she had wanted to savour this recklessness until her old age. However, as Bill had moved out of the alley, whispering 'I love you', on his way to beating the young policeman to the ground for smiling at his girlfriend, Glenda's distress had been mingled with shameful happiness: the terror of her pleasure had unequivocally ended.

A panda car had come screeching around the corner. Bill had paused and casually waved goodbye to Glenda, as if he were just popping down to the shop for a pint of milk. Then he disappeared over a fence, and two policeman scrambled out of the car and chased after him. A third policeman helped his injured colleague to his feet and dabbed at his bloody face. They had both stared at Glenda who was still in the alley, shaking and tearful. She had stood in silence, accepting their jibes and innuendoes. These were nothing. They were not talking about her. The person they had referred to no longer existed. That person had died an instant death of remorse and self-loathing, and been reborn just a moment later for the sole purpose of criticising herself for the rest of her life.

Chapter Three

Jim Wilson was twenty-seven, slim, with short, dark hair and brown eyes. His cheeks were pale and smooth, with only the faintest trace of beard-growth around his chin and on his top lip. His mouth was thin. It ran across his face in a weak pink line, tapering into two grey shadows at each corner. It gave him the aspect of someone who listened more than he spoke.

It was Saturday and he was standing in the middle of town holding onto a bus shelter as a wave of dizziness filled his head. His mind was racing excitedly: in a flash of inspiration, he suddenly knew how he was going to kill Bill. He had worked it all out; he had the answer that would allow them *all* to begin again.

When the bus arrived he hopped on without knowing if he had been waiting a minute or an hour. He kept his head down as he paid, holding out the correct money, and walked upstairs. There was a couple sitting halfway along the row of seats to his left. They did not turn at the sound of his footsteps, but as he strolled casually past them to the front, he was certain their gaze was on his back.

The bus remained virtually empty. It jogged idly through the outskirts of town, seemingly pausing at each stop for breath. There was a pleasantness about this journey that he had never experienced on the way to work. Despite his sinister purpose, he was pleased to be out of the town.

He sat back and gazed at the flamboyant show of greenery the trees were putting on.

The couple behind him had got off soon after they were out of Brighton and the bus was now well out of town. The few people who had come on board since then posed no threat. There were so many seats that it was unlikely anyone would sit next to him.

He had no idea if the bus would pass an appropriate church and graveyard, but it was a bright cheery day, and he was happy to sit and survey each town that they passed through. This had seemed to be the most innocent and methodical method of finding a church without drawing attention to himself and, since he was in no hurry, he had decided to devote the whole day to his task.

On his way home from work one evening he had stopped at the bus depot to pick up a regional timetable. Stepping into the office and asking the controller for the booklet had felt like asking for a licence to kill. 'Could I have the Countryline bus schedule please?' had seemed such a polite way of initiating his move into this new and dangerous phase of his life.

It was over an hour before he spotted the first suitable-looking church. He smiled inwardly. The game had begun. He had fallen into a daze and was thinking about nothing in particular when, out of the corner of his eye, he spotted the small grey stone building in the distance. The road was narrow and lined with trees. A hundred yards ahead, where it climbed to a shallow crest, the church stood alone to the left. He rang the bell and walked downstairs. When he reached the front of the bus, the driver acknowledged his presence with a nod but continued to look ahead. The building grew rapidly larger as the bus raced up the hill. He stared hard out of the corner of his eye, trying to spot its graveyard. Trees masked its front side, but as they drew nearer he began to make out a spiked iron fence through the black mesh of their branches. And behind this he saw a flat area of green which was strewn with a random pattern of crooked tombstones. It seemed ideal. It was well-secluded, and from what he could gather there were no houses on this side of the hill except for the solitary cottage they had passed a quarter of a mile back. The bus neared the crest, and Jim's attention turned from the church to the road ahead. He waited expectantly for the appearance of a village or a row of shops on the other side. In a second they were over the crest and racing down the other side. He felt a kick of satisfaction in his stomach when he saw nothing except a lone bus stop a further fifty yards down the road. Jim alighted, thanking the driver without looking at him, and began to walk in the same direction that the bus had been travelling. The bus drove off and he slowed to a snail's pace, until it had disappeared over the crest. He then spun round and walked excitedly up the hill.

He had already decided that if there was anyone in the church grounds he would say he had stopped on the spur of the moment to have a look at the building. He had toyed with the idea of bringing a piece of paper and a couple of crayons so that he could pretend he wanted to take some brass rubbings, but immediately realised that it would be wiser to say as little as possible: anyone he met would be more likely to remember a face if they could recall the subject of the conversation than if they had merely exchanged a few pleasantries about the weather. The church was very small. The graveyard, enclosed by iron railings, was to the left. Where it ended, open meadowland ran away to a spread of low hills. There did not appear to be anyone around. Jim tried the church door. It was locked.

He walked to the gate of the graveyard. There was a chain and padlock locked around the fence but not the gate. He lifted the latch and walked in. The gate did not squeak; he touched the hinge and felt oil. It was vital that the church was out of the way, but more importantly the graveyard had to be in use: burying a body in the turned earth of a recently filled grave would not be the hard part; nor disposing of the displaced soil. Discovering how often a funeral took place, and then being able to get everything ready within a week, would be the problem.

He stood by the gate and looked around for an indication of any recent burials. The grass was patchy and clumps of long weeds spiralled into the air. The carving in most of the headstones had been smoothed by the weather. He walked in and ambled towards the back, checking the dates as he went. Died 1971, died 1947, died 1894, died 1963: names with messages below, dates of birth, and rotten bodies and piles of bones under his feet. Within thirty paces he was at the far fence. The most recent date of death he had seen was 1974. A feeling of failure came over him. A perfect, quiet spot like this, and as far as he could see there had not been a burial for years.

It *was* quiet. He imagined that it was night, and that he had already killed Bill. He would have driven there with the body in the back of Roger's van. He paused in his thoughts and waited for a reaction. He remained calm except for a slight twinge in his stomach when he thought of throwing the body into the hole he had dug. It was not nervousness, but excitement. The mood of that night ahead was alive in his mind: the sound of the owls hooting their complicity as he carried a cooling corpse through a two hundred year old gate; the moon obscured by thick layers of cloud, which would bring the sky so low that it would nearly touch his head; the sweat and toil of the dig. He was deep in thought when a soft voice called behind him. He swallowed and paused to compose himself before reacting.

The voice called again, but even more tentatively this time.

A small man with a slicked-back head of white hair was standing by the gate. He was wearing a black crombie. The large check of a yellow and black scarf showed from underneath its upturned collar. From a distance his white hair gave the impression that he was well into middle age. But as Jim approached, the smoothness of the man's skin and the clarity of his blue eyes brought his features into the focus of youth. Jim lowered his estimation of his age by twenty years.

The man was open-mouthed and expectant. 'Good morning,' he said with a smile.

'Good morning.' Jim adopted an unsure reflection of the man's pleasant air. He took his hands out of his pockets and stood with them by his side, but immediately sneaked them back as the man spoke again.

'It's a beautiful day, is it not?' There was a trace of Irish in his accent.

Jim looked up at the pale, cold sky. The sun was shining, but it was a weak, watery glow.

'It's wonderful,' Jim said. 'Perfect weather for a day out.'

'Are you not from round here then? I don't think I've seen you before.'

Quickly Jim replied, 'No. I've come over from Portsmouth for a couple of days visiting friends.'

'Locally?'

Jim tried desperately to picture his bus map, but his mind would not co-operate. 'No, not really. Just passing through in fact. I saw the church and thought I'd have a quick look around.'

The man looked at the church and then back at Jim. 'We don't get too many people here at the best of times. Even locals.'

'Really?'

The man tugged his scarf down to reveal the white band of a vicar's dog collar. 'Local godfather. Michael McGuire, at your service, if you'll excuse the pun.' He held out his hand.

Jim greeted him with a shake and a nod. 'Holmes. Jim Holmes.' He was pleased with that. He had not hesitated. Feeling confident, he gestured to the church with his head. 'So are you opening up or closing?'

'Neither. I have to confess that I had a phone call from one of our elderly residents. She came past on the bus some minutes ago and she was worried that there was someone prowling around here.' He chuckled and a spray of smile-lines spread from the corners of his eyes. 'I told her it was probably nothing but she had a problem with a burglar last year and has been a little edgy ever since. I promised I'd hop onto my trusty bicycle and give the place a once-over.'

'I'm sorry if I've disturbed anyone. I thought it would be okay to have a look around. I tried the church door and it was locked. But this gate was open.' He was annoyed with himself. He had not heard a bus go past, nor a bicycle on the path.

The vicar smiled. 'I can understand old Mrs Gates worrying, but I can also understand your interest in my graveyard.'

Jim's mouth was suddenly very dry. His instant reaction was to look around at the graveyard so that he could swallow at this dryness. His neck was tight because of the twist of his head and the movement of his Adam's apple felt like a clenched fist being rammed up and down his throat. He forced his mouth into a wide line that he hoped resembled a smile. He looked back at the vicar.

'Brass rubbing,' Jim blurted.

There was a pause in which time the vicar's eyes widened with interest.

He continued, 'I was going to look for brass plates in the church, but as it was locked I thought I might find some nice inscriptions on the headstones instead.'

The vicar looked confused. 'I must confess I know a little about brass rubbing, of course. But as for... stone rubbing, is it?'

Jim nodded casually. 'Stone rubbing, grave rubbing, whichever.'

'Well I never!' the vicar said, throwing his head back in amazement. 'I've heard of grave *robbing*, but I must confess I've never heard of grave *rubbing*!' His laughter boomed around the graveyard.

Great, Jim thought. Really inconspicuous. A fondler of tombstones. Sherlock would have been proud.

'I suppose most people call it stone rubbing,' he said quickly before the vicar could say anything else. 'Grave rubbing, as you just pointed out, is more of a jocular way of referring to it.'

The vicar was still laughing. He threw his hands out in a gesture of welcome. 'Well young man, I'm afraid in one way you're out of luck – I haven't got the keys to the church with me. But as for the graveyard, please, feel free to look – or even rub – around.' He burst out laughing again.

Jim stood half-smiling, half-cringing as the vicar tried to regain his composure.

After a few moments his chuckling died down and he said, 'I can tell you for a fact that we've got a grave in there that dates back over two hundred years.'

Jim had the impression that someone – or something – other than the vicar, was having some fun at his expense. 'That's very kind of you.' He had obviously ruined any chance of using this church for his purpose. However, there was still a chance of getting some information.

'I hope I haven't scared anyone away,' Jim smiled. 'Except for new customers, that is.'

'Well if it's new customers for the church, then we need all we can get. But as for new customers for this square of earth—'

'That's what I meant,' Jim interrupted.

'In that case you don't have to worry about that. We stopped burials here a way back. Lack of space you see. Now they all go to the big cemetery in Brighton. The Brighton and Preston on Hartington Street. They're mostly cremations nowadays, but there's still a decent trade in burials. It's quite a place. You ought to take a look if graveyards are your thing. Acres of rubbing there. With all those stones it must look like New York City to the resident mice.' Again, he smiled at his joke.

They stood in silence for a few seconds before the vicar drew up his sleeve and checked his watch. 'Is that the time? Well, I'd better be getting along. I promised Mrs Gates I'd be down within fifteen minutes to put her mind at rest. If I'm a minute late she'll be on the phone to the local bobbies reporting my abduction. And we don't want that on such a fine morning, do we now?'

They shook hands and the vicar got onto his bicycle.

'Please, Mr Holmes, take your time. I'm off on my rounds to see the local old folk this morning, so I'll warn them about your antics.' He cycled off waving.

Jim waved back. 'Great,' he said aloud to himself, 'already I'm headline bloody news.' But he knew it could have been worse; he had just about managed to bluff his way out of trouble, and at least he now knew that the idea of a small graveyard would have to be modified a little. If the city graveyard really is that big, he thought, then that might be a definite advantage.

He left the church grounds and started walking along the other side of the road, looking for a stop back to town. On the way home Jim stopped at another two small cemeteries, but each of these also seemed to be disused. Both times he had to wait over an hour for the next bus, this after no more than a five minute tour of inspection of the grounds, and he was soon fed up with skulking around. He had virtually convinced himself that Bill would end up in the Brighton and Preston cemetery.

Dusk was approaching and a fleet of grey clouds were sailing overhead – spongy battleships that had been too long in the water. The evening breeze that accompanied them presaged the coming chill of night. Jim sat quietly on the bus. He wanted to get home as quickly as possible. It was not that the day had been a failure. Far from it: he had obtained the information he required, but as the bus rattled back he was annoyed that he had wasted over three hours looking elsewhere when he could have been in the heart of town long ago, planning and preparing. A red patch of impatience glowed on his cheeks and down the front of his neck.

Chapter Four

Jim had seen Glenda for the first time two weeks before his graveyard search. She was walking down the street and he was on the opposite pavement. He turned as she passed by and, in that instant, he knew he could follow this woman for ever. The streets were busy. Jim rushed through the crowd of unhurried shoppers and their leisurely pace seemed to be a sudden reaction to his haste. He bobbed up and down as he threaded through the plastic bags and the prams, straining desperately to get a clearer look across the road. The traffic was jammed and occasionally buses and lorries obscured his view. During those moments she would disappear like a satellite passing behind the dark side of the moon and Jim would hold his breath, anxiously awaiting her safe return. At any time it was possible that she might suddenly be gone for ever and, if that happened, he would have to live with the terrible knowledge that he had allowed her to escape from him.

Soon the consternation had become too much and Jim crossed the road. He *had* to see this girl and nobody would get in his way. He moved in a few yards behind her. His stomach tightened and he was overcome by a feeling that he was capable of doing absolutely anything he wanted. An ardour saturated his body as he marvelled at the way her hips swung as she walked. He moved to the edge of the pavement and stared at the curve of her breasts that stretched her T-shirt. He wanted her to know that he existed. It would be the only way to fill the void that was suddenly consuming him from within. She seemed to be in no hurry, yet in his mind the world was accelerating through the moments, weeks and years of the future when they would be side by side, hand in hand. He *had* to stay close to her, because he *had* to keep watching her. This must be what it meant when he had heard people say that somewhere in the world, everyone has their perfect match. Here she was, in Brighton, ten feet ahead of him.

She paused to look in a shop window. Jim stopped and checked the eyes of the men who were passing to see if they too were affected by the same intoxication. But his perfect woman seemed to be invisible to them.

His first impression was that she was not particularly pretty. But that was good. She probably did not realise how attractive she was. She had shoulder-length brown hair and a plain, bright face. But there was an allure in the way she moved that was irresistible to Jim. She was slim but rounded, hard but soft. She was elegant and she glided gently forward like a refreshing breeze. She could have been the reincarnation of all his failed relationships, yet at that moment he would still have wanted to be stranded for ever with her on a desert island.

Glenda looked around almost nervously. Her gaze ran along the shop windows and then rested briefly on Jim. She held his eye for a split second. He tried to look gently but surely; he wanted to express the desire and passion he had for her, as well as the trepidation and shyness that was suddenly rising up in his body.

She blinked and the trance was broken. She turned away and moved on.

He knew she had not noticed him but suddenly he was

nervous. A nudge of conscience distracted him: here he was following a complete stranger and he was compelled to remain near her for as long as possible without being spotted. But his only answer was to panic at the thought of colliding with an old lady if his concentration were to lapse. *She* would disappear and he would be left kneeling on the pavement stuffing tins of cat food and evaporated milk into a tartan shopping trolley.

Glenda slowed and turned into Sketchley's dry cleaners. Jim stopped behind a lamp-post opposite and leant heavily against it. He hoped against hope that she worked there. It would be ideal. She would be his visual captive and he would know where and when to go in order get his 'fix'. He could plan his destiny. There would be no unnecessary intervention of Chance.

When she appeared behind the counter wearing a green and white striped apron he clenched his fist inside his pocket and was glad that there was no God. He had not prayed for this; it was just something he wanted to happen. He owed nobody.

Jim returned to the shop on Monday. He tried not to look nervous as Glenda rubbed at the beer stain on the crow's-feet creases on the crotch of his only pair of smart trousers. The shop was silent and empty; the only sound was the muffled buzz of the traffic outside. It was small and brightly lit; a single, powerful bulb hung underneath a Chinese-hat shade. It reminded Jim of the interrogation cells he had seen in war films. The walls were white and mostly bare, except for a few colourful stars of cardboard which were filled with handwritten exclamations referring to various special offers. There was nowhere to look and his eyes were immediately drawn to Glenda.

Her head was bowed and her hair hung down over her

face. The curves of her body were exaggerated by the apron she was wearing. It was too tight for her, and she looked great in it. She glanced quickly over Jim's shoulder as if she were looking briefly at someone outside and then said abruptly, 'Standard or Gold Service?'

Jim was certain she had caught him sizing up her body. 'They're not particularly expensive,' he apologised, 'and it's only a beer stain. The standard should do.' He hoped it was the right option.

She did not seem very happy. 'You do realise, sir, that your zip is on its way out, and the top button is loose. If you just have the standard clean, you'll be back before you know it to have the rest done.'

He picked up the trousers and did his best to inspect them. He felt like someone looking over a car they want to buy without knowing the first thing about mechanics; all there is to do is kick the tyres. He pulled at the zip and looked back at her. There was an uncertain smile on her face. She was looking at him, but her gaze was distant as though it was coming from fifty, rather than five feet away. Jim steadied himself to speak, but before he could open his mouth, his eyes had suddenly been drawn to the bulge of her breasts. Panic flooded his thoughts. There seemed to be no escape. And then suddenly he heard himself speaking. The words, 'Brenda – nice name,' were bounced around the walls of the shop. He looked up at her.

Glenda was open-eyed in astonishment. 'I'm sorry?'

'Brenda. That's a nice name,' Jim said tentatively. He raised his eyebrows and gestured to the name tag that was pinned to her chest.

'Oh,' she said, shaking her head.

He pushed on, 'You're right. Why not get it all done now? I'll take the Gold Service, if that's what you recommend.' He spoke with the aplomb of somebody ordering their favourite meal in their favourite restaurant. There was a pause. He wanted to ask her what days she worked, and what time did she finish, and would she have a drink with him, and did she even like him, and was she aware that he was in the shop, a person rather than a customer? And was he simply too obvious?

She spoke. 'Erm, my name's not Brenda.'

Her words sounded flat. In an instant he knew that their intentions were wholly unrelated.

'This, er, isn't *my* apron,' she continued. 'It belongs to the other girl who works here.'

'My name's Jim,' he blurted. He held out his hand. 'Nice to meet you.'

Glenda stepped back with a start as if Jim were the horrible schoolboy in the biology laboratory who liked to scare the girls with a palmful of rats' intestines. She looked at his hand and then into his eyes. A twitchy half-smile came to her face and her gaze darted over Jim's shoulders to the door. Her smile disappeared for a moment, and traces of an expression of fear showed like permanent stains on her face. She composed herself and forced the smile back. 'I'm Glenda,' she said.

As they shook hands Jim checked her name tag. He looked up with a perplexed smile. He kept his head straight on to her so that she would not be able to see the large veins jerking in his temples. 'I don't really know how to say this. I don't know what's come over me. I mean I don't do this very often. In fact I never do this at all. But would you like to go for a drink with me? Maybe one evening after work? Maybe Friday?' They were locked in eye contact. Jim waited for her eyes to move down to the redness that was burning in his cheeks.

Glenda suddenly took a deep breath and wrote out a receipt for the trousers. Her hand was shaking slightly as she handed him the orange ticket. She did not speak but looked at Jim as if *she* were the one who had just spoken and was waiting for *his* answer. There was a long silence. Then, in a voice that was no more than a whisper, Glenda managed to say, 'Friday's late night, I'm afraid. We don't close until after seven.' Her eyes grew wide in shock, as if someone else had spoken these words from within her body. She looked down and stared at the counter. She was rigid, paralysed by nerves and seemingly holding her breath as if she were waiting for something terrible to happen to her.

It was a brush-off, it had to be, Jim thought. The girl of his dreams had said 'no' to him. He was embarrassed and had to look away. He took a slow breath, and screwed up his toes. For once in my life... he thought. Just once.

'How about after you close then?' He had said it, and he knew he would never regret this, the solitary display of boldness in his life to date. He was light-headed, and regardless of what she might say, a feeling of relief washed over him.

Glenda looked back down at the counter and again awaited the impending catastrophe. After a few seconds she looked up. Her eyes blinked rapidly. She paused for a moment as if she were summoning up her entire reserves of courage. At the end of a long, deep breath she said, 'That might be nice.'

Jim wanted to jump up and yell. 'As I said, I don't normally do this.'

Glenda was still breathing deeply. She looked exhausted. 'Neither do I,' she agreed hurriedly.

'Which pub do you normally go to?' he pressed on.

'Any pub at all. I mean I don't mind. Any pub's fine. It really doesn't matter.' She stopped speaking and placed her palms on the counter. She looked up, composed herself and said slowly, 'What I'm trying to say is, anywhere's fine. The Northern over the road might be easiest.'

'Sounds nice,' Jim said.

Sounds nerve-racking, he thought.

Chapter Five

A moment later it was Friday night and Jim was standing at the bar of The Northern with his arms outstretched, trying to ignore the unwelcome itch of perspiration. He had run there so that he could sink a couple of pints before Glenda arrived.

The pub was quiet. It was early or late, depending on whether you were still there from work, or had just come out. Apart from one couple who were talking in the corner below the television, there were only single men dotted around the bar. They were mostly locals, sitting quietly behind their pints, staring up at the flickering screen. They looked like a classroom of ageing children, sitting with hands on laps and knees together, looking silently up at a blackboard.

The barman was serving in the public bar. Jim leant an elbow on the counter and held his wallet conspicuously open by his glass. He turned, and looked out of the main front window over the road to the dry cleaners. He thought it was unusual that he had 'picked up' a girl in a dry cleaners. Then again, an unfriendly voice in his head suggested, it was unusual that he had picked up a girl at all.

'Same again, sir?' the barman asked. One hand was already on the long handle of the pump.

Jim spun around. 'Yes please, mate.'

'Hello,' a familiar voice suddenly called.

He looked around and was startled by the proximity of the speaker.

Glenda had put her handbag on the bar and was standing with her feet together and hands by her side. She was wearing her green work skirt and a white blouse, with matching green shoes. She smiled nervously and fiddled unconsciously with the strap of her bag.

'Glenda! You made me jump,' Jim said, trying to become part of the situation. 'I didn't see you come in.'

She swallowed and then said, 'Sorry I'm late.' There was a pause and she looked up at the television. 'Given up on me had you?' she said quickly. 'Taken to the TV instead?'

Jim ran his fingers through his hair. 'No! In fact I haven't been in long myself.' He held his three-quarter full pint up to show her. 'Talking of which...?' he gestured with his eyes towards the bar.

'Rum and Coke please,' Glenda said.

The barman scooped the glass into the ice bucket and then pushed it up to the optic. Jim held out a note. The barman took it without speaking and walked over to the till.

She raised her glass, smiling as if her life depended on it. 'Cheers!'

'Yeah, cheers,' Jim toasted.

'I'm sorry, but your trousers weren't ready.'

'Oh that's no problem. A good excuse for me to come in and see you again.'

Glenda's expression turned cold. He looked nervously into his glass and gulped at his beer. A second later she pulled the smile back to her face.

Jim was not convinced. He picked up his pint and took another sip. 'Fancy grabbing a table?'

Glenda was about to speak when the barman placed a rum and Coke on the bar behind her. 'Excuse me, Miss.

This is for you.' He pointed towards the public bar. 'It's already been paid for. That bloke over there bought it for you. He said he's a friend of yours.' He stepped back to allow Glenda a clearer view.

Jim edged towards the bar and leaned nonchalantly forward.

A man was staring intensely, almost insanely towards them. He was holding a pint of lager against his chest. The yellow beer stood out against his blue denim shirt. He had a narrow face, with a pointed jaw. His nose was crooked, flattened at the bridge, like a boxer's, and it stood out from his prominent cheek bones like a blunted wedge of stone. His eyes were deep-set; they looked directly, without inhibition.

Glenda turned her back on him immediately. The neatness and precision of her movements disappeared. She grabbed her bag and slid clumsily off the stool. She looked down and spoke quietly to Jim.

'I need to leave.'

Jim was transfixed by the staring face. He lowered his eyes defensively when he heard Glenda's voice, but a disquieting feeling of being studied lurked in his thoughts. 'What's the matter? Do you know him?' he asked.

'I'd just like to go now. Please!' The firmness of her voice did not brook any question. He sensed a change of atmosphere in the pub and wanted to look across the bar to see if this horrible mood was really emanating from this one man.

Glenda was staring at the ground, like a shop window dummy waiting to be moved.

'Okay, let's go,' Jim said.

Glenda turned to Jim as they stepped out into the street. She smiled nervously, swallowing before she spoke. 'I'm sorry about that.' She touched his sleeve tentatively and checked over his shoulder. 'Can I explain later? It's not a big deal, really. C'mon, let's go. We'll get a drink somewhere else.'

She moved quickly past him and he had to run to catch her up. 'Let's hurry,' she said without looking at him, 'you haven't got a jacket. You'll freeze!'

It was now mid-evening, and the roads were quiet. A car was parked on the double yellow lines opposite the pub. Its driver was pressed against the nearby cashpoint machine. The blinking orange hazard lights of her car ticked a slow beat in the silence. A few shop lights were on and their empty aisles gave the street a deserted, ghostly feel.

Jim and Glenda were not far down the road when a voice called. The shout was still accelerating when it hit them. 'Oi! Glenda! Where's your manners? How about a thank you!' The yell was loud. Much louder than it needed to be for them to hear. The voice was drunk and angry. It demanded a reaction.

'Just keep walking,' Glenda implored. Her head was low, seeking to appear as small as possible.

Jim had the same uneasy sensation of being studied that he had felt in the pub. He could still see the angular face staring at him. Glenda was nearly running, and he adjusted his stride to keep pace with her. Again the voice shouted, but this time it was accompanied by quick, trotting footsteps.

'Oi, Glenda! What are you in such a hurry for? Why don't you stop and say hello? Introduce me to your new boyfriend.' He spat the last word out with a sarcastic jeer.

Jim was scared but curious at the same time. His heart quickened, and he could feel it pounding hard in time with the sound of their shoes on the pavement. The voice called a third time. It was closing fast now. The sound of the words jerked up and down with each step as if they were all being carried in his mouth at once and were spilling onto the street in uncontrollable splashes.

'Glenda! Where do you think you're running off to like that! Stop and say hello!'

She glanced across at Jim. Her eyes were wide and staring; her skin reflected a sickly complexion of orange from the light of the street lamps. A blank look of shock was set on her face.

A sharp stab of anger pushed its way into Jim's stomach and twisted his innards. He did not understand what was happening, and later he would not be able to recollect the moment when, completely out of character, he had decided to stop and face this man. But in that instant of defiance, he did not consider his safety. The faster they walked the more frightened they were both becoming, and the more Jim's craving to see this face again took control of him. And then suddenly Jim was stooped into a crouch, waiting to be hit. The shouting man stamped towards him, but Jim could hear no sound. Glenda seemed to be shouting as well, but he did not hear this either. Jim's belligerent stance registered immediately with the man, who hardened his step and quickened his run. He was near to Jim now, and in the final few yards he accelerated and dropped his shoulder like a long-jumper driving into the take-off board. Jim shouted but no words came out. And then an explosion blasted into his face. His senses were scattered into a brief, nebulous calm before being snapped sharply back to the pain of his nose. He fell backwards and landed with a crack on the pavement. Everything then felt very soft. An uncomfortable sweetness dripped into his mouth.

Bill was standing over him, looking down with his fists

clenched. 'Get up, you shit!' he shouted. 'I hardly touched you. Get up and fight!'

Jim looked up. He was squinting as though he was looking into the sun. 'Enough. I've had enough,' he said quietly.

Jim thought he could hear Glenda shouting and see her falling. But in a second he was laying peacefully on the pavement where everything was silent. He lay back and sank into the soft concrete. He was safe now. He could relax. He knew there was not the slightest doubt that he would kill this person.

——— JC ———

The man leaves the ghost train in a hurry, looking round anxiously as he runs along the pier. He is on his way to see a friend when he sees a familiar face on the other side of the road. It is the coward, he thinks scornfully. He slows down and lets the coward move ahead of him. He is suddenly angry and does not care about the threat of going to prison, and the stupid magistrates who think they are local gods and have the right to dictate what is right and what is wrong. They can 'punish' him just because they belong to the Rotary Club. He wants to punch them and see if they will personally escort him to prison. He would like to see them try.

The traffic noise in the town is suddenly unbearable, and the people walking past him seem to be shouting and screaming, just to annoy him. Anger hardens his fists. He is still agitated about the events of the morning but is desperate not to lose his temper. He stares as the coward passes: he wants so much to run over and... He does not know what. He is confused and does not need another argument, especially at this time. He needs to straighten things out in his mind.

He darts into a Wimpy Bar and sits in the window seat. He orders a tea from the smiling young waitress. He gazes through the glass at the road. The clamour of the outside world is now reduced to a drone. He stretches his legs and tries to calm down. He cannot escape the fear that he has overstepped a boundary from which he will never be able to return. Why on earth did he go back into the ghost train? Why the fuck did he have to ruin a good day? The sight of the girl clinging to the dirty floor in the darkness pounds into his thoughts as the waitress places a pot of tea in front of him. 'No,' the man says quietly. And then, 'Why?' as the next memory follows hard on the trail of the first.

'It was tea, wasn't it?' the waitress asks in confusion.

The man has not noticed her presence and she walks away uncertainly.

Now he can see himself laughing and flicking a lit cigarette butt onto the cowering body in front of him. He is saying, 'Hello, I'm back.' He thought he'd sounded polite, even concerned, but he realises now that it was the controlled voice of a happy torturer. He has poured himself a cup of tea and has the cup to his lips. The liquid scalds his tongue and rips down his throat like barbed wire. He does not notice the pain. The girl's face is occupying every ounce of sensation he has in his body, as she has done for so long. She is crying now and her lips are quivering as if someone were passing an electric current through them. She is so beautiful, even like this. He was convinced that she was smiling and pleased to see him. He did not notice her terror; he just stood in front of her as the involuntary spasms of fear shook and shook her body. She was slumped against a wall and crying wretchedly, but no sound came out. She was paralysed. He had taken her strength by just looking at her with that inane grin on his face. He came closer and touched her shoulder; half touching and half wanting her to stand up. He wanted to kiss her so much – even through her tears, he still believed that he was the one who could make everything all right. Not the coward; he could not look after himself, let alone anyone else.

He tries to imagine the two of them holding hands and then kissing. But he cannot. He is not jealous of that wanker.

The man clears his mind. He thinks about the sea and the clouds, and can hear seagulls all around, invisible in a big sky. It is a nice day and he is walking on the beach feeling the warmth of the sun on his clothes as if they have just come out of the dryer. And then in his mind he is suddenly back in the ghost train. Everything is dark and the girl has freed herself from her paralysis; she is standing two feet in front of him, crying so desperately that she can hardly breathe to speak. But she does: 'I would rather be dead than be touched by you. I would rather be dead than be touched by you. I would rather be dead than be touched by you. I would rather be dead than be touched by you.' Her eyes are screwed shut and she keeps chanting the same words, like a mantra to ward off evil. The man drops his head. His body is drained of strength and energy. He walks away. His entire life has been ruined in the space of a two second sentence.

A little boy at the table opposite looks over his hamburger. He smiles at the man. His smile is concerned and worried. He seems to be sad for the man. He must know that the tears in the man's eyes have shocked and hurt him; he must know that it is the first time in his life that the man has ever cried.

Chapter Six

Jim awoke feeling stiff and lethargic on Monday morning. He ambled into the kitchen to make himself a cup of tea. He had decided before going to sleep that he would go back to the pub that night and kill Bill. He had no regard for *him*. He merely represented all the beatings he had taken at school; the innumerable angry faces in the pub to whom he had backed down in arguments, when what he had really wanted to do was produce a gun from his pocket and blow their heads off. The least he could do was to stand up to someone this one time.

Suddenly he picked up the kettle and began to smash it against the wall. When he saw that there was a hole in the plaster he became even madder. He punched his fist through the door of one of the kitchen cupboards. He bit on his lip and stamped so hard that a sharp, worrying pain stuck in his heel for a moment. He pressed hard on his nose. The pain grew so that it was still there when he took his hand away. It felt good. He was annoyed that this bastard who attacked him was not near to him then. He would show him what pain was. He would not stop at a poxy broken fucking nose.

Later, at work, Jim was sitting in the van with his friend Roger. He had explained what had happened to him and was now trying to stop Roger from getting too mad and insisting that they went hunting for whoever had attacked him.

Roger was a self-employed delivery driver. Jim had been working for him on a cash basis for a few months but they had known each other since junior school. He was not particularly tall but he was thickset and strong. He had always been like Jim's older brother, and had stuck up for him so readily and so often that occasionally Jim wondered if Roger created situations so that he was also able to resolve them. He was well-known for his good humour. He invariably had a broad smile on his flat round face and liked to make a joke of everything. But he did not find this situation funny. He was frowning, pulling at his short black hair.

'I walked into a door,' Jim said.

Roger ignored him and took a long puff of his cigarette.

'We'll talk about it later,' Roger said as they pulled over. 'This is it. The delivery is some kind of medical chair, quite big.'

They strolled up the shingle path to the front door. 'Muurling' was written below the bell. Roger pressed the button.

They waited in silence for a minute and then Roger rang the bell again. They were both lost in thought when the door opened and had forgotten the chair. The sound of the latch being turned shocked them and they spun round quickly as if they had been caught doing something wrong. A waft of stale air drifted out and then a hand, before a small woman appeared. She had the gaunt look of sickness. Her thin skin hung in slack folds from her jaw and it was so wrinkled that it looked as though it had been screwed up wet and left to dry. Her hair was uncombed and it lay flat on one side and her eyes were flooded with redness. She leant against the door frame with one hand on the latch. The tight-drawn sinews of her bony forearm betrayed her determined grip on the door knob.

'I don't want this chair, you know, but the doctor insists I have it. I suppose he knows best, but I don't like it.' She spoke without looking at them. 'Anyway, if you would be so kind as to take it through to the dining room I'll go and make some tea.'

When they were in the end room they leant the box on its side against the chimney breast. Immediately they started to look around, as they always did whenever the customer was not present, in a Sherlock Holmes-like game of detection.

It was a large room with patio doors which led out to a long, balding lawn. There was a heavy oak dining table pushed against the wall. A single bulb hung in the centre of the ceiling. There was no other furniture in the room, except for a padded wooden footstool which was also tucked under the table, and a small sideboard in front of the patio doors. An old-looking radio and two framed photographs were on top of this. The walls were bare except for one picture which hung in the centre of the chimney breast. Jim and Roger headed straight for the pictures on the sideboard.

'Clue number one,' Roger announced, pointing at the first picture. 'Black and white photo, young man in uniform.'

'Clue number two,' Jim called in a hushed voice. 'Young couple on wedding day. Also black and white.'

Roger walked over and peered over Jim's shoulder. Suddenly Mrs Muurling was in the room with the tea and Jim had stuffed the picture up his jumper. Roger stifled his laughter as he turned and took the tray from her. He put it down and moved to the chair with Jim. It was out of its box and they stared expectantly at it as if they were waiting for it to speak its first words. It looked out of place, surreal and threatening. The bright steel tubes which made up the arms and back were dressed in flaps of stretched black leather that gave it a futuristic and tarty appearance. Jim took an immediate dislike to it.

Roger broke the silence. 'Well, you gonna try her?' he invited hopefully.

Mrs Muurling edged towards the chair and started to inspect it. 'It doesn't look anything like the picture the doctor showed me.' Mrs Muurling was breathing hard, staring vaguely at a space above the floor, trying to catch her breath.

Roger was filling in the necessary paperwork. Jim sneaked a glance at the woman. He did not mean to catch her eye. He was certain that she knew he had the picture up his jumper. He was desperate to run away and bury his thoughts in the distraction of the pub. Lunch and then home for the day. That was all he wanted out of life at that moment. As long as he could get away soon he would post the picture to her and that would be that. His eyes met Roger's and he motioned to the front door with a flick of his head. Roger took the hint.

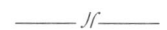

———*JI*———

When Jim got home that afternoon, he placed the picture in the drawer beside his bed and then telephoned Sketchley's. He was so confident about killing Bill that night that he was not at all surprised when he finally managed to persuade Glenda to have a meal with him later on. At first she had been insistent that she could not come, but Jim was unrelenting.

As he removed his overalls, the image of a lonely old lady came to mind. He decided that he would take the picture back to Mrs Muurling as soon as he could. He would make out that Roger had taken it and would apologise for his friend's behaviour.

He ate early that evening and on the stroke of the six he left his flat with a kitchen knife under his jacket and walked into town.

The night was dark. The moon had not yet risen, but the curved glow of its imminent ascent shone like a silver rainbow on the horizon. The air was fresh and cool and he was pleased to be outside. Jim welcomed the darkness. He saw himself as Humphrey Bogart ducking through the backstreets of Marseilles as he made his way towards the seafront. It was a nice night to be on a mission. Cut the guts out of this bastard and then relax with Glenda in the restaurant. Life really was that simple.

When he reached the pub, he peered through the window of the public bar. A nervous thrill ran through his body when he saw that Bill was playing pool. He leant back against the wall and composed himself. He tried to control his breathing and relax but his heart was pounding fast. He touched the knife for reassurance and then looked back in.

The pub looked bright and unwelcoming. The tatty stools along the bar were empty, as were most of the plain tables and chairs. The bare walls echoed the sound of shuffling feet as Bill and his opponent moved around the pool table. A fake log fire in the corner seemed to be the only thing in the room that possessed the quality of life.

Jim had already decided that he would make his move when Bill was on his way home. He would follow him, and when it was quiet he would close the gap in a sudden rush and rip the knife into his back. As he was dying he would kick him into the gutter and laugh. Bill would be convulsing with fear and agony as his blood swelled the litter and leaves in which he would be lying. In the Western films he had seen it was considered wrong to shoot anybody in the back. It was seen as the cowardly way to gun down a man as it meant near-certain death. Jim's heart palpitated at the thought of forcing the knife into *him* and watching the blood ooze out onto his hand.

'Fuck the ethics,' a voice in his mind called. 'Certain death is good. Think of us. We must live.'

Jim pushed the knife against his stomach. He felt the prick of the sharp point and pushed a little harder. He considered cutting himself so that he would be able to plead self-defence if he got caught. He could wrap the knife in Bill's hand to get his fingerprints on it and... A car screamed along the empty road blowing a deafening *cucaracha* horn. Jim spun around in time to see a pair of red lights disappearing into the distance. On cue, a dog barked and a light in a flat opposite came on. Suddenly what he was doing was real. It was a potential nightmare rather than a romantic daydream. He could be caught. He would be taken away from Glenda. And what if he was not caught, but failed? Someone like Bill would not show mercy on a person who had tried to stab him in the back. Jim's head began to spin as a series of terrible scenarios came to life in his mind. He panicked and dashed across the road. Soon he was sprinting down to the seafront as fast as he could. He did not slow until he had reached the promenade where there was the security of cars, lights and people. His lungs were screaming for air but he did not come to a halt until he had reached the beach. Through his panting he listened intently for *his* steps, but heard none. He looked nervously around and when he was certain he was safe, he squatted down to recover his breath.

He stared at the coloured lights of the Palace Pier. There were people out there, playing video games, eating fish and chips and enjoying being together. He could hear the pop music from the buzzy speakers and was drawn to the anonymous life it signalled. His breathing slowed and he closed his eyes to relax. He concentrated hard but he knew another enemy was coming. He turned.

The ghostly jumble of the broken-down West Pier skulked to his right. It terrified him. He caught a glimpse of the collapsed and forlorn black iron out of the corner of his eye. And then it did not matter if he was looking or not. An image of the past filled his mind. He was younger, standing shivering on the beach while his friends were running around on the pier's rotten decking in the darkness. Their bravado had made him want to cry and run away. He wished he had the courage to swim out and climb up the rusty ladder on the side; the guts to be like them and exist in their world. Their distant voices taunted him, 'Come up, chicken! Swim out and come up!' But he had just stared at them in silence, hoping they would come back to shore soon, and hoping they would not tell him too many times that he was afraid. He hated himself for wanting one of them to have an accident. That way they would suddenly see how reckless they were being; that way they would know what he already knew; they would understand fear and danger. But none of them ever did, and they all assumed his precaution was cowardice. 'Come up, chicken! Swim out and climb up!'

A wave broke and rushed up the pebbly shore to Jim's feet. He shook himself free of his memories. He turned away and headed home. 'So it won't be a knife then.'

Chapter Seven

Glenda was already having a drink at the bar when Jim walked into the restaurant. She was wearing a knee-length black skirt and a big black jumper. She smiled with a closed mouth when Jim walked in and extended her hand to greet him. He made up an excuse for being late and ordered a large brandy.

'I'm glad you could make it,' Jim said.

'To be honest I nearly didn't come. Especially after last week. But... I just need to be out,' she said with deliberation. 'I just need to do something different.' She took a deep breath and was unable to hide the trepidation in her voice. 'To try and live a little.'

Jim nodded uncertainly and took a mouthful of his drink.

The restaurant was Glenda's choice, and not at all what Jim had expected. The contrast between the plain brick facade outside and what assaulted him as he walked through the door had unsettled him. The walls, tables and chairs looked as though they had been decorated by a group of six year olds who had been given buckets full of brightly coloured paint but no brushes. The lights were dimmed and each of the tables sprouted numerous candles which had been pushed onto three inch nails hammered through from underneath. A nest of coloured wax had accumulated around each one, and more candles had been fused to these at various angles, so that each mound now looked like a spiky psychedelic bomb that had no intention of exploding.

They had finished their main course and had just begun their second bottle of wine. They were getting on well and there had only been a few noticeable lulls in the conversation. They had exchanged the usual necessary information about themselves and had attempted to laugh at each other's jokes. It seemed exactly how a proper date should be. And so Jim was amazed when he heard himself spoiling the mood by saying, 'How's the eye?' The red swelling on her cheek was the first thing he had noticed when he walked in. He had promised himself that he would not mention it.

Glenda brought her hand up to her cheek.

'It's fine.' She spoke quietly, but with a firmness to her tone that bordered on defiance. Her expression was blank, considered: a good poker-face.

'He hit you after he punched me,' Jim said with resignation.

Glenda did not reply. She sipped her wine and then watched the path of the glass as she replaced it on the table.

'Glenda, I know there's more to this than an angry ex-boyfriend. I'm sorry for asking, but I can't get it off my mind.' He looked for a reaction but there was none.

'There's nothing more,' Glenda said quickly. 'You were there, you saw what happened. There's nothing more.' Her lips were pinched and pressed tightly together. She reached for the gold cross on her necklace and brought it before her eyes. She held it there for a second and then let it drop.

Jim's father had often hit him for coming home cut and bruised when he had been bullied at school. Although his mother had always cleaned him up and told him everything was all right, she would soon become distant when his father came in from work. It seemed so long ago, that he had nearly forgotten these people. They were nothing more than the memory of a dream. But the sense of fear and helplessness had remained.

'I remember before I was hit,' Jim said, 'and then a little while after. But there's a gap in between. He obviously hit you in that time. I don't want to be nosy, and I certainly don't think it's my business to know what happened just because I got caught in the middle. But I get the impression that there's something not very nice going on. Useless as I may be, I might be able to—'

'I don't want you to get involved,' Glenda interrupted. 'You're a nice bloke, I don't want to see you get hurt.'

'So there's a chance it could happen again?'

Glenda picked up the dessert menu as if to change the subject. Her nervousness had suddenly been replaced by an anger that she was trying very hard to control.

'And what about you?' Jim asked. 'Has this happened to you before?'

She did not answer.

'And will we see each other after tonight, or is this really a way of saying sorry but goodbye?'

She looked him in the eye. 'Do you really still want to see me after what happened?' For the first time there was a trace of emotion in her voice.

Jim didn't know if he was scared or happy. Being hurt scared him, but he knew that kind of pain would go away. Being alone scared him more.

'Listen, Glenda. I'm here because I want to be. I didn't like what happened the other night, but I still want to see you. If we're going to go out again, you've got to tell me what's going on. I want to see you again, regardless. No conditions. Unless it's just my imagination we seem to have got on okay tonight. In fact more than okay. I feel comfortable. I'm not bothered about what happened, or what might happen, I'm just happy now.' He felt cool, as if he experienced pain and danger everyday. He was waiting for one of his friends to appear and scoff at his laughable behaviour.

Glenda was studying him. Her eyes moved around his face as though she were looking for something she had not seen before. 'Have you ever been in love?' she suddenly asked.

Jim was surprised by the question but answered immediately. 'I can remember thinking I was in love when I was at school. In fact at the time I was pretty certain I was. Why?'

'You haven't been in love since then?'

He glanced around the restaurant, checking there was nobody close by and then said, 'Probably a hundred times and never.' He laughed but then stopped when Glenda did not smile. 'I've liked a couple of girls a lot,' he offered soberly. 'Maybe once or twice.'

'Okay, that first time. What told you that you were in love?'

'What do you mean?'

'I want to know what made you think you were in love at the time. What changed in your life? How were you different?'

'Symptoms?' Jim asked with raised eyebrows.

Glenda was wearing her poker-face again. She nodded once.

Jim sat back in his seat and folded his arms. 'Er... symptoms.' He looked up and tapped his foot. 'Unwell, I suppose. I think more than anything I felt ill. Lovesick you could say. I lost my appetite—'

'Your concentration?' Glenda interrupted.

'Definitely.' A picture of Mandy Fairclough came into his mind. For a moment he was seventeen, and it was summer. It was a warm evening and he and Mandy were walking on the beach. He wanted them to be the only people left in the world. 'I lost interest in most other things I was doing at the time. I stopped playing football, forgot about schoolwork, my friends. I wanted to be with her all of the time.'

'So even when you weren't with her you thought about her?'

'Of course. Why do you want to know all of this?'

Glenda did not answer immediately. Her lips were slightly parted and her head was tilted to one side. Her right hand was still touching her pendant. She spoke wearily. '*Please*, answer these questions. I'm trying to explain what's going on but I'm not very sure how to.'

'Okay. Go on.'

'How did the relationship finish?'

Jim had never told his friends that Mandy had sent him a brief note telling him it was over. He expected them to all laugh behind his back and so he had told them that they had finished 'by mutual agreement'. Later at home, he had sat in his room and cried hard because someone had rejected a part of him that he had never given to anyone else before.

'Dear John letter.' He smiled uneasily.

'And after that?' she said calmly. 'Did you try to see her? Call her?'

'I never tried to call her. My pride or something like that had been hurt too much. But I do remember I used to wait at the end of her road... just so... so I could see her and...'

Glenda's eyes were fixed on him. 'Go on,' she said with growing confidence.

'Well I used to go to pubs she used. I wanted to speak to her.'

'And then?'

Jim rapped his temple with his knuckles. He bowed his head for a few seconds to hide his blushes.

'She saw you outside the shop and knows you followed her,' an unruly voice in his mind said.

'What an idiot!' Jim said looking up. 'I'm so slow. It just didn't seem that obvious. This guy Bill, he follows you, right? It's no coincidence he was at the pub?'

'It's my fault, really. The Northern used to be his local but I thought he'd stopped going there when it changed hands. He'd been banned for causing trouble, so I heard. I thought it was the last place he'd be.'

'But he follows you anyway, right?'

Her anger disappeared, and her usual frightened expression returned. She nodded once.

'You finished with him and he won't let go. Is that it? Like I was... er, or maybe as we've all been. But not quite so harmless?'

'Four years ago.' She swallowed and brought her hand to her pendant. 'I only went out with him for a few weeks. Don't ask me why. Four years. I can hardly believe it.' She shook her head, far away in thought. 'We'd split up and I didn't think anything of it. We hadn't got on very well to say the least and I thought he was as glad to see the back of me as I was him. I didn't see him for nearly a year after that, not even a call. In fact I'd virtually forgotten about him until one day after college.'

'You were at college? Where?' Jim asked.

'Here. At the poly. I'd stayed behind in the library to finish an essay on the computer. I spent a couple of hours typing my notes up but then remember suddenly rushing out because it was late. I was worried that I would miss the last bus. It was cold and dark and I was alone at the bus stop. I had only been standing there a minute or so when a hand suddenly grabbed my face from behind and dragged me back into the college car park. The hand was rough and dry and it reeked of cigarette smoke. It gripped so tightly so that I could hardly breathe. I was terrified. I felt so weak. I had always thought that in a situation like that I'd be able to put up a good fight, but I couldn't move. And then the next thing I knew I was being thrown against the fence and a dirty-looking man was running around in front of me waving his arms and singing, and I was thinking, Run now! Run! But still I couldn't move. He was laughing but his eyes weren't. It was only then I realised it was Bill. He'd stopped dancing and moved closer. He looked awful. His head was shaven and there were little cuts all over his skull. His clothes were soiled and torn. He looked like a tramp. He inched forward and then suddenly grabbed me by the shoulders. He forced his mouth onto mine. I could smell the stale sweat of his clothes and taste the alcohol on his breath. He pressed his lips onto me for a few seconds before pulling back and starting to dance again. Then he ran off, shouting, "Remember I'm back, slag! Remember I'm back!" As his voice faded into the distance he continued to shout the same thing. Then I was running as well, away from him towards the town and the safety of a taxi. I was crying with anger as much as fear, and I was desperately trying to spit the touch of his lips onto the pavement. That's where it began.'

Jim had been staring at Glenda while she spoke. She had looked different – unreal and detached. Like a dead body that has been drained of its blood, it could be anybody or nobody, because it is no longer the person you knew.

'I'm sorry Glenda,' he said. 'I had no idea it was like that. And here's me worried about how my eyes look.'

Glenda's mouth smiled, but it was not her smiling. She did not seem to want to leave the thoughts just yet.

'There's more, isn't there?' Jim asked.

She looked down and nodded.

He reached across the table and took her hand. 'Do you want to tell me?'

'Are you sure you want to know?' She stopped herself short and fought back her tears of anger. 'Look where it got me. Think where knowing the truth might get you.'

Jim was scared and ashamed. For a moment he wanted to walk out of the restaurant so that he did not have to get involved. But he looked at Glenda and knew he cared for her more than anything in the world. If he was going to stand up to his fear and devise a way of killing *him*, she would be his inspiration. 'I don't know how I can help. Maybe just listening would be something, but I do want to do whatever I can. Sod the coffee. Let's go, shall we?'

Outside a three-quarter moon was high in the dark blue night sky. It was fresh and the air was still. The only sound was the squawking of a seagull perched on top of a nearby parking meter.

'Do you want to go to another bar?' Jim asked.

'I don't really fancy anywhere public. We could go back to my place, but I never know if...'

'If you don't mind a bit of mess, we could always go back to mine,' Jim said.

Glenda was still distracted. 'Let's go to the taxi rank then.'

———*Jf*———

As they walked up the stairs to Jim's flat he tried to remember how he had left it when he had gone out. He slowed his pace, giving himself time to remember the things he did not want to find when he walked in. The pile of washing-up, the clumps of clothes here there and everywhere, the staleness of the air. The more he remembered the slower he climbed.

'Sorry about the mess,' Jim said as they walked in. The world of his thoughts manifested itself perfectly in the flat.

Glenda waved an uninterested hand.

He tugged a couple of cans of lager out of the fridge and sat beside her on the settee. 'Sorry, it's lager or water. Or maybe the same thing,' he joked, offering her one of the red cans that had a silhouette of a Viking emblazoned on its front.

Glenda cracked hers open and took a sip. 'Lager's fine,' she said.

'Are you okay?' Jim asked. 'You're certain we weren't followed?'

'Pretty sure,' Glenda replied. 'He should be working tonight so I'll be okay for now. It's just later. The odd occasion when I see someone for a drink he's usually waiting for me when I get back.'

'And tonight?' Jim asked.

'Tuesdays, Wednesdays and Thursdays he works at his dad's chip shop on Preston Road. Thankfully tonight is a relatively safe night. And I chose the restaurant we went to because he wouldn't be seen dead in Hove. But that doesn't mean I don't expect him to appear at any time.'

'I know the Preston Road chippy.' A sobering release of nerves came over Jim. He had been there many times. He stood up and walked to the radio that was perched on the radiator opposite. 'Shall I put some music on?'

'I'm not really bothered,' Glenda said, looking up. 'If you like. But I'm quite happy to talk instead. This is the first time I've been out with a bloke for a while. I used to have quite a good social life. I wasn't always the shy nervous idiot I am nowadays.'

Jim opened his mouth to protest, but Glenda stopped him with a raised hand.

'It's okay,' she said. 'I'm only joking, I think.' She shook her head. 'Joking's something I've always tried to do.'

Jim sat down and opened his beer. After a long silence he said, 'What you were talking about earlier – do you really want to tell me the rest?'

'I've never really told anyone before. It's been such a weight and I've wanted to so much, but I've never wanted to get anyone involved. Once, my father nearly discovered the truth. Bill came to my house and virtually threatened to beat us both up. Dad was shocked, but I said that he must have just been a passing nutcase. I was so worried that my parents would find out. Or even worse that Bill might follow them and...' Her voice trailed off. For the first time there were tears in her eyes. 'They would be so sad for me if they found out. I couldn't bear it. I can't bear to see them upset. That's why I've never told them what's really going on. As I said, once you begin to understand the type of bloke he is, especially after what happened last week, you'll be involved as well. I don't know if I could bear that.'

Jim felt special. His stomach fizzed and his scrotum tightened to a happy walnut. He had no idea why Glenda would choose to tell him of all people her most intimate secrets. But he *wanted* to be involved. Above all he wanted to be involved. He nodded and closed his eyes for a second in which time he imagined hugging Glenda. He opened his eyes and locked onto her gaze and said very calmly, 'Please tell me. I want to know. I think I'm already involved.'

Glenda wiped away her tears and took Jim's hand. 'I'm sorry about this, but I've had enough. I've got no one to turn to. The more it goes on, the less I feel I'll ever free myself from it. Even the police have told me there's not much they can do. At least that's what they said the last time I saw them. That was a couple of years ago and I suppose I've resigned myself to my situation.'

'Police?'

'They told me cases like Bill are quite common. He's "obsessed" with me as they say. Follows me around, waits outside my house, rings me at work. They call it stalking. There's only so much the police can do. They told me that if things got really bad I could take out an injunction against him. But that would be a private action and I couldn't afford the costs. I've shown the police the letters he's sent me, but because they were either typed or cut out of newspaper words there's nothing they can do. Meanwhile notes like "Hi, slag, you're going to have to kill me before I stop", keep arriving at my door.'

'And the violence? The swollen eye?'

'I've tried everything, or rather I used to try everything. But in the end it all seemed futile. He's only been violent towards me twice. He's not as stupid as he looks and he knows what he's doing. It began that time at the poly after he'd just come out of prison. He served nine months for a GBH offence which happened a week or so after we'd split up. He blames me and said that he wants revenge.' Glenda suddenly got up and walked to the window. She stared outside.

The memory of Bill's angry eyes came to Jim. An uncontrollable fury was rising within him. 'Are you okay?' he asked.

Glenda turned slowly as though she had spent her whole life composing herself and had got it down to a fine art. There were no tears now but she was still very upset. Her jaw was clenched, as were her fists, and she walked woodenly back to the settee. Jim was mad and he'd only been hit by the bastard.

Staring at nothing, Glenda said, 'Why me? What have I ever done to make him want me to suffer so much?'

Jim shuffled on his seat and was about to offer some words of consolation when Glenda shouted through her teeth, 'What gives him the right?'

'Strength' was the word that came immediately to Jim's mind. He hated himself for reducing her years of problems to the potency of that one word. He took her hand and squeezed his reassurance.

Glenda went on, quietly, almost to herself, 'Doesn't he think I've spent hours looking into the mirror at myself trying to find something that could account for his obsession? I wouldn't say I'm ugly, but I'm certainly not pretty. I'm a little overweight, certainly with a tummy I wish I could get rid of. And I could do with some exercise on my thighs and backside. I smile a lot, but mostly that's nervousness. And when I look too closely at myself, searching for wrinkles, I see a faint moustache that makes me feel like a man. Hardly an attractive package, is it?' She was whispering now and shaking her head gently. 'Oh, but there's one thing I forgot to mention. I've always had good teeth. There. That's me. Good teeth! Like a horse you'd buy.'

'Don't talk like that!' Jim protested. 'There are a hundred reasons why someone would like you. Personally I can think of just over a million and I hardly know you. Stop putting yourself down.'

'So I should be pleased he's mad about me? I should feel better that I've got the qualities that literally drive a man wild with desire?' She was shouting and stopped abruptly when she saw Jim's imploring look.

'I'm sorry,' she said, squeezing his hand. 'I shouldn't go on. I don't want you to think I'm taking it out on you. It's just that I've never been able to talk about it directly. Certainly not to a man,' she said tentatively.

'Please, Glenda, I'm here. I want you to tell me.'

Glenda smiled. 'I need to live, Jim, that's what I need. I want my life to be my own again. I need to know that all men aren't like him. There's got to be something good waiting for me away from this situation, something that I can enjoy without the fear for a while. I'd give anything for that. I need to know that I can defy him. Six months ago, I'd have shrunk behind the counter when you asked me out, or called the police, or both. But I've simply had enough. I've honestly reached the point where I can't go on as I have been any more. I have to take some chances. It's going to be difficult and I'm petrified. But if I don't do something soon, I'll go mad. I'm not going to let him strangle me from a distance.'

Jim put his arm around her. They were both a little drunk now and Jim was emboldened by the conviction of her speech. 'I just want to help,' he said with every ounce of understanding he could muster. 'I don't want you to worry about me. Despite what happened the other night I can look after myself.' He put his arm around her and she laid her head on his shoulder. It was a picture he had seen many times in films. The hero comforts the heroine. She sleeps, while he is awake and strong. He protects her and formulates brave plans and risks everything for her... but he knew these heroes' hearts would not be pumping as fast as his was at that moment; their palms would not be cold with sweat and they would not have to sneak long, nervous breaths while the jerky expansion of their chests betrayed their anxiety. Jim knew he was neither strong nor brave. He was intimidated by Glenda. Her eyes were not frightened when she talked about Bill. There was no tremble in her voice. She had the resigned air of someone who has been beaten but will never be defeated. Her will was strong and she knew it.

It was after eleven when they first kissed. Jim guessed the time as his lips were on Glenda's because there was a sudden increase in activity outside. The pubs were turning out. He hated himself for noticing this but he was taut with self-consciousness. It was not just the voices outside he could hear; the thermostat in the fridge had just cut in to bring its temperature down. Its low buzz filled his reddening ears. His heart was still beating fast and he heard its double-time accompaniment to the bellowing breathing sounds that were amplified by his swollen nose. With his small, but pronounced ears, blocked nose and ham-fisted grip on Glenda's back, she would soon realise that she was in fact kissing an Indian elephant.

Glenda pulled away. 'Are you okay?'

'Fine,' Jim nodded. 'You?'

'I'm glad I was able to talk to you. This seems a bit strange, feeling relaxed and close. But it's nice though. I'd forgotten *how* nice.' She smiled.

Jim kissed her lightly on the eye and then he wished he hadn't because it seemed so ridiculous. 'Do you want another drink?' he said quickly. 'Another Viking? They're not bad when you get the taste.'

Glenda shook her head.

What now? he thought, what now? He looked at her and

smiled casually. 'I'm meeting some of my friends at my local next week. Maybe you'd like to come along?'

'Sounds nice,' Glenda said, lost in thought.

There was a brief silence before Jim said, 'In fact, I think I might grab a beer myself.'

Glenda took his arm as he moved to get up and pulled him towards her. 'I'm not sure how to say this, but... do you mind if I stay tonight?'

'Fine.'

'Fine. What does fine mean?' the unruly voice in his mind shouted. 'Make a move, you idiot, or she'll see you for the wanker you really are!'

Jim spoke. 'Of course.' He nodded. 'I'd love you to stay over.'

'Stay over!' The unruly voice laughed. 'What, like a slumber party!'

Glenda took his hand and brought it to her cheek. Jim was aware of the warmth and softness of her body pressing against his. He closed his eyes and kissed her. He felt his hand moving to her breast. Her body responded to his touch.

The unruly voice began a practice run-through of the names of the 1966 England World Cup football side.

———— ∬ ————

The man leaves the Wimpy. He threads through the shoppers in the busy streets towards where the girl works. It would be so easy to walk into her shop and start up a conversation.

He smiles at the memory of a date they once had. They had been out to a Berni Inn. It was nothing expensive: there was a special 'early birds' deal, but they had enjoyed it a lot. Afterwards they had gone to the pub for a few beers. When they returned to the girl's house, she realised that she had forgotten her keys. They walked around to the back garden and decided that the pane in the back door would be the best way in. By the time the window was broken, a pair of policemen had arrived unnoticed and had sprung on the man and the girl from nowhere. The old lady next door had telephoned the police the moment she had seen them 'snooping around', as she phrased it when she apologised to them both the next morning.

The man sighs. That was when the old lady seemed to like him. He was a young man like any other. He loses his smile as he thinks about the old lady. He hates her now. He is upset that nowadays she dislikes him so much. She does not know anything about him. How can she make such a judgement?

He wants to be near someone close, someone whom he can trust. In fact anyone friendly would do. He feels alone and cheated. He does not know many people. He spins around, looking and thinking hard.

Chapter Eight

It was Sunday and cold. Jim had just woken up and was looking at his clock-radio. Eight forty-three. He stretched out his hand and hit the snooze button. He reached to the other side of the bed. Glenda had gone. His memory was fuzzy, as was his head that morning.

They had got drunk and ended up making love for the second night in a row. He had wanted her to stay but she had insisted on calling a cab. The memory of last night thundered into his mind. There had been no arguing with her; she was worried and had insisted on leaving. When the taxi came they had exchanged a perfunctory, even cold kiss and she had left. Jim had sat up for an hour drinking and wondering if she had left because he was so bad in bed. A feeling of guilt came to him. He dismissed it and turned onto his side. He closed his eyes and his mind began to drift.

He did not see how anybody could like Sunday mornings. He was used to waking up at about seven o'clock with a hangover, feeling as though he had just stepped off an unpleasant fairground ride into a bottomless pit. It seemed natural that the weekend should be punctuated by the mini-deaths of intoxication on Friday and Saturday nights. This, naturally, would be followed by a day of purgatory. Aimless wandering around his flat, listening to the endless, anaesthetising babble on the television and radio in between bouts of voracious feeding. He would feel haunted by a feeling of being detached that grew increasingly disconcerting as the day went on.

As if to add insult to injury the afternoons would slide slowly and frustratingly by, like an old man crossing the path of a cinema projector. Sometimes he would gaze out of the window at the passing cars. He would think about the empty pub the night before, and wonder if these cars were full of people who had stayed in so that they could 'save' themselves for the thrill of browsing in the garden and DIY centres, or the privilege of spending their hard-earned in the local superstore.

And then it would be evening. The dark, swampy nights, the well-attended church services on television would reinforce the Sundayness of everything. The hangover would be no better but the thought of a couple of 'straighteners' at The Stanford Arms would nurture his flagging interest in the day. A brisk walk, four pints and then bed. Soon he would be waking with a clear head. A rebirth that is morning. He would be given a second chance. Again.

He felt positive. I'm doing it today, he thought. I'm really going to go and see her and give her back her picture. He rushed to the bathroom.

Mrs Muurling's road was quiet. It was just after ten o'clock. Jim turned into the drive and walked to the door. He took a deep breath and let it out slowly. He reached up and pressed the bell. His heart tapped a little harder as he heard slow steps approaching along the corridor. He automatically moved back off the doorstep and ran his fingers through his hair. He swallowed at the dryness in his mouth. The saliva had been soaked up by the sponge of greetings he had crammed into his mouth on the journey over, 'Hello... do you remember me? I just thought I'd pop in to check the chair. How are you? I believe I stole a picture of you and your husband and I'm taking the piss by bringing it back and expecting you to be pleased...'

Two minutes later he found himself bending over the black chair, checking its various moving parts in an effort to look professional while trying to regain his composure. Mrs Muurling had not appeared surprised to see him. She had not stared at his injury as he had expected, but had offered him a cup of tea. He made some excuse about the condition of his nose and eyes, certain that she would soon mention this. But she acted as though there was nothing wrong. She left him to inspect the chair and went through to the kitchen. A few minutes later she came in with the tea.

'It was two sugars, wasn't it?' she asked.

'That's it.' Jim nodded. He took a sip. His eyes searched around the room and he glanced at the empty space behind the lamp on the sideboard.

They sat sipping for nearly a minute before Mrs Muurling spoke. 'So is the chair okay?'

'It's fine,' he smiled. 'I've checked the screws and the bolts and they're all okay. It seems to be in perfect working order.'

'Unlike me, eh?' she chuckled. She gripped her armrests and shook. 'It certainly feels solid enough. You and your mate did a good job. I'll be okay on this for a while.'

'Thanks for that,' he said putting his cup down. He could feel the sentences bubbling in his mind like a chemical reaction. He spoke. 'I'm really sorry about last week.'

Mrs Muurling looked up but remained silent.

Jim was not sure if she had been waiting for this apology

and was now giving him time to continue, or if she did not have a clue as to what he was talking about. He went on. 'I mean, when we came to deliver the chair. I'm sorry we had to rush off so quickly but—' He faltered hoping she would not cast an accusing glance towards the lamp.

'*You're* sorry?' Mrs Muurling interrupted with a totally unexpected smile. 'What have you got to be sorry about? There's no need for an apology. I'm the one who should be sorry for asking you and your friend to put the chair together for an old bat like me. It was very kind of you. No, I'm the one who should be sorry.' Her face was long and thin and her smile took away its sharpness.

Mrs Muurling stood up and put her cup on the table. She walked to the chimney breast and reached up to straighten a picture. Suddenly she was breathing hard and she sat down heavily.

'Are you okay?'

'I'm fine. Just catching my breath.' Her solemn expression had returned. Her head was bowed but despite the heavy breathing she looked so much better than she had done the week before. He wanted to ask what was wrong with her but knew the question would be as awkward in sound as it was in thought. She looked up and caught Jim staring at her.

'I understand your curiosity. But I'm quite well really. The doctor insisted that I had this. The black leather doesn't really blend in, does it? It's not really me.'

He became sad and nodded. He looked out of the patio doors. The thin, spiked arms of the overgrown bramble bushes were tapping on the glass in the wind. It looked cold, like a Sunday.

'I'm afraid I've got a confession to make,' Jim said suddenly.

'That sounds rather serious,' Mrs Muurling said putting down her cup.

'It's something I've done and I'm not proud of.'

'Nothing to do with those black eyes of yours? I hope you're not in any kind of trouble. Not a jailbreaker or anything exciting like that? My neighbours would have a field day if they found out I was harbouring a criminal!'

Jim missed the irony in her voice. 'No. No, nothing like that.'

'Shame really,' Mrs Muurling mused. 'A cat burglar or a serial axe killer would have been nice.'

Jim quickly rehearsed in his mind. His stomach was knotted and he knew the only way to relax was to speak.

'Well, go on then.' Mrs Muurling smiled.

Jim swallowed hard. He pulled the picture out of his inside pocket. 'It's this,' he said flatly. 'It's yours. I've come to return it.'

'But...'

'I really am sorry. My mate and I play a stupid game of detection when we get to a new house. We try and work out a little history of the customer from their possessions.' He spoke quickly, nervously, hardly pausing for breath. 'I was looking at this photo when you walked in. I didn't know what to do so I stuffed it up my jumper.'

Mrs Muurling took a sip of her tea and then placed her cup on its saucer. She stared thoughtfully at Jim for a few seconds and then said: 'And so?'

'And so? What do you mean?'

'And so,' she stressed her words, 'what did you discover about me? What's *my* history?'

Jim was not sure if there was irony or humour in her voice, or both. 'Well, we didn't really get that far. As I said, you walked in.'

Mrs Muurling nodded. 'Spoiled the fun did I?'

'We didn't mean—'

'I'm joking, don't look so worried.' She smiled and sat forward slightly. 'Really, don't worry. I appreciate the fact that you came back. I mean, I wasn't about to come after you with a vengeance, was I?'

'Thank you,' Jim said, relieved. 'I've been feeling so bad—'

'How about making it up to me?' Mrs Muurling interrupted. 'You seem like a trustworthy young man, and I'm getting too old to waste any time with polite preamble.'

Jim realised he was nodding.

'This is only a request,' she went on. 'I mean it's not legally binding. Anyway, let's forget all that rubbish.' She fixed a stare on Jim. 'I need a man, and I need one now. Sixty years ago, my husband Tom and I were married. We spent our honeymoon in Cornwall. He had the idea of us each writing a letter to the other on the first day of our marriage, and burying these in a casket that we would dig up on the first day of our retirement. That's what we did. But Tom died before he retired and the box is still waiting for me. I don't want it to be left forgotten with my death.' She stood up and walked towards the kitchen. She stopped at the door and said quietly, 'I just need some help. I need to borrow someone's youth and energy.'

He was not sure he understood what she was talking about, but his youth and energy was suddenly excited. He jumped up and ran to the kitchen. 'It sounds confusing, but yes, I'll help.'

'You're not just feeling guilty and saying yes are you?'

'I could be, but I'm not. I really mean it. I brought the picture back didn't I?'

Mrs Muurling went to speak. Her mouth formed words

but no sounds came out. She brought a hand to her face and held it on her cheek with her fingers outstretched. Tears came to her eyes and her other hand came to her face. Eventually her words came out, but quietly, almost in a whisper.

'You really mean it?'

'Of course. I'd love to help. You tell me how I fit into your plan, tell me what to do and Bob's your uncle.'

'It suddenly seems such a shock. We don't know each other and you really want to help?'

Jim nodded in excitement. He could see it now: himself, Mrs Muurling and Glenda on an adventure together. 'I can't wait!'

'I really am very grateful.' She looked down and wiped her eyes. When she looked up again she said, 'You *really* mean it?'

Jim's mind was racing ahead. He and Glenda could have their own casket.

'Let's get this bloody show on the road,' Mrs Muurling shouted defiantly. Her raised voice sounded strange, almost comical, like the pretend words of a child. 'You don't know what it'll mean to me if we could...' She stopped, aware that she was on the point of breaking down. She stood up and turned towards the kitchen. 'Tea!' she said with forced brightness. 'Another tea! I'll do that first; we can talk after. Just let me get the kettle on.'

Jim walked to the back window and stared out into the garden. He heard the sound of her stifled weeping in the kitchen. A deep feeling of satisfaction rooted him to the spot. 'I can borrow a car from my friend Alan in the pub. I'll ask him. Glenda my girlfriend can come as well, if you don't mind someone else on the team.'

'Of course, your friends are welcome. But we might not

even find the thing. It could just be one great disappointment for all of us.'

Jim walked into the kitchen. 'And what about the contents? What did you write?' Jim said positively.

Mrs Muurling looked away and then back at Jim as if she were waiting for some recrimination. 'Nothing much,' she said. 'There's nothing momentous in there. It's just a part of our past I'd like to have back.'

'You prepare yourself and I'll organise everything.'

Chapter Nine

Glenda had spent some time at her parents' house in Rottingdean. She had returned to see Jim on Friday night only to announce suddenly that she was leaving Brighton for good. 'To get away from him.' It was as final as that. She had a sort of a smile on her face as she said these words, and briefly this dispossessed her of the usual shocked expression that came over her whenever she mentioned the future.

Jim's heart sank. Was it need or love that bubbled queasily in his stomach? And was it rejection or envy that overcame him as she laid out her plans for her new life? His mind worked quickly, wondering whether he had any place in these plans.

'I'll call you tomorrow,' Glenda said. 'Maybe we could do something, sneak out somewhere?' The fear had left her eyes.

'If you like,' Jim said unsurely. 'I'm going to see my friend Mrs Muurling again tomorrow. You could come along if you had nothing else to do. I know she'd like to meet you.' Jim could tell by her expression that she was not keen. 'I'll ring you after work anyway. We can talk then.'

Glenda kissed him on the cheek and left.

He jumped up and clenched his fists. The word 'fuck' repeated itself noisily in his mind. He ran to the window and drew the curtain back slightly so that he could just peep through the gap. Glenda was stepping into a cab and then closing the door. Then the car was moving away and he had opened the curtain completely and was staring at the orange cloak of light that hung from the street lamp. A tinny voice in the background was talking about how an earthworm has three linings of tissue in its stomach, and that its stomach only has the one opening for ingestion and excretion. He turned away from the window and switched the television off. Glenda would not have to run away if Bill were no longer a threat to them. She could go back to the poly in Brighton, he could sleep soundly in his own house and everything would be fine. The decision he had made *was* final. Kill Bill; really do it. The thought worried him less and less, especially now that he had no choice. It made so much sense. After all, if Glenda ran away, Bill would soon find someone else to torture, and so he was doing that person a favour as well.

Chapter Ten

Roger had been trying to convince Jim to go for a drink with him in town ever since Jim had been beaten up. At first he had not tried to disguise the fact that he wanted to find Jim's attacker and 'see if he wanted to pick on someone his own size'. Jim had told him that the matter had been forgotten, but Roger would not let it drop. Eventually Roger just parked his van around the corner from The Northern and said to Jim that if this person was really not a problem then it would be okay to go in for a couple of beers. Jim wanted to protest. He did not need to do this at all – yet he knew it was something that he *should* do. A plan was already forming in his mind that would remove the need to avoid such fearful situations. But Roger was insistent. Jim could see Roger enjoying the role of tough guy. He was the kind of man who wanted to kick his way through the saloon swing doors, with his head held high, making the hero's entrance – turning heads and silencing the piano player. Everyone would be intrigued, the prelude to yet another showdown with yet another 'baddie'.

Roger lit up a cigarette and they pushed their way through the door to the saloon bar. Jim felt a lightness about his body. He walked in without looking around and ordered two pints. It was his show of indifference. He kept his back confidently to the enemy, showing complete disdain.

Roger's words struck a chord. 'What kind of tough nut is going to drink in an old man's bar like this?' In his heart Jim knew that his brave show was little more than bravado.

They had been pushed into the bar by the irrational force of simply being men. Roger had always fought at the first hint of a personal insult, and he knew that he owed it to his masculinity not to back down to another. But suddenly Jim really did not want to be there. He wanted to leave, and was more than satisfied that they had at least stepped foot in the bar.

Roger finished his beer. 'One more?' he asked, glancing around the bar. He had not shaved for a couple of days and a large black hand of stubble gripped his chin.

'This is a waste of time,' Jim said. 'How about we make a move back to The Stanford?'

'Just one more,' Roger insisted. 'And then we'll go.'

Jim nodded. It seemed all right. Roger picked up his coat and walked towards the door.

'Where are you going? I thought we were having one more.'

'It's dead in here, let's go into the public bar next door.' Roger seemed convinced that the danger of confrontation was over. His shoulders were now relaxed and his eyes were once again alive with wrinkles. He wanted to enjoy his beer. His 'job' was done and he led the way next door.

The public bar was swollen with drinkers. The moment Jim was enveloped by the soft wall of cigarette smoke at the door, and carried in its haze through to the bar, he knew Bill was in the room. He hoped that he was overreacting by creating a situation out of nothing, but if it were possible to make things come true just by thinking about them, then this was surely the one time when it would work.

Roger handed Jim a pint and walked over to the pool

table. He added a couple of coppers to the short line of coins on the edge of the table for a game. Jim followed him, glancing furtively either side of the path Roger made. He checked faces and then quickly looked away, sipping his pint as a distraction before looking back to check another group of people. Roger moved to one side and Jim's gaze continued to the dartboard on the opposite wall. It locked on the cocky, laughing face walking back from the chalkboard towards his opponent. Of course it was Bill, he realised the same time as his adrenal glands did. The pointed jaw and sharp nose looked in Jim's direction. Jim turned and walked quickly back to the bar.

Roger came over. 'We should be on soon: there's only a couple of games in front of us. If they're playing doubles by the time they get to us I'll take one of them up. But it looks like it'll be singles.'

'To be honest I'm not that bothered about a game of pool.' He leant casually against the bar.

'How about darts?' Roger asked.

'No, I'm all right with my beer. I'm pretty tired. I just feel like taking it easy.' He swallowed hard at his pint.

By the time Jim and Roger had finished their third pint it was Roger's turn on the pool table. He walked over and picked up his penny. He dropped it into his jacket pocket and then rummaged in his jeans. He called to Jim. 'Fifty pence piece. Have you got one?'

Bill had walked over to the pool table and was looking down at the line of coins. He spoke to Roger.

Roger was on his haunches by the coin slot. He stuck his hand out as Jim approached. He laughed and gestured to Bill with his head. 'This joker reckons he's on next.' Roger laughed again: a deep, satisfied guffaw. He introduced the coin into the slot. 'Ours were the only pennies in the line.

I've told him but he won't listen.' He racked the red and yellow balls alternately into the black triangle. When they were all in, he rolled the triangle back and positioned it over the black marker dot.

Jim and Bill looked at each other. Bill looked indifferently at him, like a bored butcher looking at yet another carcass. He winked and then spoke quietly but with assurance. 'I'm on next. And then my mates are.' He spoke directly to Jim. Then he looked over his shoulder to his two friends, now standing right behind him. He spoke to Roger again. 'You can pay if you like, mate, but we're on next.'

Roger raised himself up in front of Bill. 'You're on after me and my mate,' he said calmly. 'No arguments.' He reached for a cue. 'So if you don't mind...' He waited patiently for Bill to get out of the way.

A girl in her middle twenties wearing a pair of jeans and a white blouse was standing at the end of the table. She held a pool cue in one hand and a cigarette in the other. She was tall and thin, over-dressed and overly made-up for the pub. Her high heels boosted her above most of the heads around her. 'So which one of you two mugs is on next? I won and it's winner stays on,' she said testily. 'You can't both play. I haven't got all night and there are other people waiting to be beaten. So one of you get on with it.'

Bill snapped loudly at the girl. He did not turn to her as he spoke, but continued to stare at Roger. 'Shut it, Jane! I'm on next. You just shut it!' His sudden shout silenced the chatter in the bar.

The girl took a puff of her cigarette. 'I'll shut it when you stop bleating and sort your date out with your boyfriend there. Once you've done that you can gaze into each other's eyes all you like.'

People on the nearby tables cast interested glances

towards the first of the inevitable Friday night arguments. Jim stepped back two paces into the crowd. Bill turned to the girl.

'I said shut it! That means fucking shut it! Got it? Shut your fucking mouth!' He snatched the cue from her. 'I'm on and it's my break. You sit down and stay out of this!'

Roger looked up at Bill with mild amusement. 'Okay mate, you've had your fun. Time to move aside now unless you're playing instead of your lady friend.' He looked over to the girl and smiled. She smiled back.

'Nobody's asking the slag anything,' Bill said. 'I'm on, and that's the end of it.' He stamped his foot on the ground and stormed to the white ball at head of the table.

A quietness had come over Roger. He had the calm air of a patient teacher. He was smiling and shaking his head at the predictability of the situation. He walked towards Bill.

Bill dropped his cue and let his hands fall to his side. He moved away from the table. He glared cold-eyed at Roger and said: 'You want an argument you little shit, you've got one! Come on then, let's see what you can do.'

The tension had quickly spread around the bar. People sat motionless with their heads down so as not to involve themselves. Those closest to the table had drawn their chairs out of the way. Jim knew that if a fight broke out, Bill's two friends would no doubt join in, and also knew that he would be expected to do the same.

Roger and Bill were now face to face. Roger was still smiling calmly. He looked as though he was about to present Bill with an award.

Suddenly there was a loud crash accompanied by a flurry of shouts and then a dumbstruck silence. Bill was slumped face down on the pool table, groaning, with one hand holding the back of his head. Jane had taken another cue from the rack and had smashed it over the back of his head. She stood motionless with the split remains of wood in her hand.

'Never call me slag again,' she said. Her voice was shaky but her chin jutted forward defiantly. One of the customers let out a tentative titter, and then another joined in, and then one more, until the whole bar was filled with expansive, relieved laughter. Roger bowed courteously to Jane. She curtsied back.

The laughter stopped as Bill got up. He smiled. He seemed to have forgotten Roger, and studied the grinning faces that surrounded him. An instant later he had spun on his heels and thrown a hard, fast punch at Jane. He caught her full in the eye and she crashed to the floor. Bill's friends were suddenly upon him and dragging him out of the pub. Roger made to go after them, but Jim rushed forward and grabbed his arm.

'Don't, Roger! The girl. Let's look after her.'

Roger yanked his sleeve from Jim's grip. 'Leave it Jim. I've got to go. He deserves it. He's got it coming.' He moved towards the door.

Jane had been helped up and was suddenly standing in Roger's way. Her skirt was wet with beer and one side of her blouse was filthy from the floor. She held an arm out. 'Don't!' she said firmly. 'Don't go, it's not worth it.'

'How can you say that after what he did to you? He's got it coming.'

She held Roger's arm. 'I know he has. Has done for a long time. But not you, not now.'

Roger was about to speak but Jane cut him short. 'Nasty pieces of work those three. You never know what they're carrying, but it's always something. I've known them too long.' She was alarmingly unruffled and spoke as though she had 'been there' and 'done that' many times before. She picked up her coat and walked out.

Roger looked around at the stunned faces in the bar. 'What do I do?' he said helplessly. 'Shall I go for it?'

Jim led him to the bar. He ordered two pints.

'Forget it Roger, it wasn't your fight.'

'But it was. She got hit because of me.'

'She was standing up for herself, not you. She did what she had to do and that's the end of it. Forget it. It *wasn't* personal, it could've been anyone. He won't remember your face, just as he doesn't know what the next person he hits will look like.'

Roger looked hard into Jim's eyes. 'Was that the bloke who hit you?'

Jim looked away and shook his head. 'No. I'd remember a face like that.'

'Because if it is...'

'Look, Roger it wasn't him, I'm telling you. If you're upset, worry about the girl, not me.'

Maybe worry about yourself as well, Jim thought.

Chapter Eleven

Brighton and Preston cemetery was indeed perfect. Six weeks after he had first been there, Jim returned during the day to confirm what he already suspected. He had taken a bunch of flowers so that his presence would not be noticed. What could be less memorable than a man with flowers in a cemetery?

The only information he now required which he thought could not be obtained quickly by stealth and observation, was what time the cemetery was closed to visitors. This was an easy phone call. The side gate was never locked, it seemed, and should he not want to be disturbed by an actual burial taking place, the funeral services themselves were always completed by 3 p.m. in the winter, and 4 p.m. in the summer. There were hardly any burials any more, the lady on the phone had continued; mostly cremations because of the lack of space. The number of burials was down to about four or five a week. There was a new, larger site out of town that had recently opened to cope with the overspill.

That was good enough for Jim. There were no houses at the top end of the road leading to the main gate and only one either side of the junction with the main road. Of the burials that had obviously taken place recently, he estimated that at six ceremonies a week, the flattest mound of earth was over four weeks old.

He checked one of the recent burials and was pleased to see that the rain had not yet made the earth sink. Removing and replacing the earth should go unnoticed. Obviously there were plenty of sites. He would not make the decision of exactly which one to use until a couple of days before he killed Bill.

Choosing the method of doing this had taken some thought. He had spent night after night pondering the steps that would have to be taken to work out Bill's routine. He would need to be familiar with where he lived, whom he saw, where he was most likely to be at any given time. But hardest of all, he would need to find a way of luring him to somewhere secluded. The dangers were obvious. Not only would he have to do it as precisely as possible, but he would also need to protect himself. The idea for disposing the body had come in what he considered to be a flash of brilliance. All he had to do now was make contact with Bill. He would not have to make his face known. For all Jim knew he could be spying on him now. He had been very careful in his movements recently and was banking on the fact that Bill would be too preoccupied with stalking Glenda to waste time on scaring him. The idea of using Glenda, directly or indirectly as a lure, began to gestate in his mind.

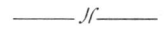

———— *Jf* ————

Jim was shocked to return home and discover that an intruder had sprayed a threatening message over one of the walls inside his flat. He rushed outside immediately in case *he* was still there.

His street suddenly felt alien and unwelcoming. He looked around at his building and realised he was shaking. He perched himself on the wall and checked for signs of him. He looked up and down the street and strained to look into the windows of the parked cars. At any moment he expected to see a smiling face staring back at him. If Bill knew where he lived, then he must have been followed. He was angry. Nobody should know where he lived unless he wanted them to. The thought of Bill prowling around his flat infused him with panic.

When he had calmed down and was certain that nobody was watching him, he stole back into his flat.

The stale smell of tobacco was in the air and he imagined Bill strolling confidently around blowing great draughts of smoke ahead of him. Jim looked at the floor as he walked through to the lounge. Bill would have trodden on the same carpet. Jim wanted to shout with outrage at this literal invasion of privacy. His stomach turned as he looked up and saw the message again.

On one of the walls in the lounge, big letters read, BE CAREFUL, WANKER.

Pictures had been taken down from the wall and were resting against the skirting board. Bill had moved furniture to give himself access to spray the wall. But what Jim had not noticed before, and what he now found so chilling was that *he* must have been so relaxed and had such presence of mind, that he had even taken the time to punctuate what he wrote.

Jim surveyed the room. There were more shadows than he remembered and there seemed to be new areas of darkness in every corner. The unconscious bubble of safety and invulnerability that he normally knew on his home ground had been pierced by *his* entry. The structure of his home suddenly seemed to have been dismantled. The walls of the rooms were now no more than bricks placed on top of each other by someone; these had been sealed by a carpeted floor and low, concrete ceilings. The windows were small, thin sheets of easily broken glass held shut by flimsy stays and tiny screws. A single lock and two hinges kept his door closed to the outside world. It was no refuge. His mother could break in. He lived there because of an arrangement to give his landlord money; dozens of people had lived there before him and dozens would do so afterwards. There was nothing unique about his existence, except that while he paid his rent he knew he was supposed to have the exclusive right to this tangible portion of space. But that was the way things were supposed to be, not the way they were. What did someone like Bill care about rules and laws?

Chapter Twelve

That night, Jim went to the pub with Roger for a few pints. Throughout the evening, and each time he went to the toilet, he tried to telephone Glenda. He had told his friends at the pub that she would be there tonight to meet them. It was getting late, and Jim was becoming increasingly desperate to contact her. He rang her three times but each time it was engaged. By now his friends were starting to make fun of him and asking him if he had been 'blown out'. He tried to smile at their jokes.

He was thinking about the conversation he had had with Glenda on the phone earlier. He had spent half an hour persuading her to come to the pub. Bill had appeared briefly outside while she was on the phone. Jim was aware of this even before she whispered it to him because of the sudden change in her tone. At first she had been enthusiastic about going out, but the instant her voice dropped, so did her energy. She said quietly that she wanted to stay in. Jim had offered to pick her up in a cab, but she did not like the idea. He then suggested that she could meet him at the end of the back garden if that would be safer. And before she had time to reply he heard himself offering to come round and 'have a word' with Bill if he was still there. In the pause between his words and her refusal, which seemed to last tens of seconds, the pub's phone number came to him like the solution to a mathematical puzzle. If she accepted, he would have no choice but to phone Roger from a call box and ask him to 'happen' to be in the area at a given time.

There it was: he was scared again. The pause had never existed; she spoke immediately after he had.

'No don't do that, but thanks anyway,' Glenda said, a split second after his offer.

Fear flooded to his knees and he hated himself once more for being afraid. Eventually she had said that she would be at the pub by nine. By ten fifteen he was standing permanently by the phone, punching frustratedly on the buttons in the hope that he would suddenly hear the hollow ringing. Yet again the beeps of the engaged signal came to his ear, and yet again he hung up and tried again. He had only drunk two pints, since he had realised he might have to drive, and was now ready to go. Roger must have sensed that something was wrong and was already walking over with his van keys. He said that Jim could borrow the van if he wanted to go and pick her up, and a couple of tries later he was on his way.

On the way back from the hospital the night he had first been attacked by Bill, Jim had been too shocked to take any notice of where Glenda lived. He remembered the road but was unsure of the number. It was either twenty-five or fifty-two. He arrived at half past ten and drove slowly up and down once. There was a line of about fifty terraced houses running along each side, broken up every ten or so by narrow alleys that shrunk into the dark gaps between the houses. All the houses looked the same; lights showing behind different coloured curtains. Doors closed and silent. There was nobody in the street.

He parked round the corner and began to walk as casually as he could. When he reached number twenty-five he glanced in through the gap in the curtains. He caught a glimpse of a figure moving and hesitated before stopping. He backed up a couple of paces and looked up and down the road. He was just about to step into the front garden when he noticed that an old lady was staring from the top window of the house next door. She was holding the net curtain back and was looking unswervingly at Jim. He dropped his head and walked on. However he viewed it, he was spying. He was Peeping Tom, and she had seen him. He felt her gaze follow him down the street and was glad when he turned the corner. When enough time had passed for the old lady to have lost interest he crossed the road and began to check the other side.

The upstairs light of the old lady's house was still on but she did not appear to be at the window. He moved slowly, with his senses keen like a prowling cat, straining to look at everything in his field of vision without ever facing what he was studying. When he was opposite the old lady's house her curtain twitched and he dropped his gaze. In doing so he caught sight of a silhouette out of the corner of his eye. He lowered his gaze to the line of cars on the side of the road. The smooth line of saloons was broken by the square edges of a pick-up truck. There was a person in it, looking towards the house next to the one where the old lady was still at her window. It was a he, and the he was smoking a cigarette.

Within a couple of seconds Jim was level with the truck. The head turned as though the person had heard his footsteps. Jim had not noticed the sound of his walking before, but now each pace clopped onto the pavement as noisily as a horse's hoof. He just managed to avoid the eyes of the angular face in the car, but he could feel them staring at him, recognising him, he thought, moody and dangerous, ready to strike. He quickened his pace. At the end of the road he crossed without looking back. When he stopped around the corner his heart was racing but not pounding hard. He coughed, and a dry spray of nervous breath flew from his mouth. It was undoubtedly Bill, and if Jim had noticed him, he was sure that Glenda would have done as well and would definitely not be leaving by the front door. Jim pulled up his sleeve and looked anxiously at his watch. It was ten thirty-five. Glenda was trapped. If she still intended going to the pub her only way out would be via the back garden.

Jim dipped his head and crossed the road. He slipped into the nearest alley. The orange light of the street lamps was cut off at an angle by the front house like a wedge of cheese sliced by a wire. The light soon tapered off into pitch darkness. Jim walked blindly with his hands outstretched until he reached the end of the alley where it was a little lighter. He turned left and made his way along the path at the bottom of the back gardens which ran parallel to the road. This was dimly lit by the occasional light shining through bedroom curtains and kitchen blinds. The intriguing outline of a silhouette moved behind a frosted bathroom window. Jim paused for a moment before moving on. The path was overgrown and he stepped carefully through the long gate of dense branches that clung unnervingly at his trousers. He awaited the obligatory sound of a dog barking or perhaps cats fighting or even people arguing. But he heard nothing except the precise crack of breaking twigs and the suction of mud underfoot. He counted the gardens, and when he had reached the tenth house he stopped. The upstairs lights of the eleventh were on. The old lady's house. He muttered a few words of encouragement to himself. He blinked rapidly as he stared into the slate-black window panes of what he believed to be Glenda's house. He checked up and down the alley and a few seconds later checked again. After a third look he stepped over the picket fence that lay on its side like a disused piece of railway track and tiptoed to the back door. Still no dog, no prying eyes, no police siren. His worry was subdued by the spike of excitement that prodded him forward. Twenty to eleven. The green luminous hands and dots on his watch seemed to be floating above his wrist and magically following it around.

He knew that he should walk away and call Glenda tomorrow. But the excitement quickly returned and urged him on. He stooped and cupped his hands over the back window. A thin bar of light shone through the gap at the bottom of the door ahead. He rapped lightly on the glass. He looked around again, waiting for one of the neighbours to rush out brandishing a cricket bat. After a few seconds he tapped again, but louder. Then he knelt and tapped a third time. He heard a sharp click but was not sure where it came from. He scrambled onto his hands and knees and squashed himself behind the old fridge that was standing by the side fence. The snap of a light switch? But there was no light. He crept out from behind the fridge and peeped into the kitchen. It was black and empty. Suddenly he heard the click again, and then again. He moved quickly behind the fridge. The sound was coming from the path. It was the snap of twigs. The steps came closer, but were moving slowly. This person was definitely looking. The feet stopped. Jim curled himself up on the damp grass and brought his knees to his chest. He stared intently towards the end of the garden through the gap between the fence and fridge. Slowly a figure became visible, like a shadow being poured into a mould.

'Who's there?' a man's voice said. 'I know there's someone here. I saw someone come round.'

Jim realised he had been holding his breath and let it out as quietly as he could.

The voice spoke again, almost in a friendly way, and at the same time a funnel of light spouted from the kitchen and cast a dim crescent onto the garden. The tone of the voice changed suddenly. 'Who's there? Is it you, dead meat?' The figure stopped speaking and remained still.

Jim was coiled tightly and he feared the slightest change in position would give him away.

'Kill the bastard. Kill the bastard,' his mind taunted. 'Kill the bastard or else take this crap for ever.'

The figure raised an arm, obviously communicating with the person in the house. His fist was clenched and he held it out like a military salute. He laughed, but not so loudly that the person in the house would be able to hear him. He waved half-heartedly and then dropped his arm by his side before turning and walking away.

When the sound of the steps had faded Jim jumped up and peered into the window. He was breathing quickly and tried to calm himself so he would not appear scared.

Glenda was still looking towards the end of the garden. As Jim came into view she jumped and screamed in a whisper, 'I'll call the police!'

'It's me! Jim!' he said urgently. 'Quick, let me in!'

Her eyes were frightened and her mouth was open ready to shout again. She edged towards the door with her arms folded, squinting to see outside.

'It's me, Glenda. It's Jim. Let me in.'

She opened the door and hurried him through to the lounge. She drew the gap in the curtains together and turned the television up. Jim sat on the brown settee and

Glenda sat opposite him on an upright wooden chair with her back to the window.

'Sorry about the surprise,' Jim said after a moment. He brushed at his trousers. 'Sorry about the mud as well.'

Glenda was wearing a long white bathrobe. She pulled it tightly down over her knees as she sat down. She was still open-mouthed, breathing hard, as though she had been running. Her hair was wet and beads of water ran down the side of her face like sweat. She looked at him in astonishment. 'I saw Bill outside. I'm sure of it. He was out there.'

Jim shrugged his shoulders. 'I know, we nearly had a little run-in. But he's gone now. He didn't see me come in, I'm sure of that. I came around the back because I didn't want to cause any trouble. Your phone was off the hook and I was worried. I know you said you might not come, but I was just... well... worried.' He looked at the window. 'Especially with our friend out there.'

Glenda stood up. 'I appreciate your concern, but I can look after myself. You'll only make things worse by coming here. If you two get into another fight I'll be the one who'll suffer in the end. He'll get mad, and the madder he gets the more jealous he becomes, and the more jealous he becomes, the more he follows me.' Her eyes were dark and enraged although she was speaking in a whisper. 'Jim, I thought we were just a bit of fun, nothing serious...'

'We are,' Jim agreed, 'but I was just a little worried, that's all.'

'I enjoy the time we have together, but...' She paused and then said calmly. 'This is just casual, isn't it. I thought you understood. I'm glad of your company, I've been transformed since we met. It's great hiding a secret from him. But he is still there,' she pointed outside, 'and a secret affair is all we can be.'

'Well I'm sure he's gone now,' Jim said. 'And he won't be back tonight, not with me here.' He sounded like a child speaking lines written for Clint Eastwood. His hands were shaking and he thrust them into his pockets. 'And things are fine for me as well, Glenda. I understand, I *really* do. You don't have to worry about me. An easy life, that's all I want.'

'I can live with things as they are at the moment,' Glenda went on, 'but I don't want to rock the boat. I don't want to get hurt. I don't think you liked it much yourself, did you?'

That comment spoke to Jim's depths, the place where there was no disguising the truth. He stood up. 'Do you want me to leave? I don't mind, just say,' he said petulantly.

Glenda came over and took his hand. She was barefoot and was not wearing any make-up. Her skin looked fresh and young and her eyes were clear. He put his arms around her and pulled her close.

'I'm sorry, but I was worried about you. That's all. I didn't mean any harm.'

Glenda did not resist the hug. She spoke quietly from behind his head. 'I appreciate it. But getting him mad doesn't help me.'

'Would it be better if I went now?' Jim said. 'I really don't want to cause any trouble. But as I said, I was worried. I won't do it again, honest.'

'I think it might be better.'

He tried to find some regret in her words.

'Why don't you come with me? We could sneak out the back. We've missed last orders but maybe we could get a curry or something? It'd be a great laugh, and then at least you'd be away from him. We'd both be away from him,' he added.

Glenda stared at him for a few seconds. Jim could feel the tension rising before she spoke. 'I thought you understood.' She paused. 'You of all people should know. You shouldn't ask me these things. I'm not doing anything while he's around. I really like you, but...'

But what? he thought. He waited for her to continue but she did not. 'I'm sorry,' he said feebly, 'I just thought you might like to get away from here for a bit. I thought a break might be nice. I'm only asking for your sake. I want you to have a nice time, that's all. I just want everything to be all right for you.'

Glenda took his hands and kissed them. 'I appreciate it, I really do. It seems strange having someone else in on my horrible secret.' She closed her eyes and inhaled slowly. Her chest swelled against his. 'But one day I'm determined to be free again. That's going to happen.'

Jim pulled away and looked at her in amazement. 'What do you mean?'

Glenda closed her eyes and nodded. A long tear snaked down her cheek. 'I suppose my only choice is to run away. With him here there's no chance of that. I would give everything up for my freedom. My family, my friends, his life...'

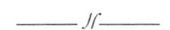

———*Jf*———

The girl is in the man's thoughts again as the bus draws into the town centre. In just two stops it will be outside her shop. This time she will want to see him. He is still full of the television programme he saw late the night before about relationships. He would not normally watch something like that, but for some reason it caught his attention.

'Give her space,' he recites to himself. 'Give her space and allow her to be herself. She has her own personality. Allow it to be free.' A sudden flush of anxiety makes him sweat. Give her space, he thinks. If I don't, she will only run away. It is inevitable. He tries to strengthen his resolve so that he will appear relaxed and open when he sees her. But the idea of her having a new boyfriend infuriates him. Especially a coward.

The man sweats more as his guilt makes him remember some of the times he has gone to her house to 'talk'. He has always lost his temper. He grips hard on the seat in front of him and begins to shake it. He is so annoyed with himself for losing his temper at those times. Why couldn't he just talk? Listen and be reasonable; that's how he wants to be with her more than anything.

The person sitting on the seat in front turns around to see why it is being shaken so violently. He asks the man what he is doing and tells him to stop it. His tone is aggressive.

The man is still thinking about the girl and it is a few seconds before he realises that there is someone shouting at him. His instant reaction is fury. A surge of power fills his body, and at that moment he is not scared of anyone or anything in the world. He knows there is no reason to be. The worst that can happen is that he will be physically hurt. Or he might even die. Where's the fear in that? He is about to thrust his chin towards his fellow passenger, flash his enraged eyes and spit out a challenge to get off the bus and fight when he realises the bus has stopped outside the girl's shop. He does not want to cause trouble here.

He sees the girl in the shop. She is talking to a customer and cannot see the bus, let alone the man staring like a sweaty schoolboy out of the window. She is distant and beautiful. He wants to work things out with her so that he can be near her.

The bus pauses as people get on and off. The man is about to stand up and walk off when with a cringe he remembers the ghost train that morning. It was stupid of him to follow her in, he knows, but he wanted to talk to her so much. He is mad that he lost his temper and looks around with embarrassment in case anyone has read his thoughts.

The bus pulls away and the man sits back. The person in front has turned away. The man's indignation has gone. He must learn to relax. He is proud that he did not smack the person in front of him.

Chapter Thirteen

Jim and Glenda had spent the evening in The Stanford Arms and then gone for a curry. Jim had finally introduced her to his friends and they had spent most of the evening chatting at the bar. Glenda had mentioned that she had been to a few travel agents and was looking forward to going away soon.

Back at Jim's flat Glenda was standing by the window staring out at the road. Jim brought in two cups of tea and set them down on the table in front of the sofa.

'Tea's up,' he said, sitting down.

Glenda looked over her shoulder and then back out of the window. 'Thanks,' she said listlessly.

'Are you okay?' he asked.

She had not been very keen about coming back. Now he was getting the impression that he had press-ganged her into being there.

'Is there something wrong? Didn't you enjoy tonight?'

Glenda came and sat beside Jim. She cupped her tea in both hands and took a sip. 'What makes you say that? I had a great time. Your friends were really nice.'

'You seem a bit distant, that's all. Have I done something?'

Glenda put her tea down. 'No it's nothing, I'm fine. Maybe I've had a bit too much to drink.'

'Three rum and cokes?'

'Well maybe it was the food, then. I don't eat curry very often. Perhaps it was that. It certainly didn't seem to agree with Alan, did it?'

'I don't know why they don't just serve it on the pavement outside and cut out the middleman.'

Glenda smiled weakly at Jim's joke. She picked her tea up again. 'I'm sorry,' she said. 'I shouldn't have come back. I'm not very good company tonight. I don't know what it is, but you're right, I don't feel too good. I'll be okay tomorrow.' She looked over the lip of her cup at Jim. 'Would you mind calling me a cab? I'd quite like to get home, if that's okay. I think I just need a decent night's sleep.'

She smiled. Jim knew he understood the innuendo: even if she stayed she would not be in danger of missing a night's sleep through lovemaking. They had made love a total of twenty times on nineteen different occasions. He had never felt comfortable in bed with Glenda, but knew that would all change once they could spend time together and relax properly. He took her hand. 'I'll call you a cab now,' he said, defeated.

Jim picked up the phone and before he had brought it to his ear the unruly voice in his mind said, 'All you understand is that she wants to leave the country because she hates you. She's not going home tonight. She's off to see another man.'

Fifteen minutes later the doorbell rang. He walked Glenda to the cab and they kissed goodbye.

'I'm really sorry about this,' she said. 'I'll call you tomorrow. You mentioned going to see Mrs Muurling. We could go tomorrow night, maybe.'

'Okay, we'll talk tomorrow. I've got to speak to Alan. He's got a car and he's going to come along as well. He's agreed to do me and Mrs Muurling a big favour,' Jim said, trying to sound cryptic.

When Glenda's cab had pulled away, Jim went back in and called another cab. It arrived within a few minutes. He leant into the passenger window and told the driver to go to Glenda's address. Jim jumped into the back seat and pulled out his wallet. He began to look through the old bus tickets and betting slips he found in there in an attempt to appear occupied and so avoid a conversation with the driver.

The voice in his mind would not keep silent. It imbued him with a feeling of satisfaction. 'She's up to something,' it told him. 'She doesn't want to be with you. What can you give her?' His excitement was forceful. 'You'll find her out and be proven right. Maybe the whole thing is a joke and she loves Bill and they're having a bit of fun with you!'

But he was conscious of his betrayal. Testing her was wrong and cruel, he tried to convince himself. What on earth am I up to? he suddenly thought. This is just what *he* would do. On the spot, Jim decided that if he trusted her and did not go to her house, then everything would be all right. It was one of those spontaneous superstitions that he did not really believe but to which he was nevertheless bound. It was the same as avoiding the cracks in the pavement on the way to school so that he would pass an exam; or managing to get changed before a song on the radio ends so that a date works out well.

He leant forward to tell the cabby to turn around, but as he made eye contact in the mirror he quickly looked down at the bus ticket he was holding. It was the one from his cemetery search. Suddenly he was angry. He saw Bill's face and heard the unruly voice in his mind as Bill's taunting voice. He touched at the bump to the side of the bridge of his nose that was now a permanent reminder of their encounter. He screwed the ticket up and put it in the ashtray.

'Change of plan,' Jim said. 'Could you take me to the Lewes Road. I can't remember where exactly, but I'll know when we get there.'

It was a ten minute walk to the cemetery from where Jim asked the driver to stop. He walked up the steep hill of Hartington Road with his hands in his pockets and his head bowed. Soon he reached the imposing iron gates to the cemetery that spanned the cul-de-sac to his left. It was a cold night. There was no cloud cover and the moon gave Jim the company of his shadow. He walked through the gates and was suddenly struck by the bright light shining from a pair of marble tombstones in front of him. They stood out like fluorescent bars of soap. Jim stared at them as if in a trance. They glowed like beacons and he felt drawn to investigate; to see what kind of person deserved such conspicuousness in death. But a gust of wind blew and his skin tightened with goose pimples of cold and apprehension. He moved quickly off the path onto the grass and began to thread through the mass of monuments and headstones. The graveyard was vast; indeed as the vicar in the country church had said, 'like New York to the resident mice.'

Within a minute he came across a recent burial. A large mound of earth was heaped in front of a modest stone cross. There was no epitaph, simply a name and an inscription: 'Frederick Johnson. Beloved husband.' Jim kicked at the earth and a cascade of dirt fell down over his shoe. He glanced around and then fell to his knees. He scooped at the mound with his hands. The earth came away easily. After a few handfuls he began to scrape the dirt he had pulled away back onto the mound. A thought struck him. The countless shovelfuls of earth he intended heaping on the grass beside the grave would no doubt ruin it, and make it obvious that the site had been tampered with. He would have to bring a tarpaulin with him onto which he could dump the earth while he dug. He remembered now: the two funerals he had been to, and those he had seen in films, all used plastic sheeting to surround the grave. He was encouraged that his mind was on the task and moved further into the cemetery. He passed one of the luminous marble tombstones and was tempted to stop and read it, still drawn to the light. But another spontaneous superstition told him that if he managed to avoid reading any of these, the murder would go smoothly. A wrench of nerves pulled in his stomach as the word 'murder' came to mind. I'm at the scene of the crime, he thought confidently. It *will* happen, and here, and soon. He felt his eyes being drawn to the large black letters of the marble tombstone and he wanted to look. But soon his legs had taken him past and his attention was drawn to the next recent burial. He cut across to the opposite perimeter. He began to walk faster as his excitement grew. He counted each new burial mound. Five, six, seven, eight! At the far end of the cemetery, furthest from the gates and street lamps, a low wooden fence was lined with a single row of bushy trees. He looked over the fence expecting to see a housing estate or some shops, but there was nothing except for a jumble of interlocking allotments stretching into the darkness. This was only broken after about a hundred yards by the dim lights of some houses. This *was* perfect. Another idea suddenly sprang to mind; he could use the tarpaulin to wrap the body as well as for protecting the grass. His mind was racing. He had grown immeasurably in confidence over the past ten minutes so that he felt invincible; he wished he were burying the body that night. This satisfied him. He now knew he would not be afraid. He could go through the ordeal without cowardice. For the first time in his life he experienced what seemed like bravery.

Chapter Fourteen

Mrs Muurling had baked two cakes. She had cut them into neat triangles and placed four pieces onto matching china plates. A crisp white linen tablecloth covered the table in the back room and a doily lay under each of the plates. She had brought two chairs through from the front room and had positioned the seating arrangement in a neat semicircle around the table in the lounge. Tea was waiting for them when they arrived. The front door was open, as were all of the windows. The curtains were drawn wide and a warm breeze explored the house, acquainting itself with each room for possible visits in the future. The difference was startling. Gone was the sad air of neglect, as was the claustrophobic mustiness that seemed to have been stained into the furniture and carpets.

Jim introduced Glenda and Alan to Mrs Muurling and then they all sat down and looked out at the flat crop of the recently mown lawn through the patio doors.

Mrs Muurling was looking well. Her hair was tied into a tight bun and she was wearing make-up and a brightly coloured flower-print dress. She wore matching strings of pearls around her wrist and neck. At first she seemed a little apprehensive about being in company. But Alan's ease of conversation soon created a comfortable mood. Alan was in his early forties and had long dyed-black hair and a straggly beard. He always wore a bandanna around his neck. His brother-in-law owned The Stanford Arms, where he was barman, so he had a job for life.

'How did you all meet?' Mrs Muurling asked.

Alan took the initiative. He spoke quickly and almost without punctuation, like a child telling a parent about something exciting. 'Me and Jimmy go back a long way. The bar in fact, alcohol and philosophy rather than law. Me and Glen only met a few days ago in the pub. Short and sweet, eh Glen?'

'Me or our acquaintance?' Glenda said with a smile.

'Good one.' Alan nodded. 'Good one.'

Jim was worried that the conversation might return to his bar habits. 'Anyone for more cake? Tea?' he said.

'Perhaps in a minute,' Mrs Muurling said. 'But first, Jim, you never did tell me how you and Glenda met. Don't tell me, in a pub.' She chuckled. 'That's how me and my husband met. Well, at a fair really. Not far from the beer tent. He liked a drink, and I have to admit I'm rather partial to a little tipple myself.'

'A dry cleaners. We met in a dry cleaners,' Glenda said, glancing at Jim with obvious embarrassment. 'I was working there and Jim came to have a stain removed from his trousers. Hardly *Dr Zhivago*.'

'Beer stain, hopefully, Jimmy boy?' Alan interjected.

Jim ignored the comment. He knew he was blushing and would even have welcomed another of Alan's facetious comments to take the attention away from himself.

Mrs Muurling saved him from reddening further. She said to Glenda, 'Have you worked in the dry cleaners long?'

'A few months. It's nothing permanent. I'm in between things at the moment.'

'Talking of being in between things...' Alan produced a half-bottle of scotch from his jacket pocket. He unscrewed the top. 'I'm dying for a little snifter. I'm driving, but what the hell.' He stood up and offered the bottle to Mrs Muurling's teacup. 'Mrs M. Join me in one?'

'Tea and scotch hardly go. Then again neither should stout and champagne and I've had a few of those in my time. Go on then, Alan, why not?' She put her hand up quickly to stop him pouring. 'But only if everyone else has a drop to keep us company.'

'Don't mind if I do,' Glenda said, thrusting her cup forward.

Jim also offered his cup to the bottle. He was looking at Mrs Muurling in disbelief. He was proud to know her. She smiled at him. 'Thank you', she mouthed.

'You certainly know how to pick the babes, Jimmy boy.' Alan toasted with his cup.

Jim nodded. It was one of the best feelings he had ever had. It was like being in the centre of a wonderful world and he was its creator.

'And what do you want to do with yourself?' Mrs Muurling asked Glenda when they were all sitting again. 'When you've finished with the dry cleaners I mean.'

Glenda glanced at Jim and then said, 'Funny you should ask. Only today I applied for some colleges to do a degree course.'

'What a cow,' the unruly voice in Jim's head said.

He tried to smile as he asked a question but was fighting the anger he could feel coming. 'Which ones?' he said as lightly as he could.

Glenda swallowed. 'Erm, Nottingham, Liverpool, Manchester and London.' She sipped at her tea and shuffled on her seat.

'What about poor Jim here! Leaving him all alone?' Alan joked.

'Did you think about the local colleges?' Mrs Muurling asked. 'They're supposed to be very good.'

Jim listened intently for the answer. As Glenda spoke it seemed to him that he was watching her on television. For a moment nothing seemed real.

'I just fancied a change, that's all. I've lived in Brighton for a long time. I wouldn't mind seeing another part of the country.'

'Bitch!' the unruly voice shouted.

Jim spoke to Mrs Muurling to change the subject. 'I told Glenda and Alan about the casket. They're the help we're counting on. It looks like all systems are go. We can set off almost any time.' He could already feel the scotch numbing his lips. But only after I kill Bill. I'll be happier then, he thought. Then we'll go. Set Glenda free to be with me first.

Mrs Muurling stared back at Jim without any expression on her face, like a poorly painted portrait. Then a tear came to her eye. She brought her hands to her mouth and spoke. 'I don't know what to say. I mean, this is something I wish I could deal with myself.' She lowered her head. 'But I can't. Please don't feel obliged to help. I know you're probably all very busy. But if you really mean you'll help...' She wiped some tears from her cheeks. 'I just don't know what to say. I really am very grateful. You're all so kind. You don't know how much this means to me. I can't believe it.'

Alan stood up. 'You're a cool gal, Mrs M. As far as I'm concerned if you need a little help, I've got the wheels and they're all yours.'

'Me too,' Glenda said.

'But we don't even know each other, I mean...'

'That's what's so unreal about it,' Alan said with a broad smile. 'This is living. We're doing it. Let's make plans now! I've never been to Cornwall either.' He took a swig of scotch straight from the bottle.

Jim sat back in relief. He looked over at Mrs Muurling and she mouthed 'thank you' again. He stood up and took her hand. He said, looking her in the eye, 'It's my pleasure.'

Glenda and Alan were smiling.

Part two is on course, he thought. It won't be long, thank goodness. Just the killing and then it can all end.

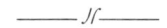

———— Jf ————

A pregnant woman is sitting across from the man on the bus. She has a child with her and three bags of shopping. As she gets up to leave the man jumps up to help, but a man nearer has beaten him to it. They wheel past him. The man smiles at the toddler whose entire being is concentrated on the choc ice she has glued to her mouth. He goes back to his seat with his head down thinking that everyone is watching him.

The man never did manage to have a proper conversation with the girl about the abortion she had. He was never able to tell her how sad he was; and how much he would have loved their child, and how safe he would have made their lives.

It was about that time when he started following her.

The lady with the child waves at her helper as the bus pulls away.

The man sticks a cigarette in his mouth without lighting it, ready for his stop.

Chapter Fifteen

It was the end of May and not getting dark until nearly nine o'clock. The shroud of anonymity that the cold, dark nights of the winter months afforded had disappeared almost overnight. Suddenly the trees were in flower and the sun shone whenever it could. The town was busier. The drudgery in the steps of people going about their daily business was gone. Weary looks were exchanged for bright, friendly smiles that spread like a revelation. Everything happened longer and later, especially the number of people visiting the graveyard. This would be swelled by the addition of the fair-weather mourners. Older people who perhaps were not up to making the journey in the winter.

Jim and Roger were sitting in The Stanford Arms having their lunch. The pub was nearly empty.

Alan was talking to a customer a little further along the bar. They had the racing pages of the newspaper open in front of them and Alan was sipping a Bloody Mary. He came over and said hello before pulling them their usual pints.

'Why not call the office, Roger,' Jim said, 'see what the chances of any drops are.'

'Let's finish these, and if they haven't called by then, I'll turn the damn thing off,' Roger suggested with the mischievous grin that told Jim he had already made up his mind.

'I can't argue with that. Anyway I've got a few things to do this afternoon, I could use the time.'

'You not staying for a few beers?'

'I'd love to but,' Jim's mind raced to choose the right excuse, 'I'm a bit skint—'

'Don't worry about that, I'll get them in. I could sub you a few quid if you need it,' Roger interrupted.

'Also I said I'd help my auntie. She's getting some new furniture. She needs a hand moving it. I was thinking, Roger,' Jim continued casually, 'if you're not going to be using the van this afternoon, maybe I could...'

'Borrow it?'

'If it'd be all right. I might be back quite late though. She's got a shitload of stuff to move.'

'I won't need it until the morning. Look, sod it. I'm turning the mobile off. The office can whistle for us if they can't find any work on a Monday. If I'm not too shitfaced I might pop past your place tonight and get the keys, otherwise just pick me up tomorrow.' He dangled the keys in front of Jim. 'Have fun with your auntie,' he laughed.

Jim ignored Roger's sarcasm. It was like the pieces to a puzzle falling into place as they fell out of their box. Jim got up and walked to the end of the bar and called Alan over.

'What's up mate?' Alan asked as he sidled up.

'Mrs Muurling,' Jim said. 'You still on for going down to Cornwall? I was thinking about this weekend. What do you reckon?'

'You bet! She's great. I reckon this means a lot to her. It'd be great just to be part of it. Can you imagine! That box has been down there over fifty years. What a feeling if we find it.'

'If,' said Jim gravely. 'That's what I'm worried about. What if we can't find it? And what if he wrote a load of old crap...'

'She just wants to know. That'll be good enough for her. You always think you'll tie up the loose ends of your life as you go along. But people rarely do. It's too easy to put things off until another day. There's another day. Even the day before you die, that's just another day. But in this case the thing is cut and dried. Get there and read it. She's got the eyes, and all she needs is our arms and legs.'

Jim nodded as he took in what Alan said. 'You're right. I suppose I'm just nervous. I'm worried for her, you know? I'm sure it'll be all right.' He paused and then spoke the words he had rehearsed earlier. 'Listen, Alan. I've got something to say to you that you must promise *never* to repeat to anyone. No matter what. It's not serious, but it's important to me that I can trust you with this.'

'Shoot, Jimmy. I'm all ears and promises.'

Jim hesitated. Roger was waving his glass for another drink. Alan turned around. 'Lean over and pour it yourself. You've done it enough times when I haven't been looking!' Alan shouted.

'As I was saying,' Jim continued, 'what I want to say or ask is, if, for any reason I'm not around at the weekend, I want you to still go ahead with the trip. I'll call you Thursday anyway, but let's just say I don't and nobody has seen me. Will you promise that you'll keep what I've just said secret, and still go? Glenda's booked the hotel, it's all paid for.' He handed Alan a slip of paper with Mrs Muurling's number on it. 'Take this just in case. If she asks anything, tell her I had to visit someone who's ill or something like that.'

Alan took a deep breath and blew it out slowly. 'What's with this "if I'm not there" deal? Sounds pretty heavy to me.'

'It's not a big deal, honestly. Just something that might keep me away for a couple of days... Family matters,' he added. 'You know what it's like. But I need to be sure that you'll still help Mrs Muurling.'

'I'm not sure where you're at, but as I said, I'm in. I wouldn't miss it for the world. You'll definitely be there, but then again you might not. That's cool.' He gestured along the bar with his head. 'And the gang? What do they know?'

'Nothing. As I said, it's no big deal. But I'd like you to keep it under your bandanna all the same.'

Alan tapped his nose with his forefinger and nodded. 'I'll be hearing from you on Thursday, if not before.'

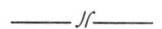

Jim drove the van the twenty miles along the coast to Eastbourne. He nosed inquisitively around the short one-way system a couple of times, orientating himself with the layout of the town before parking in a quiet street on the seafront.

It was a warm day, yet the sandy beach was nearly deserted. A long row of cars were parked on the promenade. They faced the sea and a few were occupied by old couples gazing at the scagulls playing above the small waves. He crossed the empty road and walked past a group of fish and chip shops, bed and breakfast houses and small, stripy souvenir shops and headed away from the front.

There was a small car accessory shop just around the corner from the promenade. 'NUMBER PLATES WHILE U WAIT' was printed on four number plates hanging on a board outside. It was an old shop with a hand-painted wooden board above the large, cluttered front window. Jim pushed the stiff door open. A loud brass bell reverberated on its spring and was still ringing when he reached the counter. It was dim and noticeably cooler than outside. Jim had a quick glance around before handing the man behind the counter a slip of paper with a registration number he had made up.

The man was old and hunched at the shoulders. His thin grey hair was greased neatly back and he wore a shirt with a tie under a pullover. He pushed his round spectacles up on the bridge of his nose and held the note out at arm's length. 'Both plates?' he asked, eyeing Jim. 'Front and back?'

'Yes please,' Jim replied politely. 'I also need the holes for the screws drilling exactly ten inches apart at the front and eleven and a half at the back.' He was pleased with his attention to detail and hoped the piece of string with which he had measured the gap between the screws on Roger's van was accurate. 'How long will that take?'

The man was writing in a notebook. 'People normally ask how much they will cost first,' the man said almost to himself. He walked to the end of the counter and consulted a list that was hanging from the wall on a red piece of string. 'Standard will be one hour. I can just squeeze you in before lunch. And they are eight pounds and ninety-nine pence the pair. With the holes, how about we call it a round tenner for cash,' the man said without a smile.

Jim paid and headed around the corner to the builders' merchant he had seen. It was a large, busy centre. Jim felt out of place in his clean clothes when he saw the cement- and paint-covered builders walking around. A man behind the counter caught his eye. Jim smiled and mouthed, 'just looking', before darting into one of the aisles.

The darkness of the cemetery seemed a long way away compared to the austere fluorescence of the modern building. Bins of stainless steel bolts shone beside heavy bags of galvanised nails. Black buckets were filled with wooden-handled hammers and trowels hung from a long string, like socks on a washing line. Printed rectangular signs hung down from the high ceiling above each row. Jim found a low trolley and headed for 'TOOLS'. He stopped at the shovels and looked at the prices. He was surprised by how expensive they were. They were hanging by the handle from a horizontal metal pole, and as far as Jim could see they were all the same. He moved towards a selection that was highlighted by a pink arrow on which 'Buy of the Week' was written. Jim unhooked one of the green and silver shovels from the rack and began to study it. He felt the smooth, plastic handle and ran his hand down to the shiny metal blade. He smiled at the thought of burying someone with a 'Buy of the Week' and placed it in his trolley. He moved on, walking meticulously, trying to calm his excited mind as he pondered the prices of the various items to which his eyes were drawn. After a few minutes, he found a twelve foot by twelve foot black tarpaulin. It was larger than he had wanted and not green as he imagined it would be. But black seemed okay. It was the only one left and he threw it onto the trolley. He began to inspect nearly every new product he came across. It seemed that everything he saw could be of some use. But he had only brought seventy pounds cash with him and that was going to have to do. Seventy pounds for a broken nose, a ruined shirt, a frightened girlfriend who was about to leave town and the trouble and cost of repainting his lounge wall. Seventy pounds in exchange for *his* life. That seemed to be the buy of the week.

He came to the bathroom fittings aisle and found himself staring into a mirror. He smiled. His face looked strange, as if he were looking at a brother he had never met. He grinned. I'm nearly a killer, he thought. Bill's face came to mind. His stomach tightened. The unruly voice agreed. 'Why not tonight?' they said in accord.

He paid for the shovel, tarpaulin and dust sheet and took them back to the van. He had been tempted to buy a hammer, but he had held one for weight and tested it for reach and was not entirely happy. The impact would be too precise, covering too small an area. He decided to stick with the original idea, the English version, not the American. A cricket bat, rather than a baseball bat, from the first sports shop he saw, was the final ingredient.

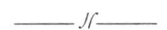

———— *Jf* ————

That night Jim rounded the corner of his road and headed towards the chip shop. It was raining lightly. A thin haze of drizzle hung from the street lamps. He hurried into the breeze. His hair was soon wet and he turned his collar up in unconscious deference to his Hollywood screen idols. He would confront Bill. He was confident. Tonight *was* the night.

It was hot inside the chip shop, but in contrast to the wet of outside, Jim found even the fatty atmosphere of The Ocean Platter quite heartening. He passed the long queue of people waiting for takeaways, and nodded at the small Greek man behind the counter. He walked through the white Formica alcove to the tables out the back. He was trembling as he lowered himself into his seat: he would have to eat so that he had a reason for being there, but he was sure he would not be able to swallow his food. His mouth was dry. It was hard enough to swallow air. He picked up the menu and peered cautiously over the top of it. Everything seemed safe. The owner was smiling and busily punching orders into the cash register. His wife was beside him shovelling scoops of chips in and out of the deep-fry, every now and then accompanying them with a dripping yellow hunk of battered fish.

Jim put the menu down and sat back with a minor feeling of relief. At least he had decided what he was going to eat. The owner wrapped another meal and then looked through the alcove. He caught Jim's eye and raised his brows in a friendly question. Before Jim knew it, he was ordering.

'Er, yes. Cod and chips... and a cup of tea,' he added quickly in anticipation to the question that was about to fall out of the owner's mouth.

The chip shop was simmering with a quiet haste. Everybody was trying to edge their way closer to the counter.

Three brightly dressed youths were standing at the front of the queue. Two of them were leaning against the counter waiting for their order, while the third, who had already been served, was standing by the alcove busily stabbing his bag of chips with a wooden fork. They were laughing and joking together. Occasionally, as one of the two boys by the counter spoke to the third, the other seized his chance and threw his hand into the bag of chips.

'Look at that massive spider up there!' one shouted in exaggerated amazement. He pointed to the ceiling behind the third boy's head.

'Cor! That's unbelievable!' the second added. He looked up with even greater astonishment. 'Have a look at that, Dave! Go on, it's bloody amazing.'

Dave smirked. 'Oh really!' he said ironically. 'I bet it's enormous! I simply have to take a look.' He opened his eyes as wide as he could and followed the line of the pointed fingers.

Suddenly there was an explosion of action: darting hands grabbed at Dave's chips. Giggles and happy shouts cut into the air.

Dave darted ahead of the others. On reaching the door, he produced the saveloy from among his chips and with a sudden spin and thrust of his hips he jabbed the flopping sausage to his crotch.

'Sunburnt king dong!' he stated as if he were a magician embarking on a series of tricks.

His friends were momentarily stunned by the accuracy of the imitation. But their dismay soon turned to appreciation as they rushed at him in a playful attack. Dave quickly pulled the saveloy away and juggled it from hand to hand, pretending that for his second trick it had become a stick of dynamite. Playing to the audience, he stepped over to the window ledge and slid it into the roaring mouth of a gorilla-shaped World Wildlife Fund charity box. A few moments later they could be heard clattering down the street. Their cheery voices had soon been diluted by the blowing wind. All ears drew back inside the shop. Attention turned again to the sound of the hot oil.

According to Glenda's timetable Bill should have been there over half an hour ago. He's not coming tonight, Jim thought thankfully.

'Leave then, you coward,' the unruly voice scoffed.

Jim pushed his plate to the centre of the table and slid

his chair back. The classroom-like screech of the wooden legs ripped through the air. He looked warily around. The owner was looking over. Jim gestured with his head to the money he had left on the table. The owner nodded and continued to serve.

On his way out, Jim's eyes were suddenly drawn to the saveloy that was still in the mouth of the charity box. A moment later, he had one hand on the gorilla's head and the other clasped around the saveloy. As he plucked the two apart, a voice, with the hollow resonance of an echo, boomed in through the door.

'You perverted sod! Hey, everybody! Look what we've got here! A sicko putting things into animals' mouths. Is that the only was you can get your fun?' Bill was standing in the doorway. 'You sick bastard!'

Jim's hands were glued to the gorilla and a shiver of vulnerability came over him.

A murmur of interest sounded from the queue. There was a rustling of feet as the people behind him begin to break rank and turn to see what was happening.

Jim turned to face Bill. He met the uncompromising gaze that streaked towards him. Jim dropped his hands and opened his mouth to speak. His mind squirmed as he fumbled ineptly to piece together some words of defence. His planned speech about a meeting seemed ludicrous. 'I just...' The many answers that had flooded uninvited into his mind also seemed ludicrous. He looked around the shop for help.

Open faces watched him. They waited for an explanation.

Jim rushed to the door. Bill was standing solidly in his way. His arm was extended with a flat palm showing, like a policeman stopping traffic. Jim bowed his head and tried to burst past him. But in an instant he had been pulled outside and was pinned to the wall. Bill gripped his collar. He spat his words into Jim's face. Jim craned his head upwards, trying to look away from the gusts of Bill's dank breath.

'You think you're so clever, don't you! What are you doing? Come to spy on me have you? Well you don't look so clever now, do you? You pathetic shit! Are you looking for another slap, dead meat? What on earth can she see in you?'

Jim tried to shout, but his voice was hiding.

Bill laughed maliciously. 'You little shit! Get out of here! Keep out of my sight! I'm not even going to waste my time punching that frightened look off your face.' He pulled Jim with both arms and threw him onto the street. His face grew cold and hard. 'The next time I see you, if you even so much as look at me you're dead.' He spat into Jim's face.

Jim's legs buckled and he fell. He did not have the will to pick himself up. He lay there looking at the fuzzy outlines of the figures that were sweating through the misty shop window. He heard laughter; Bill's noisy, satisfied cackle. After a few moments he managed to pick himself up and automatically checked his elbows for cuts. His arms ached from the whack of concrete. He wanted to run away. He definitely needed a drink. Jim was about to go when for once his mind spoke as one and told him to stay. There could be no doubt; he could not waver from his course.

Bill stood with his arms folded in satisfaction. He grinned and seemed happy.

Jim smiled inside. For an instant he even thought he liked this person. He was thankful. At that moment, more than ever before, his life had focus and meaning.

Bill's grin turned sour. 'Fuck off! And I mean now!'

'We need to talk,' Jim said quietly.

'You need to fuck off, more like.'

'We need to sort some things out.'

'What, like your face!' Bill laughed.

There it was again. Jim liked him. Bill's scorn made Jim stronger.

'We need to talk about Glenda.'

The sound of her name enraged Bill. 'You leave her the fuck alone!' he yelled. He rushed at Jim.

Jim tried to avoid the punch but was suddenly falling onto his elbows. He dabbed at where he had been struck.

The unruly voice shouted, 'Fuck the pain! For once in your life *do* something!'

When Jim saw there was no blood he went on more boldly, 'I've got a message for you. It's from Gl... er, *her*,' he emphasised. 'She wants to meet you. To sort things out. She wants to meet you tonight.'

'What do you know?' he shouted.

'She wants to meet you. By the old pavilion in the Patcham Place rec. At midnight.'

'What the fuck are you talking about? The park, midnight. Why Patcham Place? It's miles away. Why midnight?'

Jim checked to see that nobody from the chip shop was watching. 'Look, it's got nothing to do with me. I'm just the messenger boy.' Putting himself down made him feel good. 'All I know is she wants to meet you. She said something about wanting to be alone.'

Bill eyes narrowed. He stared at Jim as if he were straining to look through a thick fog. Jim thought he saw the trace of a smile in Bill's eyes.

'You keep her as far as I'm concerned.' Jim shrugged. 'It's obvious she doesn't want anything to do with me, mate.'

Mate. The unruly voice liked it.

'She said she might be going away soon,' Jim said with growing excitement. 'If you're that interested, go and meet her. Nothing to do with me. I bring messages and I get a slap for my trouble. I've had enough of this. I'm out of here—' Another 'mate' perhaps? Why not. 'Mate,' he said.

Jim turned and headed off, making sure he was cowering and rubbing the side of his head.

Chapter Sixteen

It was nine o'clock when Jim got home. He parked the van a few hundred yards away from his flat and stood beside it. He was glad that the drizzle had not lasted long. The earth would hardly be wet. He took his jacket off and cooled himself in the evening breeze. Sweating had been the only release for his nerves. He listened to the hypnotic sound of the wind in his ears. He bowed his head and closed his eyes. After a few moments he looked up and held his fingers spread in front of him. They were steady. He went through his checklist. Screwdriver, number plates, shovel, tarpaulin, dust sheet and bat.

He saw a picture of himself digging in the cemetery. There was no reaction. He felt perfectly relaxed. He tried to make himself nervous by thinking about being in a dark isolated place with Bill. But the nerves did not come.

When he was back in his flat he called Glenda. After several rings she answered.

'Hello?' Her voice was hesitant.

'Glenda. It's me,' Jim said.

'Oh hello,' she said with audible relief. 'How are you?'

'Fine. You? You sound a bit flat. I thought you were seeing your parents in town today.'

'I did.'

'How was it?' Jim asked. 'Did you have a good time?'

Glenda was silent for a few seconds. He thought he

heard a sniff. 'They went on the tour bus,' she said quietly. 'I didn't want to go. I went on the pier instead.' She paused again. 'I went on the ghost train.' There was silence and then suddenly she had burst into tears.

'Glenda! Glenda! What's wrong? Why are you crying, tell me!' Jim panicked. 'He's not there, is he? I thought he was working tonight!'

Glenda managed to hold in her sobs. She spoke slowly as if she had just learnt the English language and the words were difficult to say. 'No, he's not here. Not now anyway.' She blew her nose and then said, 'I'm fine, honestly. I'm just a little tired.'

'Are you sure?' Jim asked. 'You sound dreadful.'

'I'm fine, really.' Glenda paused. 'What are you up to? Will you come over?'

Jim wanted to go and see her so much. Her invitation sounded welcoming. Both of them sitting in front of the television, relaxing and enjoying their solitude. But above all he responded to her desire for him to be there. He had wanted her to ask him this for so long now. Finally, despite her fear, she wanted him to be with her. This would be the beginning of a proper relationship, more than just sex and the odd date. It would be the start of love; her love for him. He was momentarily overwhelmed and began to grin. For an instant he had forgotten that he was going to kill someone that night. 'I'd love to, but I can't,' he said, remembering. 'I want to more than anything, but I've got a couple of things to do. Really important things.' He waited for her response but it did not come. 'Tomorrow?' he suggested apologetically.

'I understand, it was just a thought. What things have you got to do?' Glenda said coldly.

Jim ignored the question. 'I really would like to see you.

I just can't explain why at the moment. You'll have to trust me.'

'It's okay. It's not a big deal. I'm pretty tired now anyway. I'll probably have an early night.'

Jim heard the uncertainty in her voice. If you can hear me, he thought as loudly as he could, I'm doing it tonight. And what's more, I'm doing it for you. I know there is something wrong, but soon it will all be okay.

'Glenda, you won't get away if you try to leave me,' the unruly voice whispered. 'I will not allow it.'

He flushed and spoke out loud to dismiss these thoughts. 'So you're still on for giving Mrs Muurling a hand with her casket? Alan's got the car. We're thinking about going this weekend.'

'When exactly?'

'Friday morning,' Jim said confidently. 'It'll be great, I promise.'

'I'll need to organise a day off.' She hesitated. 'Things are getting me down a bit and I could really use the time away from Brighton.' Her voice trembled. It sounded like they suddenly had a bad connection.

'Of course, I understand.' He wanted to say that by the time they got back it would be all right for them to make love outside the chip shop. If she wanted she could have a queue of Casanovas waiting outside her door, without fear of consequences, from Bill at least. The beady-eyed old lady looking from her top window would be the greatest of her worries after tonight. A nudge of conscience urged Jim to finish the conversation. 'Look, I've got to go,' Jim said, 'but I'll organise things with Mrs Muurling and call you tomorrow. I've sorted the hotel in Padstow. Can you do me a favour without asking why?' he said matter-of-factly.

'What?'

'Keep all of your curtains closed, and if he comes around tonight, whatever you do, don't let him know you're in. I need you to promise this.'

'What do you mean?'

'Will you do that? Just trust me and do it, please. I've just got a feeling.'

'I'd do that anyway.'

'How about we go out somewhere nice tomorrow. What do you say?' Jim suggested. 'Pub, cinema, meal, anything. You choose. I'm easy.'

'We'll see,' she said with resignation. 'But...' She had nothing more to say but was obviously hovering on the line, unwilling to put the phone down.

'I'd love to chat, Glenda, but I've got to be somewhere. I have to go.' He said goodbye and placed the receiver down gently. He shook his fist and a sudden strength filled his hand.

Chapter Seventeen

It was a very dark night. The low cloud from the earlier shower had not passed. The wind had dropped and it was humid. The weather forecast had said that there were storms approaching.

Jim was wearing a black T-shirt and jeans. He parked the van behind the pavilion and changed the number plates immediately. He did not worry that Bill might see the van. If he came he would certainly be looking for Glenda. And after...

The pavilion had been abandoned for as long as he could remember. It stood in front of a small area of parkland which was shielded from the main road by a barrier of squat elms whose outspread branches were now heavy with leaves. Behind the pavilion a steep escarpment rose over three hundred feet to a lookout point at the top.

The dirt track to the pavilion was unlit and, once out of the van, it was several minutes before Jim's eyes became accustomed to the faint light of the moon behind the broken clouds. He took up position behind a tree on the far side of the pavilion. He was about four yards from the corner of the building and had a clear view of the approach road and the field. He walked the few steps to the area of ground in front of the pavilion where he hoped Bill would stand. He kicked away twigs, stones and litter that might give away his approach. When he was satisfied, he stepped back behind the tree. He was holding the cricket bat tightly with both hands. He weighed it for use, swinging it gently in front of him. Without thinking he practised a swing against the tree. He tried to stop the bat a fraction before impact but misjudged. The bat bludgeoned its way through the air. Its path was suddenly cut dead by the dull thud of wood against wood. The impact sent a jarring pain through his hands to his shoulders. He was impressed with this and stared in fascination at the ivory whiteness of the wood.

There were squirrels everywhere. One appeared a matter of inches from his head. He swung round with his bat raised, holding his breath, searching in front of him for a dark shadow. He had expected to see Bill there, holding a gun or a knife. The squirrel darted up the tree. A few minutes later he heard a scuffling sound a little way off. He checked his watch. Eleven fifty-eight. He listened hard for the sound to continue. For a second it disappeared. He held his breath again. He stretched out his hand; it was trembling, but his mind was clear. It was okay that his body was afraid, it did not understand the reasoning of his mind.

The sound returned. It was closer, and then closer still. A succession of footsteps grew increasingly louder. His eyes had now adjusted to the darkness and he kept his gaze fixed on the front of the pavilion. He peered with one eye from the edge of the tree to the area of grass just in front of him. A moment later a figure appeared in front of the pavilion. It stopped and looked around.

'Glenda? It's me.' Bill put his hands in his pockets. 'Glenda! Are you there?' There was a smile in his voice. 'Oh, Glenda! Where are you?' He kicked at the grass and paused before moving towards Jim's tree. He was no more than two yards away when he stopped.

Jim could hear Bill's breathing and was certain that Bill

would hear his. Jim trembled as he released each lungful of air, convinced that his body was going to shatter into a hundred pieces. Suddenly what he was doing seemed ludicrous. He had not seriously considered that he might be the one who could be killed. He felt weak and the bat felt heavy and dangerous. He was desperate for Bill to leave. He was scared, but this time he was certain that his legs *would* work. They would carry him away faster than he had ever moved before; possibly faster than anyone had ever moved before. They would take him further and for longer. He would become the only person who had run away for ever.

Bill kicked at the grass again. He spoke. His voice was quiet but it sounded like the terrible roar. 'Come out, come out, wherever you are,' he chanted. He paused for several long moments and then said, 'You're not here are you, Glenda? Or are you here with that wanker boyfriend of yours? Why doesn't he come out if *he* wants to talk to me?' He was enjoying himself, it was a good game. 'Or maybe you could both come out and see me?'

Jim forced himself so tightly against the tree that he was certain he would push it over if he stayed there much longer. He shut his eyes and pleaded in silent capitulation for him to leave.

And then another voice sounded from behind the pavilion like an answer to his prayers. It was familiar, but it was hard-edged and cold. The voice was accompanied by fast steps which stopped as they recognised Bill's presence. Jim chanced a look from behind the tree. Bill had turned and was facing the direction of the new voice. The figure stepped forward into the moonlight. He was a few yards in front of Bill and he stood firmly with his feet planted wide apart and his arms folded. Jim caught his breath as he saw

Roger's concentrated face. He realised why he had not recognised the voice before. Roger was drunk. He sounded detached and dangerous. He spoke again.

'Fancied a nice evening walk did you?'

Bill leant forward and stared for a moment. 'It's you, isn't it? The pool queen? What the fuck are you doing here? Was this arranged so that you could get me all alone? Have your wicked way with me?'

'What do you want with my friend?' Roger said calmly.

'Which friend is that?' Bill sneered. 'I didn't think an idiot like you had any friends.'

'I saw you earlier, outside his house after the pubs had turned out. I followed you here. What were you doing there? How do you know where he lives?'

Bill laughed. 'I know where a lot of people live. I might even know where you live. I do a bit of following myself. Perhaps I'll come and visit you one day. But only if you're a very good boy.'

Roger did not change his tone. It was restrained but challenging. '*What* were you doing there?'

Bill laughed but then stopped abruptly. 'Fuck you!' he said. 'Fuck you *and* your boyfriend.' He stepped towards Roger. 'You're going to be sorry you ever came here. I wanted to wrap a cue around your head in the pub that night. Now you'll have to make do with my fists instead.'

Roger dropped his hands to his side as the two of them squared up. Jim had expected him to sway if he were drunk but he appeared steady and in control. They were a couple of yards apart, shifting weight from foot to foot, assessing each other, waiting for the first move. Jim took a step forward, but before he had even moved out from behind the tree, they had begun to fight.

Bill and Roger could only see punches and kicks. They

scrapped like a pair of wolves, snarling and tearing at each other with no consideration of loss. They flew around in circles as each tried to gain an edge. Roger was the shorter of the two men but he was powerful and unyielding. He tried to get inside Bill's defence but his darting attacks were being kept at bay by the taller man's reach. Bill jabbed quickly and accurately, sending Roger's head snapping back. Soon Roger was wiping blood away from his swelling left eye and was concentrating hard on seeing his target. He rushed at Bill, suddenly grabbing him and punching furiously at his head. Bill pulled his head away to avoid the punches and in an instant had stepped back and thrown a hook that sent Roger crashing to the floor.

Bill said calmly to Roger. 'Where's Glenda then? Or is this just your personal vendetta?'

Roger stood up and took a deep breath in preparation for another assault. 'I don't know what you're talking about,' he said slowly, 'but I think I've just made this my personal vendetta.' A moment later he rushed at Bill and they were fighting again.

Roger now had Bill in a neck-lock. He was shouting as he squeezed. But, with a quick flick of his back, Bill threw Roger to the ground. He stepped forward to kick him but stopped. 'I think you've had enough,' he said. He withdrew a couple of paces. He was now talking very quietly. His voice was sad and hurt; it sounded as though he was the one who had been beaten. 'Some stupid trick of yours this is. I really did need to see Glenda. I just wanted to tell her a few things, that's all.'

'I bet you did, you bastard!' Roger shouted. He was now on his feet again – if a little unsteadily – and was about to attack when Jim dropped the bat and rushed forward.

'Stop, Roger! It was me! It was my idea. Stop it, he'll kill you!'

In an instant, Bill had spun around and was facing Jim. He nodded. 'I thought you might be behind this somehow!' He motioned over Jim's shoulder and laughed. 'Behind the tree, eh? That's just your style, isn't it?'

Bill was already walking away as Jim spoke. 'Just leave my mate alone will you, it's nothing to do with him. I'm the one you need to beat up.' Jim looked across to Roger and, in a split second that would live with him for the rest of his life, he was certain he was at his parents' house, following his grandfather downstairs. Finally he knew he would see death.

Roger shouted agonisingly and rushed after Bill. The swinging arms and boots of his body were suddenly frozen and then thawed with a splash as he dived onto Bill and sent them both tumbling onto the concrete of the pavilion's patio. They had hold of each other's throats and were forcing their hands to squeeze harder than their own neck was being squeezed. They were locked together in a motionless, desperate effort to survive and defeat. Their eyes stared disbelievingly, as if what they were doing shocked them but they were unable to stop what had started.

Bill rolled onto his back and pushed Roger into the air as if he were bench-pressing a kitten. He shouted angrily and shook Roger violently. And then, very slowly, the anger left his face and he said in a whisper, 'Fuck this. Fuck all of this.' He lowered Roger, took his hands from his neck and spread his arms wide. He lay his head on the ground and began to laugh.

Roger still had hold of Bill's throat and, as the laughter grew louder, he became more determined. Bill nodded and slowly closed his eyes. A moment later, Roger was repeatedly smashing Bill's head onto the concrete.

Jim heard the same resounding thud that the bat had made against the tree. He was panting heavily as he bent down to grab Roger's shoulder. He stared disbelievingly at the silent face that was stuck to Bill's motionless body. For a moment Jim was convinced that he must have hit him with his bat. He snapped himself out of his shock and looked around. Everything was normal. He looked down at the body and tentatively kicked at its shoulder. There was no movement. He tapped the head with his boot. It rolled a few inches on its neck. Its eyes were closed and its mouth was fixed in a stunned smile. Jim prodded at the head again and then kicked the body in its side. Still it did not move.

Bill appeared to be smaller – or perhaps Jim was now twice his height? Whatever the illusion, it seemed impossible for them to be so far apart when he knew they were not. So this was what being dead was like? It seemed so undignified. He went to kick it again but stopped himself. He could kick as hard as he liked but the body would never understand why he was doing that. *It* would never feel pain again. He could laugh at it, but its ears would not hear; and he could call it names but its feelings would not be hurt. There was nothing at all he could do to it. He experienced a brief moment of anger and loss.

The sound of a squirrel moving through branches broke him from his distraction. His mind quickly began to clear and he was soon prepared for what he had to do.

'What the fuck have I done?' Roger said. He was now standing in front of the body holding his hands clasped behind his neck. He spoke again, his voice was barely audible, like a penitent's confessional mumble. 'I've killed him, I can't believe it, I've killed him.' He prodded at the body. '*Is* he dead?' He grabbed Jim. 'Is he dead? What have

I done? What the fuck have I done!'

Jim knew he was dead and was glad. He was calm. It seemed as though he had been preparing himself for this sight for as long as he could remember. He shook his head and smiled inside as he spoke. 'He's just unconscious, Roger. You knocked him out. He'll be round in a minute or two. Don't worry, mate. Take it easy, he'll be okay. Just try and relax. It's going to be all right.' He reached out to Roger. 'Are you all right?'

'No I'm bloody not!' Roger shouted.

'Okay, Roger. Just try and take it easy,' Jim said quickly, assessing Roger's injuries. 'You want to get some ice on that swelling.' He turned Roger away and coaxed him towards the pavilion. 'Look, you'd better leave now. I don't want you two maniacs going at it again when he comes round. Then one of you *really* might get hurt. I'll see that he's okay. You get home and clean yourself up. I'll sort this out. I'll wait for him to come round. I'll call an ambulance if he needs one and then bugger off before they arrive. I promise you, I'll sort it out. He won't be any trouble.' He stopped and moved directly in front of Roger. He looked hard into his eyes. 'Not a word though, to anyone. Just in case. We weren't here, okay? This never happened. This bloke will keep his gob shut. He's that type. And so will we.'

Roger nodded. Jim turned him and pushed him gently away. 'I'll see you tomorrow.'

Roger was still mumbling as he stumbled off towards the main road.

As Jim walked back to the pavilion he was aware that he was more shocked at seeing how upset Roger was than at having witnessed a killing.

Before long he had wrapped the body in the tarpaulin and had dragged it to the van. He humped it into the back and dumped the bat and the torch beside it. He closed the back and got into the cab. He sat for a moment in silence and then suddenly banged the steering wheel in anger. He still could not believe it. *He* was actually dead but he had not killed him, yet he would still have to bury the bastard. He became mad and tears of frustration flooded to his eyes.

The drive to the cemetery took no more than a second. Another second later he had parked the van and opened the back. He hauled the long cylinder of black plastic out and bounced it onto his shoulder in a fireman's lift. As he walked through the gate and threaded between the gravestones to the far perimeter, he could not stop thinking about how light the body was.

When he reached the grave he balanced his torch on the headstone and unrolled the tarpaulin. He dragged the body to one side and made a mental note of the shape of the mound of earth. He ran back to the van and returned with the shovel and bat. 'Hello, Mr Falmer,' he said as he started to dig, 'you might be lonely down there but you'll soon have some company.'

He attacked the earth with the sharp shovel. It plunged into the yielding ground. He pushed down hard on the wooden handle and, at the point he felt it would go no further, he pushed a little bit more, each time squeezing a couple more inches of thrust and of satisfaction. The more he pushed, the harder he felt compelled to work. After an hour of digging Jim was three feet down. He had taken off his shirt and was dripping with sweat. The clouds seemed to be even lower and he was sure that it had suddenly become extremely hot. The pile of earth he had removed seemed incredibly large and he was thankful that there was going to be enough room on the tarpaulin. He worked incessantly and without thought of fatigue. His mind was blank except for the intense, studied concentration of shovelling. The push, the effort, the pull, the effort. He was removed from the world of uncertainties. For those hours he had only one function. He would be able to consider the choices, the consequences, later.

Suddenly a hollow knock sounded like the snap of a hypnotist's fingers. The crack of metal on wood surged into his hands like an electric current. He clambered out of the hole and walked over to the body. He dragged it to the graveside. He had expected it to be colder. It's a warm night, he thought, but he'll be cold soon enough.

Jim rolled the body in and tossed the bat on top. Suddenly there was no sense of elation or revenge. He was not even satisfied that he had robbed the man of his dignity by dumping him in a twisted heap like this. There was just death and shock. Nothing and everything. He began to fill the hole.

Just over three-quarters of an hour later, when he was satisfied that the mound of earth was the same shape as before, he folded the ends of the tarpaulin and pulled the excess earth into a bundle. He dragged it aside and inspected the grass for damage. It was flattened, as he had expected, but otherwise there seemed to be no sign of his presence. He hauled the tarpaulin towards the back fence. It became elongated, like a balloon full of water. He pulled hard but was still mindful not to leave a trail of earth. He was now returning to his senses, and began to worry about being caught. There was a small cluster of trees and a depressed strip of stony earth running along the fence. He opened the tarpaulin and began to shovel the earth into this trench. When he had done this he walked quickly to the van and threw the tarpaulin and shovel in the back.

Change the plates back, he thought, then dump the

tarpaulin anywhere away from the cemetery.

It was now 4.30 a.m. There were no lights showing from the houses opposite the gates. He pulled into Hartington Road and drove away slowly. Three hours sleep, and then pick Roger up for work. He could not wait for it to be the next day. Everything would be bright and real.

Chapter Eighteen

The man gets off the bus and walks down to the seafront to think. He sits and watches the waves crash, aware that he has to be at the chip shop in ten minutes for work.

He is calmer now, but has not managed to shake off the uncomfortable feeling of uncertainty that has been with him all day. He turns to look at the pavement behind him and watches a pair of blond-headed tourists hurrying by. They have rucksacks with foreign writing on it – Swedish or German perhaps? He keeps his eyes on the road and watches a few cars and a bus pass by. His gaze falls on the funeral parlour across the road. He does not think about his real father immediately, but the memory of him is standing patiently in the wings of his mind.

Soon he is not looking at anything at all, but is a boy, standing in the family front room on the day of his father's funeral...

His uncle finishes his brief address to the small gathering of family members, and opens the door to let them file out to greet the growing crowd of people walking through the corridor to the garden. The boy is looking out of the window, staring at the people standing on his dad's front lawn; they are treading closer to the row of velvety pansies and pink roses than his father would normally have let them. His uncle puts a hand on his small shoulder.

'Here they all come, son, here they all come,' he says wearily. 'Your aunt's seeing them in. You best get yourself out the back now and make an appearance, lad.' He lets his hand slide down the boy's arm, and gives his elbow a light squeeze of reassurance before

following the others to the kitchen and out into the back garden.

When his uncle has gone the boy edges warily to his left, until his body is obscured by the thick curtain at the side of the paunched bay window. He holds the dusty material across his face like a yashmak and peeks out at the steady stream of cars stopping at the gate.

The front room has the stiff quality of Sunday best; a dry, musky air of disuse that reminds the boy of the boredom of his grandparents' monthly visits. It is a distant smell that comes from another time and which possesses the hazy recollections of family get-togethers, cigar smoke and drunken laughter. The room has seldom been used at all, except for special visits. Christmases and birthdays – 'special-room days' his mother called them reverentially. It is certainly the first time that the boy has ever been left alone with his father's sprawling collection of military models that are still arranged in precise colonies over the sideboard and chest of drawers.

The light is off and the windows are shut, dampening sound outside into an edgeless muffle. The boy feels safe in his own friendly world. So safe that he wants to stand behind that curtain for ever and will away the future. But however hard he tries he can see it coming. Even now he sees it as they walk into his house, past the half-open door behind him, along the narrow, pictured corridor, through the cluttered kitchen, out onto the fresh green of the close-cropped lawn, and up to the trestle tables covered with white bed-sheets and paper plates. They will grab at chicken drumsticks and crustless quarter-sandwiches and pile them onto paper plates that are decorated with red napkins folded into neat triangles. He sees it as they chew with hungry mouths, talking with measured respect, all the time filling plastic beakers with yet more beer and wine. They will all be keeping an eye on the poor little lad, of course, nodding condolences over shoulders and giving him woeful pats on the back until, one by one, they have had enough of the numb, mechanical existence that is the hangover of death and choose to go. They will leave more gradually than they came, hanging on to the sorrow of the day, until it will be reluctantly released like each final handshake at the door, both holding firm and sincere, both unsure when to let go. And then the wake will be over and finished with, for ever; the hands will be empty and the door will be slowly closed.

The boy sits down in his father's reclining chair by the chest of drawers. He slides out the ageing family photograph album from the small row of books in the bottom cupboard and places it on his knee. He lifts the leather-bound cover gently open with respect for the stiffness of its long spine.

The boy's occasional glances into the past have usually been driven by the youthful vanity of growth. He has wanted to show off the comparison between the burgeoning of his adolescence and the small-boned child of his younger self in the photographs to the indulgent gathering of family and friends on a 'special-room day'. He has sat at his mother's knee and watched the grown-ups' faces light up at the sight of each captured frame of time, while waiting patiently for the dawdle through the years to reach the colourful clarity of the present so that they can then go out into the garden and play the game of cricket that his father has promised him.

He handles each plastic-covered page with great care, as if he does not want to disturb the subjects with his clumsy touch. The faces are still bright and alive; they have endured and will continue to endure their fate beyond their being. The boy smiles as forgotten moments come alive before his eyes: his father is sitting with a fishing rod by a leafy river-bank, wearing his favourite cap and looking over his shoulder at the camera with a frown after a day of fishless angling. 'Dangling' he called it, because of his usual lack of success. Next, his grandparents are in typical deckchair pose on the beach. His grandmother's head is bent, concentrating on her knitting, while his granddad, with trousers rolled up to the knee, is holding a bottle of beer up to some passers-by. And then, his mother and father are standing arm in arm in front of their first house, looking so young and so proud with the boy's large-wheeled pram in front of them.

Willow, their ghostly white cat, has its tail in the air and is rubbing a whiskered cheek against the front door in the background.

Suddenly the door opens and his uncle walks in. The boy bobs to the surface of his trance. He closes the album and looks up. His uncle's cheeks are red with wine. He pulls his handkerchief out from his top pocket and dabs his shiny forehead. 'You should come outside, lad, get some sun. It's a beautiful day.'

'Looks a bit hot,' *the boy says.*

His uncle looks down. He knows it is not a beautiful day. The boy places the album back on the chest of drawers and then looks back at his uncle. He does not want to make it hard for him, he just does not want to go out, not yet. 'These dark suits aren't exactly beachwear,' *he says, tugging at his stiff lapel.*

His uncle nods with a half-smile. 'I suppose we're lucky though. Better that it's sunny and they're all out there rather than in here. They forecast rain this morning.' *He pauses a second.* 'It's cleared up nicely.'

The boy likes his uncle and can see how sad he is. He looks up and returns his smile. 'I'll be out soon. I just want a bit longer.'

'It's just me and your auntie were...'

The boy understands. He realises he has been selfish, letting them do all the work. He feels an urge to be with them. He does not understand why his mother has not come to his father's funeral, nor will he ever. 'It's okay uncle,' *he says, getting up.* 'We'll stick together. Safety in numbers, eh?'

'That sounds like a good idea. And a quick bite to eat in the kitchen on the way out.' *He winks.*

His auntie is racing in and out of the house, replenishing supplies of food and drink, directing people to the toilet, and sinking the odd glass of sherry out of sight of the guests. Her hair has lost the immobility it was given in the salon earlier, and now hangs flatly down from under her black hat. The boy and his uncle stroll into the kitchen.

'You'd better watch yourself with that sherry, Carolyn,' the uncle quips. 'Before you know it you'll be using a sausage as a straw!'

'Do something useful, you two,' she says coldly.

'Better give her a hand, I suppose,' his uncle whispers. 'You grab those, will you lad, and offer them around in the garden.'

The boy takes the bowls of crisps and peanuts and, after a slow, deep breath, walks outside.

The small lawn is being trodden down and pierced by about sixty pairs of polished shoes and sharp heels. Jackets and coats are piled over a pasting table that is doubling as a cloakroom at the end of the garden. The sun is now hidden behind greyness, but it is still warm and the sultry afternoon feels heavy. The lawn was mown that morning and unraked clumps of grass are strewn around the garden. Their damp, earthy fragrance hangs in the air. Occasionally a light breeze blows through the scene and the women with larger hats put hands up to them automatically without interrupting their conversations.

The boy finishes his rounds and takes the bowls back to the kitchen. His aunt is pouring some sherry into her plastic cup. She looks up as the boy walks in.

'Just a small one now that all the food's finished with,' she says, turning away from the boy. She screws the cap back onto the bottle and takes a sip. She looks disapprovingly at the label. 'I don't want to waste your mother's good stuff. Nobody can tell the difference by this time anyway.'

The boy goes to the cupboard beneath the sink and pulls out a frosted-glass bottle of Spanish sherry.

'You might as well drink it,' he says, offering her the bottle. 'It'll only get left there with the scouring powder and washing-up liquid.'

Her eyes dart to the bottle and then back to the boy. She hesitates and stares at him. 'I'll be okay with this.' And then adds: 'I'm not a *great drinker, as you know.'*

The boy pulls a plastic beaker from the tight stack on the worktop and cracks the seal of the expensive bottle. He holds the beaker up, asking the question with his eyebrows.

'You don't want to end up like your mother, do you? She's probably legless somewhere now. I don't know. I always told your uncle his sister would be the death of us. What are we going to do with you now?' She takes the bottle from him and pours herself another drink.

The boy still has his beaker raised.

'Anyway, you're not old enough.' She smirks.

The boy grabs the bottle back. She raises the back of her hand to him. He lifts his chin and stares at her without fear.

'Please do,' he says impassively.

She lowers her hand and turns away.

'Today,' he states as he pours the sherry, 'fourteen is old enough.' He raises his beaker and takes a lip-wetting sip. He has not drunk sherry before. His tongue licks at the fruity bitterness. He takes another larger mouthful and swallows hard. He feels the liquid sinking warmly down through his chest. 'Is this better than that cheap stuff you were drinking?' he asks.

His auntie does not reply.

The boy sets his beaker down onto the worktop. 'I'd better go and find uncle,' he says, distancing himself from his drink. He glances out of the back window at the dark sky. 'It's going to rain, and they'll all be coming inside soon. We don't want him to get caught in the rush.' He pauses and stares at nothing for a moment. Then he turns and looks at his auntie. 'I want him to come back,' he says very calmly. 'I don't want him to be gone for ever.' He takes her arm and turns her to face him. His grip is hard. 'But I know he can't and he never will.'

He understands for the first time in his life that he will never be scared of anyone. He continues, 'I know you don't like my mother.'

He stares hard into her eyes. 'But don't you ever speak badly of her again.' He releases her arm and pushes through the back door into the buzz of the crowd.

The man shrugs off these thoughts and heads off for his evening shift.

Chapter Nineteen

Nothing had felt real at work the next day. Roger had been subdued and worried. Even when Jim had told him the story he had carefully rehearsed, Roger was still distraught. Jim told him the whole story about Bill and Glenda. He said that this was justice, and he was just sorry that Bill had woken up a few minutes later and stumbled off. He said that what Roger had done was right. Roger was still uncertain, and his doubts seemed to increase when Jim made him swear never to mention any of what had happened to anyone. Roger agreed.

Jim had arranged to meet everyone at the cinema. He and Roger had finished work early, and Jim had taken a stroll down to the seafront to kill some time. It was cloudy and getting dark, but there was a half-moon low in the sky. Its reflection lit a narrow white channel along the sea from the horizon to the shore. This skidded closely over the choppy waves, being broken at the edges as it rose and fell over each bump of sea. Along the beach, the metal arms and wheels of the funfair were empty; they were silhouetted against the neon reds, blues and greens of the lights on the Palace Pier.

It was Thursday, and busy. The usual early evening rush back from work filled the roads. Everyone was in a hurry to be the first to burst out of the clogged roads that led from the heart of Brighton.

Jim had always enjoyed the bustle of a crowded town. He belonged to the confusion. Until that night he had always felt secure whenever he was in its midst but, as he walked back to his flat, he felt strangely detached from these surroundings. It was as though they had become too familiar to him; like living with someone who no longer loves you, and realising that you feel more isolated when you are with them than when you are alone. As he continued to stare at the activity around him, the streets began to look hostile and unwelcoming.

When he got back to his flat he checked his watch. It was seven forty. He was meeting Glenda, Roger and Alan outside the cinema at eight. It was late, and it had been pointless returning. He was going to have to leave within a couple of minutes if he wanted to be there on time, but a sudden and overwhelming desire to be in the warmth and safety of his room had filled his mind. He looked at the steaming cars jammed in the road outside, and then beyond them to the viaduct, and beyond that to the black-blue of the sky. Yet the flat did not seem so welcoming and he looked around not understanding why he had wanted to return.

The night was now staring back at him. He turned away from the window and walked briskly to the door. He stepped out onto the landing. Light from a naked bulb threw long bars of shadow down the stairs from the wooden banister above. A wave of anxiety came over him. A moment later it had disappeared as if a sweating phantom had passed right through his body. He brushed a hand at his wet brow and snatched at a deep breath. A flurry of heartbeats rose and popped in his chest like a plume of bubbles rising in water. His legs felt weak but full of energy. He raced down the stairs and burst out into the open air. The fresh sea breeze gusted into his face. He sucked eagerly at the clean taste of the salt. For a moment he was distracted by the noise of the traffic and the clawing and crashing of the waves in the distance. He thought of the West Pier and the rusty ladder on the side dipping into the sea. He shuddered. The unswerving truth about the murder came to him. He was part of it and he could go to jail. But worse than that was having to accept that he had not done it himself. He was destined to live with this lie. His marriage to Glenda would be a lie, as would their children and grandchildren. His existence was now nothing more than a lie.

He marched off towards the cinema in search of any diversion. Ranks of people threaded nimbly past him, moving instinctively on, heads down in their shopper's rush. He looked at his watch. He was late and began to run.

The others were inside the foyer when he arrived. Glenda looked odd, as if a stranger had borrowed her body and was occupying it for the night. She had been unresponsive on the phone earlier, but the invitation to the cinema and the thought of getting out of her house for a while had caused a sudden rush of enthusiasm. Jim had mistaken this for affection. He pecked at her cheek while the others were buying the tickets and said that she looked nice. Glenda was wearing an old pair of jeans and a sweatshirt. Her hair looked as if it had not been washed for days. She looked down and shook her head.

As they went to their seats, Jim filed into the row first. Immediately he wished that he had waited and taken the seat nearest the aisle. It was hot, and he was still sweating from the run. But the others were now jammed in behind him and there was no time to change places. The titles of the main feature were already on the screen. The pre-film hubbub quickly died out and was replaced by the rustle of hands in cartons of popcorn.

After about twenty minutes, the hard pounding in Jim's chest returned. It was a violent thump that soon spread down into his stomach. He tried to convince himself that he had not yet recovered from the run. He was still sweating and had stripped down to his shirt. But despite the fact that he knew he was not particularly fit, he also knew he should not still feel as breathless as he did. The beating was stronger than before. The thought of it covered him in a flush of prickly heat. He was restless and he shifted uncomfortably in his seat. The heat of the crowd of bodies filled the cinema. The air was dry and rough. He dabbed a finger at his wrist. His pulse was firing in sharp bursts. It stopped agonisingly every couple of seconds before starting again, but even more quickly each time. He tried to defend himself against the deep concern that he might be going through the first stages of a heart attack. As the thought took hold in his mind, the physical evidence soon became irrefutable. He had been present when his uncle had suffered one; he remembered the pained, terrified look on his red face. He clutched his chest, frozen and twisted like a gargoyle. He had looked disbelievingly at Jim before collapsing on the sideboard. He had died instantly. Jim wanted to go to the toilets to see if his face was the same colour. He stretched his legs out and then brought them quickly back. He shuffled on his seat.

Glenda leaned over and whispered, 'Are you all right?'

He wanted to jump up and escape the suffocation of the darkness and the proximity to so many people. He now believed he would die if he did not get outside quickly. He grabbed at another deep breath.

'Are you sure you're okay?' Glenda whispered.

'I don't feel too good. I've got to go outside for a bit. It's too hot in here, too claustrophobic. I can't breathe properly, I need to get out.'

'Do you want me to come with you?'

'No. No, I'll be fine, I won't be long. I just need to stand outside for five minutes.'

'Are you sure you're all right? I'll come if you like.'

The conversation was like an incomprehensible exchange in a dream. Jim thought he was dying and here he was excusing himself politely in a cinema. His words were quiet but sharp. He edged along the row with restrained urgency. He concentrated hard and hoped that he would make it to the aisle without screaming. He tried to smile at the concerned faces who stood up to let him past, however, at the same time he felt detached from his body, as if he were being dragged through the crush between the backs of the seats and the people's knees, with no control over what was happening.

He walked quickly up the aisle and broke into a run when he got through the door to the foyer.

The usher got up from his seat. 'The toilets are to the left.' A torch pointed towards a door and a voice spoke.

There was nobody there; it was not real. Jim ran outside.

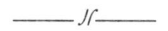

———— *Jf* ————

He did not remember much about how he had made his way to the hospital. Nor about what he had said when he arrived. By that time Jim was certain his heart was about to explode. His finger was pressed permanently to his wrist. The pulse rate was so high that it seemed as though his reserve of life were being squandered in one reckless spree by someone who had no regard for its value. He was counting feverishly, waiting for the inevitable.

The space around him was closing in and each encroachment increased the activity in his mind. His movements became jerky and perplexed, like those of a fly trapped in a jar. He recognised the forms of the objects around him but could not get close enough to touch anything that appeared to be real. He wanted desperately to hold onto something solid and permanent; to step back into the comfortable world that he had known for so long, but which now just seemed like a naive dream that he should have stopped having when he was a child. He was isolated and had been singled out to be punished.

This day was the only day there had ever been to be alive. And like the life of an insect to a human, the cycle was coming to an end before it seemed to have started. There had been nothing before; no events, no family, no friends. He had seen life for the first time as he left the cinema. Now that it had revealed itself to him, it would be over so soon.

He was sitting on something white and was surrounded by faces. They were moving around him in circles, and the faster his head spun to follow them, the quicker they avoided his gaze. They too were waiting for the end. They knew he was dying, but it did not seem to matter to them. It was his death and it had no bearing on their lives. They were only there to watch and study. When it was over their world would still be alive. They would carry on as before, only vaguely noticing his life and death as it passed them by. They would only ever understand when it was their turn for its cold, numbing hand to be laid on them, once and for ever.

As the faces closed in they brought the flimsy props of the world tumbling down behind them. This was the closing night of a performance and they were like a group of philistines smashing their way uncaringly through a carefully constructed theatre set. The faces were now very close to him. Some of them were speaking but their voices were unintelligible. Others peered silently. He tried to speak back to them, but nobody seemed to react. He was dizzy and a will-sapping weakness had spread to his legs. This was it, he was about to fall. He was about to fall.

'I don't want to die! I don't want to die!' he shouted in the silence, 'I don't want to die!'

He had capitulated and begged for mercy. He called for his parents, wherever they were, who had demonstrated a natural reign over the problems of life when he was small. And if they could not hear him he was trying to summon the force from which they drew their strength.

'I don't want to die!' he screamed again.

The faces had dispersed. They were now no more substantial than ethereal visitors who floated harmlessly around him. His focus had been drawn away from the hostility outside his body. The final moments were occurring within his mind.

Death was not a word, nor an image he could see. It was a clear sense that what was about to happen could only come at that moment. The moment, however, was not specific and had not been chosen. It simply was. There was neither salvation nor reprieve from it. Death had not followed him and then preyed on his inability to defend himself from it. It was not an enemy and it was nothing personal. It was just his moment in time to be no more. Afterwards it would be painless. There would be no worry, nor regret. Just nothing.

That was soon, but now the fear of the end came like a pair of skewers which were being forced into his eyes, so that he would see no more. And it came in the form of daggers which sliced into his ears, so that he would hear no more. And then it exerted an immense compression on his body, so that the insignificant thoughts of his mind would no longer occupy any space on the earth. He cried and was scared. He wanted to escape. But he knew he had no right. The faces continued to stare. Still they did not understand. The imminence of the clinical transition from being alive into being nothing was so terrifying that there was too much fear in his body, yet too little ability to express it. Death was greater than him because he did not have the power to react to it. Half of eternity had already sped past before his birth. He was now about to embark on a journey that would last for ever and for a split second because that was how short eternity really was.

'I don't want to die. I don't want to die.' His voice made no sound, but still he screamed, 'I don't want to die! I don't want to die!'

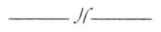

——— *Jf* ———

Jim was disorientated when he awoke the next morning. The smell of the disinfectant, the sterile decor and the sharp brightness of the day tried to engage his drowsy senses. He strained to remember the images of the unbelievable nightmare that he had suffered long ago. His body was numb but relaxed, as if he had a hangover without the sickness. He got up and drew back the dividing curtain of the cubicle he was in. He stepped out into the corridor. A small piece of the nightmare returned to him. He remembered where he was.

The duty nurse appeared out of a door and he remembered a little more.

'How are you feeling today?' She smiled.

Jim wondered if he looked different. He still did not understand what had happened.

She spoke. 'Can you still feel the sedative? Sometimes it lasts until the next day, but it'll wear off soon.'

He spoke. 'What happened to me? Can I see a doctor?'

She spoke again. 'Oh, you're well enough to go. You could have gone last night, or rather you should have, but you wouldn't leave. You were in quite a state. We weren't too busy so we let you stay. You had a panic attack, but you're perfectly well now. They're really quite common.'

He heard a voice but it did not seem to be coming from her. His mind was occupied with the nightmare. He spoke to himself, but aloud. 'I can't be fine. It can't just be over like that.' The pieces of his memory were returning, but the picture they formed did not make any sense. She was a nurse, and this was a hospital. Yet he was still alive.

'Most people are happy when they find out there is nothing wrong with them.'

The voice sounded kind. He looked at her. Her eyes were warm and they understood pain.

'I know it must have been terrifying,' she said, 'I've seen too many of these cases, and too much of the fear they cause. You thought you were going to die. You were in a state of extreme anxiety for over six hours. You were very, very... confused and scared. There's never much we can do. We don't usually sedate because these things are created by the mind. A panic attack can't kill you, but here we can't convince you of that. All we can do is wait for it to pass.'

He was certain that he had been on the point of being removed, or taken away by someone or something. Surely he did not have the right to be talking to this person after such a catastrophe? There was no sense. It had to be a trick.

'It's understandable that you're worried. When you're anxious you start to hyperventilate and this fools your mind into thinking all sorts of strange things. Then you worry more and so your heart rate speeds up. That makes you breathe even more quickly... and then it all starts again. It's a vicious circle.'

Jim was silent.

'Sorry. That's probably an understatement. But the fact is, as I said before, it can't kill you – however bad it seems. The doctor recommended that you make an appointment with your own GP. He'll be able to tell you more about it. But if you really want to see a doctor now...?'

'No. I'm okay. It's all right. I feel... a bit shocked, but...' He did not know what to say. He wanted to leave.

'Well then, I'd better get on,' the nurse said. 'As I said, just try to relax. This type of anxiety is really more common than you might realise.' She nodded her goodbye and went back into her office.

It was very early in the morning. The pavement edges were lined with endless rows of parked cars. There was an emptiness to the roads, like that of Christmas Day. When a car passed, Jim had time to watch it and wonder where it was going. When each one was gone, and its sound had diffused into the silence in the distance, he immediately felt alone. The feeling of being detached returned to him. He remembered the murder and expected to see police everywhere. But there were none. Everything should have been different, but it was not.

He walked across the grass of the Old Steine and tripped

on a mound of earth. He stopped to look down. The blades of grass quivered as the wind blew through their tip. He tried to focus on a large patch, but each time his gaze was drawn to a single blade. He looked ahead. The mass of green stretched before him into long rows of thin spikes, like a bed of living nails that he would crush with each step. It was a violent sight and he had to look away. He looked up and reeled at the thought of last night, and the night before that. He moved backwards with slow, faltering steps in the way a person who has just been shot in a film begins to die. He squinted in order to shield his eyes from the mass of activity around him. His head spun and he stretched his arms out. He felt as if he were in a sickening centrifuge. He tried desperately to reach for the safety of the centre but was being constantly drawn away from it by a non-existent force.

He began to run. Faster than he had ever run before, towards the haven of his room. After a few strides he was breathing hard and deeply, drawing in as much oxygen as possible to fuel his springing legs. With each pace he drove into the ground, trying to crush his feet under the alternate explosions of his calves and quadriceps. His knees cracked straight, and his toes clawed frantically inside his shoes in an attempt to keep him ahead of the turmoil that pursued him.

When he reached his flat he climbed into bed. It was 6.30 a.m. Roger would be round in an hour.

Chapter Twenty

Jim listened to the news on the radio throughout the day. He expected to hear his name or a description being read out by the police but there was nothing. Work passed in a silent daze. Again they were not very busy and Roger, who had hardly said anything all day, sent Jim home at two o'clock. Jim went immediately to bed and slept straight through to the next morning.

Alan came round at seven o'clock and they picked up Glenda at the dry cleaners where she had insisted that they meet her. Soon they were at Mrs Muurling's house. The front door was open and the three of them walked through to the back room.

Mrs Muurling was sitting in the black chair, clutching a small brown travel case on her lap. When she saw them she looked down for a second to compose herself, and then looked back up with a nervous smile.

'Are you ready, Mrs M.?' Alan asked. 'We're all set if you are.'

She stood up slowly and looked across to the picture of her husband on the sideboard. 'It's now or never, I think the expression is.'

Jim stepped forward. He passed her case to Alan and took her hand. 'If you're really sure,' he said. He hoped desperately that she was. He needed her to want to go. He needed to help.

'Shall I drive?' she said with a deadpan expression.

'Maybe a bit later, if you're still sober.' Alan laughed.

Jim laughed as well. It felt strange, almost unnatural. It was the first time he had laughed in over two days. He looked at Glenda. Even she was smiling. She almost looked happy.

Mrs Muurling sat in the front passenger seat during the journey. Jim had been concerned that she might be uncomfortable, but with the seat fully upright she had been perfectly happy to sit for as long as it took. They stopped twice for petrol. Each time, they grabbed a quick cup of tea and were quickly on their way again. They could all feel the excitement. Although the conversation never touched directly on finding the casket, everyone was infected with a kind of holiday spirit that gave enthusiasm to anything anyone said or did. It was a release. Separately they each relished the trip. Alan was away from the pub, and as far as he was concerned Mrs Muurling's goal of freeing herself from the past was freedom for them all. Glenda gained confidence with every mile that took them further away from Brighton.

Jim surveyed the scene. He could not help being overtaken by the mood of anticipation. As Alan had said, they would all find something different on this trip. Every time he looked at Mrs Muurling he felt a twinge of excitement, but immediately the unruly voice told him that it would be funny if her husband's note read something like, 'You ruined my life, you blood-sucking shrew.' He looked away and flushed.

He rehearsed in his mind how he would tell Glenda about what he had done for her. Surely she would be elated and grateful and would want to hold his hand? The unruly voice sneered that the freedom she now had would without doubt take her away from him. He stared out of the window comforting himself with the thought that they would be sharing a room together undisturbed for at least two days.

———— // ————

The man leaves the seafront and walks up London Road. He threads through the lines of jammed traffic and crosses the street. It is cool, and he smokes his cigarette with his hands in his pockets. He is walking fast and feels he must hurry for some reason. He is working in the chip shop tonight but he is not late, yet still he steps up his pace.

As he nears The Ocean Platter he sees the queue stretching back to the door. He is glad it looks busy. The first few hours are the worst but at least when he is working hard the time passes quickly.

He takes a last puff of his cigarette and then flicks it into the road. The glowing butt is caught by the wind and lands on the bonnet of a car in the traffic jam next to him. Automatically the man looks across. The driver of the car is mouthing some words and does not look happy. The man looks down and continues to walk. He is pleased. Twice so far he has managed not to react stupidly to other people.

He reaches the shop and strolls in. His foster mother is at the door end of the counter picking a gherkin out of a jar with some tongs. She smiles warmly at the man as he walks in. He knows she is pleased that he is there early because it will mean she will be able to go upstairs and watch her favourite soap opera for once.

He looks up and he is about to walk through to the back to get his apron when he recognises a face, and then an instant later sees a reaction he knows so well. The coward sees the man and a look of fear rips across his face like an open wound.

The man now understands why he has been hurrying, why he has been feeling unsettled.

Chapter Twenty-One

Padstow, on the north Cornwall coast, was the nearest town to the cove where Mr and Mrs Muurling had spent their honeymoon. It was late when they arrived. They drove to the hotel and booked in immediately. They were tired and within ten minutes they were all in their rooms. Jim sat on the bed nervously as Glenda walked around the room and bathroom checking things out.

'There's a trouser press. That's handy,' she said. 'I'll tell you what. You lot can have all the fun digging and I'll stay here and press all of our clothes a few times. A busman's holiday.' She walked over to the kettle and cups on the sideboard beneath the window. 'Free tea. D'you want one?'

'Not really, thanks. Are you having one?'

'Why not? I think I'll live it up a little. Enjoy my parole.'

Jim smiled inwardly. 'Go on then,' he said, 'I'll join you in a celebration tea.'

'I don't like to tempt fate. Maybe it should just be a potential celebration tea. I'm worried that we might not find the box. It would be awful. She's so excited.'

'I know what you mean,' Jim said. 'But I meant a tea to celebrate the fact that you can wake up in the knowledge that there won't be any unfriendly faces waiting outside for you.'

'Oh that.' Her expression turned cold.

'Oh that? I would have thought it'd be nice not to have

him around.' He nearly said 'have the bastard around' but he checked himself. That would have been disrespectful.

'It is. Definitely. But in a way it makes things worse, or makes me impatient anyway. I can't relax when I think about going back. He'll always be there.'

Jim held out his hand. Glenda came and sat next to him on the bed. He looked at her earnestly. 'He won't always be there...' *He's dead*, he whispered. 'Believe me.'

Glenda looked down. 'I'd love to believe that. I've tried to, but he always keeps turning up to spoil everything I plan. I hate to think about leaving and running away but I just want my life back. When this is over I'm going to book a flight to my auntie's. She lives in Canada. I'd like to see the bastard find me over there.' She squeezed his hand.

She had actually said it. 'I hate to think about leaving.' She had obviously meant to say 'you', 'I hate to think about leaving you,' but had forgotten. So she wanted to stay. He pulled her towards him. They kissed. He brought his arms around her waist. An incredible strength hardened his body. He was suddenly made of steel; invincible and capable of doing and saying anything he liked.

'Bill's gone for ever. He's dead,' he said boldly.

Glenda pulled away from him. Her eyes were wide and her mouth was open. She shook her head. 'What? How can you say that? You think that's funny?'

Jim did not flinch. 'Do you want him to be?'

'Is this some kind of sick joke? Is this your strange sense of humour? If it is, it's not funny.'

'Answer me! Do you want him to be?'

Glenda stood up. 'I can't believe this. How can you do this to me, Jim?'

'Do you want him to be dead?' He stared at her impassively, but he was fighting the urge to smile.

'I wish the bastard was out of my life, I know that for sure.'

'Dead, though?' Jim spoke quietly now, momentarily worried that he might not be able to elicit an honest reply.

Glenda turned and looked out of the window. 'What are you playing at, Jim? What have I done to you? How can you do this to me? I don't need this. I'm going away because I don't want him near me. If someone could take him away then, yes, I'd want that. I want my life back. I want to live again. Why are you doing this to me? I thought this was going to be a nice weekend. A relaxing break from all the crap we put up with in Brighton. I need this break, Jim. I really do. Just a couple of days of calm. Please don't worry me. Please!' Her voice was weary. She turned to look at him. She was drained of energy.

Jim jumped up and hugged her. He kissed her. 'I'm sorry, I'm sorry, but I had to know. If you didn't want him dead then...'

Glenda moved back a step. She had become pale in an instant. 'I don't believe it! You didn't!' She moved back further. 'What are you saying? You killed him? I don't believe it! You murdered someone? You want me to be happy? I want to go. I want to get out of here.' She was shouting. Jim moved forward and put his arms around her. She struggled but he held tight.

'Calm down,' Jim whispered. 'It's all right. Calm down.' His mind scrabbled for words. 'No... no, you don't understand. Glenda, listen. There's nothing wrong, I haven't done anything stupid. Please calm down, it's all right. Glenda, we're safe, it's all right, I promise. We're here for a nice weekend, let's not spoil it.'

After a while she stopped struggling and sat on the bed. Tears were rolling down her cheeks. The look in her eyes told Jim that she hated him and wanted to be away from *him* as well.

The unruly voice spoke. 'Kill her now. Just for a laugh. Strangle her, you could do it, easily. You're a killer.'

'Glenda. Look at me. I haven't killed anyone,' he sighed. He waited for her to react but her body was rigid. He went on, 'When I said he's dead, I meant we can forget about him. This trip is going to be a turning-point. From now on things are going to be different. You *are* going to have a new life. Please trust me, please try and believe.'

'But...'

'No buts! He's out of your life and mine, because we are going to find a way of making that happen. Glenda, I want to help you.' He paused. 'I love you.'

A look of shock shattered Glenda's fixed stare. Her eyes were glazed. She punched him in the chest. 'Bastard!' she shouted. 'Not fucking you as well! Not *two* nutters.'

Jim pleaded again and then did not know what to say. Suddenly he began to cry and turned to make the tea. 'I'm sorry,' he said quietly, without trying to conceal his tears. 'I can't help my feelings. Don't say that I'm like him, because I'm not. I care, I really do. I wish I had killed him, and if I had it would have been for you. But I'm weak. I couldn't do anything like that.' He sank to his knees and cried without restraint. Minutes later, when he had recovered his composure he said, 'Like before when I made an idiot of myself, I want to show you that I'm not like 'him'. Let's find the casket. Let's make Mrs Muurling's day, please Glenda. I'll check into another room tonight. Give you some space.'

―――― *JC* ――――

Padstow is a pretty town. The small picturesque harbour is lined on three sides by old pubs, a couple of restaurants and a number of souvenir shops, and it is still an active fishing port. The tide was in, and at least two dozen small fishing boats floated shoulder to shoulder within the confines of the harbour walls. There was a sea gate that opened into a large estuary flanked on three sides by low hills. When the tide was out, the beaches reached out over a hundred yards to the sea. During low tide the boats in the harbour lay uselessly on keel and hull. The muddy seabed was soon invaded by gangs of squawking gulls foraging in the piles of driftwood and seaweed.

Jim, Glenda and Alan found Mrs Muurling sitting outside one of the cafés by the harbour next morning.

'We wondered where you'd got to,' Alan said, pulling up a chair.

Mrs Muurling had some tea, toast and marmalade in front of her. 'I'm sorry,' she said. 'Just checking out the local scene. It was such a long drive and I didn't want to wake anyone. I was up early and I fancied a breath of fresh air.' She looked around. 'Isn't it beautiful? It's the first time I've been out on my own like this for ages. I wanted to do a bit of sunbathing, but apart from the weather I don't think my legs are up to it yet. I might book myself in for a wax this afternoon.'

Glenda and Jim sat down. The previous night, Jim had fallen asleep soundly and very definitely on *his* side of the bed. He had awoken the next morning with the embarrassing hangover of his outburst. He had apologised again to Glenda, and decided to make a conscious effort to hide his affection until she had seen the change in her situation herself. She had awoken a little happier this morning, pleasantly surprised to be away from Brighton, although she was still a little withdrawn. The thought of finding the casket had made them both shelve their differences.

'We could get your wheelchair from the car,' Glenda said, peering over the menu.

Mrs Muurling nodded. 'When we really get going that'll be a good idea.'

Jim said, 'Talking of which, how about getting on the task this afternoon? I've got my shovel...' He cut himself short, expecting the others to stare at him disapprovingly.

'Sounds like a good idea,' Mrs Muurling said. 'I'm so nervous that I don't want to go, but so excited that I feel I could run all the way there.'

'We'll see you there if that's what you decide. Personally I'd rather drive,' Alan said.

An hour later they were in the car, and within twenty minutes they had reached a tiny thatched village along the coast. Mrs Muurling remembered this as being the nearest place on the map to the cove. From there they drove slowly, as Mrs Muurling remembered the way as they went along. After several wrong turns and much backtracking she seemed to have found her bearings. The roads were the same but newer, she said tentatively, visibly becoming more excited as they rounded each corner. They drove along a narrow road for a mile or so. It ran parallel to the cliff and soon they had lost sight of the sea and were descending through a tunnel of trees.

'At the end!' Mrs Muurling pointed excitedly. 'That's it! We'll come out onto the beach. A long beach with towering cliffs either side. I remember this path. This is right. I know it is.'

From the car they could see a thin stretch of beach running the length of the shoreline. It cut a yellow crescent between the sea and the rock-strewn chain of dunes that ran parallel to the path. Either end of the cove was sealed by a high cliff. A large scoop of rock had been ground out at the foot of each one by the undermining work of the waves. They pounded constantly against the rock, throwing flamboyant plumes of foam high into the air. The crashing and clawing of the sea seemed to be everywhere.

The path entered the cove at the right. The ground was uneven and Mrs Muurling took Jim's arm. Alan walked ahead. He was carrying Mrs Muurling's wheelchair and set it down just before they reached the sand. Glenda joined him and they stood silently waiting for the others to catch up.

Mrs Muurling let go of Jim's arm and walked slowly past them to where the back door of a cottage lay face down on the path. The house was in ruins. Its roof had collapsed, and its timber frame had fallen in on itself like the poles of a wigwam. The wood was rotten except for a few small areas that were protected from the wind and rain by crazed patches of light-blue paint. The windows had buckled and been crushed as the walls had fallen in. Broken glass littered the area. After several minutes, Mrs Muurling spoke.

'This is it,' she said, without turning.

The others walked over to her.

'I'm sorry,' Glenda said.

'It's all right. I suppose I expected it to be like this. Still, it's a bit of a shock. I remember being here as though it were yesterday.'

Nobody spoke for a couple of minutes as Mrs Muurling stared, then Alan said, 'Can you remember where the casket was from here?'

'That won't be a problem,' she said, still studying the house.

'Sit down for a minute. We've got the chair here.'

Mrs Muurling moved back and Alan helped her onto the seat. 'We'd better get going soon.' She looked across to the horizon. 'It looks fine, but I wouldn't trust the weather round here.'

'I checked the forecast,' Jim said.

'Me too,' said Glenda. 'It's supposed to stay nice.'

Mrs Muurling was staring at the house again. 'It's like meeting a friend you haven't seen for a very long time and being shocked that they are so old. You don't know what to say.' She sighed. 'The thing is, your friend is thinking exactly the same thing about you. Maybe that's what is so sad. Maybe this is what I didn't want to face up to. I had pictured this scene so many times and each time it was exactly as we'd left it all those years ago. In my heart I knew it would be different; time changes everything, not just people. I knew I would be disappointed but I just didn't want to believe it. I feel so old.'

'Good memories though, I'll bet,' Alan said cheerily. 'So you haven't seen someone or something for a while. It only bothers you what they look like if you're bothered about how they see you.' He had taken his bandanna from his neck and tied it around his head ready for work. 'Eventually you both remember the person inside. After the initial shock, of course. That's why they invented this.' He pulled out a half-bottle of scotch and handed it to Mrs Muurling.

'The casket?' Jim asked.

Mrs Muurling took a long drink of scotch and handed the bottle back to Alan with a wink. She stood up and walked to the side of the house. She pointed to a tall triangular wedge of rock that stood out along from the cliff on the right-hand side. 'That rock...' She stopped and turned in shock. 'It shouldn't be underwater.' She shook her head. 'Tom dug a hole in its side near the base. It was in sand and rock. I remember it being quite deep. He wedged the casket it in with a load of rocks and put a dollop of cement on top of it all, there.' She pointed. 'On the back edge. What's happened?' She suddenly stepped forward and then stopped and turned again with the same look of shock.

A quarter of the rock was submerged. Its leading edge sliced into the oncoming waves.

'Easy. We'll wait for the tide to go out,' Alan said.

Jim shook his head.

'It is out,' Glenda said flatly. 'Low tide this morning and tonight.' She turned to Jim. 'What do you reckon? It doesn't look very deep.'

Jim walked to the front of the house. He jabbed at the line of seaweed that drew the high-tide mark. 'We're near low tide now.' He picked up his shovel and strode down the beach to the sea. He surveyed the scene for a few moments and then waded out to the rock. The water was up to the middle of his calves, and the swell of each wave forced this level up to his knees. The waves had life; their power made him nervous. He turned to go back but Glenda was behind him. He had to go on.

She edged up beside him. 'I say go for it. But your shovel's not going to be much use. We'll get Alan's pick.'

Jim turned. 'You're right.' He flung the shovel out to sea.

'That's a good shovel. What did you do that for?' Glenda asked.

'Suddenly I don't want it any more.'

'But someone might,' she said.

'They won't,' he assured her.

They had a quick cup of tea from one of the flasks they had brought and then Jim waded back out to the rock with the pickaxe. He was wearing jeans and a T-shirt, and dipped his hand into the water and began feeling for the cluster of rocks. His head was close to the water's surface and he was certain that it was suddenly going to suck him under. He trailed his fingers along the back edge, but the rock was smooth and there was no break to suggest that a hole had been dug and then patched. The sea had crept up the beach and cut into the cliffs during the last fifty years. Surely it could have smoothed a bit of cement? he thought.

He braced himself and struck the pick through the surface of the water. He aimed for the central point of the back edge of the rock. His first attempt missed the base and quickly ground to a halt in the sand. He swung again, but a little higher and felt the satisfying jar of the impact of metal on rock. The blisters on his palms distracted him for a moment. He wiped them on the back of his jeans and continued. After a few more swings they had all burst, and a row of small circles of raw skin grated against the wet wood of the handle.

Jim, Glenda and Alan worked in relay. Each dug for a period of ten minutes before handing the pick over and going to sit with Mrs Muurling. She had been certain that they had buried the casket at the centre point of the back edge of the rock, but after an hour of fruitless digging she was soon doubting her memory. She had told them that her husband had deliberately made the covering of cement quite thin because they were not going to be so young when it came to digging the box out. But it was a large rock, maybe even a different rock, she was not sure any more. And then suddenly there was relief. Mrs Muurling dropped her tea and stood up with hands clasped on her chest as Alan came to shore in the middle of his third turn of digging. He was clutching a small piece of cement. This knowledge added a hope to their work. From then on they started to make better progress. They were soaking wet, clothes drenched and hair matted from the salt, but not tired. The two who were not digging sat on the broken porch of the house in silent anticipation. They had not expected to get wet and had brought no change of clothing, yet despite the sharp breeze each of them was eager to get the pick back in their hands.

Just after midday Mrs Muurling told Jim that there was a storm coming. 'We'd better pack up soon,' she said. 'The water's getting quite high as well.'

Jim could not see any signs of a storm. It was true the tide was coming in, but the horizon was clear and bright. Glenda had stopped digging a little while ago because the waves were now above her waist, and Alan had driven off to refill the thermos flasks and get some blankets. Mrs Muurling looked cold and uncomfortable. Alan had offered to take her back but she had been determined to stay. Suddenly she seemed keen to leave.

Jim was now digging alone, working for fifteen minutes and resting for five. During one of his rests he said, 'We're nearly there, I know it. The hole's pretty big now, I can feel it. I know I'm not getting much purchase on the swing, but it's got to come soon. There can't be much more cement. It's starting to sound hollow.'

Mrs Muurling repeated her words automatically. 'Maybe we should pack up soon.'

Jim could see the nervousness in her eyes. She was trembling slightly and her cheeks were flushed. She looked edgily out to the horizon. 'There's going to be a storm. The sea's getting up. We should stop.'

Glenda took her hand. 'Jim's going to have one last try. Is that okay? Are you warm enough?'

'And then we should pack up,' she said.

Jim understood. He knew it was not the cold that bothered her. 'Alan should be back soon,' he whispered to Glenda. 'Get her in the car as soon as he is. I won't be long. It's coming out this time.'

He waded out to the rock. By now even the top half of his clothes were soaking from constantly reaching down to check on his progress with his hands. He was waist-deep, and each wave bounced the level of water to his chest. He jammed the pick into the deepest part of the whole and pushed down on the handle. He felt the grind of the metal against the rock as he increased the pressure. Suddenly there was a sharp snap as the axe sprung free, bringing with it another small chunk of rock. He did this several more times. Each time the axe penetrated deeper into the opening. Glenda looked anxiously from the beach and Jim waved a confident gesture of assurance with the axe. He hurriedly dug the point in again. He had a good hold this time. The head was obviously curved up behind the remaining wall of cement. He turned and pulled back on the handle. His shoulders were completely submerged and the back of his head was laying on the water and his hair floated on the surface. He took a deep breath and then pulled as hard as he could, as hard as he ever would. There was the grind again, but it quickly stopped as the point took an even better hold. Soon he was straining with all his might for a second time. For a moment he was completely underwater as a wave washed over him. He ignored the water rushing up his nose and sat back even further on the handle. His eyes were shut tight and the sinews in his neck stuck out. He willed the concrete to give in to him as another wave crashed over him. Salt stung his eyes and the sound of rushing water swirled in his ears. And then suddenly there was a loud crack and he lost his grip on the axe. He fell underwater and jumped up immediately, spluttering and coughing. He wanted to cry. It was over, he had failed. The handle must have broken, he thought angrily. He reached down to find it. He felt down at the rock and was shocked as his hand was unexpectedly lost in a large hole. He took a deep breath and dived under. He could not see anything and probed frantically with his hands. He touched something hard and smooth, and knocked at it. It was hollow. He erupted out of the water and gave Glenda the thumbs up sign. Within a few seconds she had rushed out and was standing next to him. He dived down again and pulled away some loose rock. Then the third time he was sliding the casket out from its compartment. Suddenly Jim and Glenda were trying to talk but could not because they were laughing so much.

They raced to the shore and held the box out to show Mrs Muurling. She was astounded. There was a look of intrigue on her face as though she were inspecting an alien artefact. She reached out to touch it but quickly brought her hand away. She looked at Jim and then Glenda. 'I need to rest first,' she said quietly, 'if that's all right. Can we go back now? The storm will be here soon.'

Chapter Twenty-Two

Jim was still standing at the window of their hotel room when Glenda came out of the shower.

The rain was lashing at the window and it drummed a rapid beat on the glass. The low rumble of the thunder was hardly noticeable as the storm moved on. The power of the lightning was dimmed to a tarnished fork in the distance. He looked out of the window again and searched for the ducks he had seen in the pond. The lightning had illuminated their silhouettes and they had been nothing more than three inanimate black blobs. But now the worst of the storm had passed they could just be seen moving in the light of a nearby street lamp. He wondered if the thunder and lightning had scared them.

Glenda touched his shoulder. He jumped slightly.

'Shall we go and see Mrs Muurling?' she asked. 'It's gone nine and she said to wake her at eight thirty.' She was dressed and ready for dinner as they had arranged.

'I must have forgotten. Sorry,' Jim said. He sat on the bed and pulled on his shoes. His hands trembled slightly as he tied his laces. 'If you give Alan a shout and tell him we're about ready to eat we can all go together. He'll be in the bar, no doubt.'

'Do you think she's opened it yet?' Glenda said.

'Do you?'

Glenda did not answer.

Jim said, 'I'll be a few minutes getting ready. I'll see you down at the bar.'

Glenda went downstairs and Jim crossed the corridor to Mrs Muurling's room. He knocked gently.

'Who is it?'

'It's me, Jim. Can I come in?'

'It's open.'

Mrs Muurling was sitting in front of the mirror brushing her hair. The casket was on the dressing table in front of her. She smiled as Jim came in. 'Are we nearly ready for dinner then?' she said.

Jim came beside her and touched the casket. It was the size of a shoe box and made of dark brown wood. It had rounded edges and its lid was held closed by a brass fastening clasp. Earlier Jim had removed a number of sheets of linen from outside the box which had been daubed with a sticky wax compound that was obviously some kind of waterproofing.

'You haven't opened it then?' Jim said to her in the mirror.

Mrs Muurling stopped brushing her hair.

'No. But I want to.'

'Would you rather I left? Me, Glenda and Alan can have dinner together. We can leave you in peace if you'd prefer.'

'I'd rather you didn't,' she said back to the mirror. 'The fact is I don't think I can open it.'

'Is there something wrong?'

'No, nothing, and I don't know why I'm making such a big fuss. There are only two letters in there. I don't know what I'm worried about. But I *am* worried, scared even.'

Jim leant on the dressing table.

'The anticlimax of it perhaps?'

Mrs Muurling touched the casket. 'I don't want to think

that, but I have to admit it's something I can't get out of my head. It's all I've considered since I knew we were coming. I know the thought of finding it was exciting, but maybe a part of me did not want to find it. Maybe I wanted to leave the past as it was. When it comes down to it, all this thing is about is a couple of old letters. I've been hanging on to the special memory of this for too long. Now it's in front of me I feel as though the rug's been taken away from under my feet. My security has gone. Part of me wants to put it back so that I will never know what's in it. Maybe I'll be happier that way. Ignorant but happy. Maybe it's better that we all keep something buried.'

Jim cleared his throat. 'And if you open it? What's the worst that could happen? You were happy together, weren't you? I mean it was your honeymoon. When else could you be happier?'

'We *were* happy. That's just it. If I don't read the letters, then I'll always have that happiness, and more. But if I read them there's no way that they can add to the happiness we had. And then whatever my husband wrote will be known and ended. There will be nothing left after that. Perhaps it's all a bit too final.'

'And so you'd rather hang on to that security. The real truth is your time together, after all. Nothing can take that away. This box, whatever ideal it represents, won't make any difference to that.'

Mrs Muurling reached out to touch it. 'If I can face up to the truth, that is.'

'Is that the real reason?' Jim asked.

Mrs Muurling slid the box across to Jim. 'Will you open it?' She drew her hands away and clasped them on her lap. Jim was about to protest when she looked him in the eye and said, 'No arguments. I want you to open it. Please.'

Jim nodded. He picked it up and twisted the clasp. He had to pull hard and there was a crack as the lid came free. He pushed the lid back on its hinges and a faint smell of dry wood and a stale smell of old paper wafted out. A very tangible sensation of the past lingered in the room for a few moments, like a fleeting memory. Jim pulled the two letters out of the casket. They were the only contents. He held them out towards her. One was smaller than the other and she stepped forward and took it eagerly. She almost snatched at it. Jim was startled and dropped the other letter. He bent down to pick it up, and when he arose, Mrs Muurling had opened the envelope and had pulled out the letter from inside. She gazed glassy-eyed at the single piece of paper for a few seconds and then dropped it and walked to her bed.

'Are you okay?' Jim asked. 'Do you want some water? Or something a little stronger? Is it the shock?' As he spoke he could not help looking down at the fallen letter. The side he could see was blank; he tried to look through it to see what was on the other side. He walked over to the bed and sat beside her. 'Do you want to talk about it?'

Mrs Muurling looked up. Her eyes were still full of tears, and she looked very worried.

'What did it say? What did he write?' Jim asked.

'It's not his letter, it's mine. Have a look yourself.'

Jim walked over to the letter and picked it up. He looked back at Mrs Muurling in astonishment. 'There's nothing on it!' He waved the piece of paper like a flag of surrender.

'That's supposed to be my letter.' She was staring out of the window, shaking her head. 'It almost makes me glad he died so that he never had to endure that.'

'You didn't write anything? This is it?' Jim realised his

tone was harsh and accusing. 'What happened?' he asked gently.

Mrs Muurling stood up and walked to the window.

The glass was beaded with rain. A game of join-the-dots was being played by the heavier drops. She put a finger to the glass and followed the progress of one line down to the sill.

'Just think. While I was warm at home during the past years, the box was often only a few inches from storms like this.'

'Your finger is close to that rain, but it is still dry.'

'That's true.' She turned to Jim. 'Is there any way to make up for something you did wrong in the past?'

'I suppose that depends on what you've done,' Jim said.

'I've been denied access to my mistake for so long. I knew where it was but haven't been able to do anything about it. The moment when I made that mistake has long since disappeared. And with it, I suppose, any chance of rectification. Maybe that's my punishment.'

Jim was silent for a few seconds. The unruly voice laughed at his nervousness. 'Why *did* you make that mistake?' he asked quietly. 'Why didn't you write anything? It's one thing to do something wrong, but another to do it when you know you'll be found out.'

Mrs Muurling smiled. 'I couldn't have told you at the time why I didn't write anything. It just seemed to be the right thing to do. Maybe I thought I was cheating time. I didn't think I would ever be old enough to retire. I certainly didn't have the guts to envisage myself as an old lady. I didn't want to store memories of my youth for something that I thought would never happen. I didn't think I would ever be found out. It was nothing to do with my husband. I loved him dearly, and if he were here now I could explain and he would understand. He would even laugh about it. He saw the funny side of everything. I just feel bad that he might have been the one standing here now, without me, without my explanation. Can you imagine that?'

'And his letter?' Jim asked.

She turned back to the window. 'Another time, I think. I'm exhausted now. I'd like to lie down for a while. I don't think I'm ready yet.'

'What about dinner? Are you coming down with us?'

Mrs Muurling was laying on the bed with her eyes closed. 'I'll stay here for a while, if that's okay. I need to rest.'

'What shall I tell the others? They're bound to ask.'

'Tell them that everything is all right. I'll speak to them later. But I'm tired now.'

'But the letters? Do you want me to tell them about those? They're bound to be excited.'

She did not reply; she was dozing off.

Jim returned to his room. He remembered the electric fire, the bars and the bones of his melting hands. He strode towards it and stamped repeatedly but calmly at the elements until they were broken. Its orange heat quickly died, and soon the twisted bars were grey and harmless.

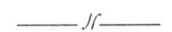

———— Jf ————

The man is ready to go to the pavilion, but first he has to check the girl's house. Outside the chip shop, there was something he did not like in the eyes of the coward. He seemed to be too unconcerned about the girl. How could he not stand up for her? What was the matter with him? The man has decided to verify his story and see if she is in.

He is outside the girl's house. It is half past eleven. If he leaves within the next ten minutes he will be able to get to the park in under twenty minutes at a brisk walk. He does not want to have to run; if this is some kind of trick he will want to be fit and full of energy when he arrives.

He stands on the opposite side of the street and screws his eyes up. He peers through the gap in the curtains of the top window. The hall light is on, and he holds his breath and waits expectantly for a shadow or a movement. He pictures where her bed is, and remembers the colour of the wallpaper. He wonders if she still has that strange picture of that weird tree by the French painter whose name he could never recall. His stomach goes cold as he thinks about how stupid he is. He wonders if she is ashamed of his lack of education as well. He crosses the road and walks down the alley to the back of the house. The kitchen light is on. The clean worktops look stark and clinical, like an operating table. He smiles at her tidiness.

He is constantly aware of the old lady next door. Luckily it is past her bedtime and he will not have to run away from the police tonight. He only runs to cut out the bother. He knows they do not really care about the girl as he does. They are just trying to put on a show. He wants to call out, or knock on the door to see if she is there. He might be able to save an unnecessary journey. If this is part of some plan there might be trouble. If the girl knows nothing about this, and he manages to avoid the trouble, it will please her and look bad for the coward. But if this is the coward's plan, she will be annoyed if he wakes her up and is seen near her house. So far he has managed to keep out of sight when he comes to try and glimpse her. Apart from when he loses his temper, that is. But that has not happened very often and will certainly stop in the future. The only reason he has watched her in the past is because he was not able to express himself before. But he will be able to talk properly tonight. She will feel relaxed near him. He will make her relax.

He does not shout, but waits another ten minutes to see if anything happens. He strains his ears to listen. He has crept up to the kitchen door and is leaning against the broken fridge. There is the sound of car tyres on the London Road in the distance. A door slams shut a few houses down and he hears raised voices. He is distracted, and tries to make out what they are arguing about. Soon the voices are soft enough to be contained by the walls of their house. The man is uneasy. He walks out of the alley and heads off to the pavilion via the coward's house.

He takes a deep breath and keeps an eye out for a gnarled tree to help raise his spirits. He will squint so that it looks blurred, the same as the French artist painted it.

Chapter Twenty-Three

A few days after returning from Cornwall, Glenda accepted an offer of a place from a college in London. Jim had tried to persuade her to resume her studies in Brighton, but the assurance in her calm words left him with no doubt that she would not change her mind.

He was desolate. Despite Glenda's initial intimation that they would continue to see each other occasionally, Jim noticed a very rapid deterioration in their relationship. With Bill's sudden disappearance, he knew she no longer needed him. Their experiences together seemed to amount to nothing more than a series of impersonal circumstances. They had met and felt some kind of attraction or need. Jim had been injured; he had risked his life and had liberated her from her tormentor. Now the only tangible emotion that endured was blame. He blamed himself for giving her this unchecked freedom which allowed her to distance herself from him.

For a few weeks Glenda had lived her life as though she were a new person. It was as if the recovery of the casket was a watershed in her life that had been a signal for her to begin again. She was full of plans and dreams. Jim knew he was not part of these. In her eyes, Bill had apparently given up and she compared her situation to someone who had been sentenced to a life in prison and had unexpectedly been given an eleventh-hour pardon. Her relief was obvious, as was her need to leave the scene of her torture. Certainly she was happier than Jim had ever seen her. Her smile was once again a pure, instinctive response. It dramatically changed the way she looked, which seemed to change the way people viewed her. Jim quickly noticed that as her confidence returned, the sudden sexual interest towards her of bus drivers, customers, men in the street and friends magnified the change. He was helpless as he witnessed this unstoppable metamorphosis. For him there would be no such transformation.

When he was quiet, brooding, he would see Glenda in his mind. She was walking and he was scuttling after her. He would run to keep up and, even though she was walking slowly, he could never catch her. She would smile and wave and Jim would scream and punch himself in the head until his fists hurt. In spite of his pain, she would continue to move forward as though he had ceased to exist.

Confirmation of Glenda's desire to leave him had come after their return from Cornwall. They had visited Mrs Muurling each weekend subsequent to the trip. Mrs Muurling was much happier and it was incredible how much healthier she had become since she had started to venture into town on her own. She went regularly to her friend's tea shop and had begun to make contact with acquaintances from long ago. Despite the fact that she still refused to open the letter, her confidence had grown in equal measure to this happiness. She kept the casket proudly on her sideboard like a store of vitality from which she could draw by sight. Glenda had even taken to visiting Mrs Muurling on her way home from work. This pleased Jim; it indicated that they shared the desire to be together, like an adopted family.

Then police 'missing persons' leaflets for Bill appeared

around town. Overnight Glenda disappeared. It was that sudden.

Jim could see the root of her uncertainty in his poorly disguised confession about killing Bill. Glenda was convinced she had seen Bill after they had returned from Cornwall. Jim had put this down to paranoia. He had reacted calmly and had assured her that she could call him if she was ever scared. He cringed at the memory of the cockiness in his voice. He had also turned up at her house a couple of times when he should have known very well that it was Bill's night to spy on her. He winced at his naivety.

He continued to ring her at home, but nobody answered. He tried her at the shop but the impatient manager was dismissive and said that she had taken some holiday and he did not know where she was. During the following week Jim caught the bus to Glenda's house every night after work. The first night he knocked on the door a couple of times and then walked around to the back garden to see if there were any signs of her presence. He trod carefully through the garden and pressed his face to the cold glass of the back window. His body was heavy and listless. He leant on the sill and rested as he listened. He returned the second night, but this time he rattled the door handle and prised at the kitchen window. As he pulled, the bottom corner of the window twisted and a section of unputtied glass ground ominously into the frame. For a moment he was both scared and excited that the pane might break. He held his breath and looked along the row of neighbouring houses, knowing that a sudden sound would be the stimulus for a volley of lights to be fired across the back gardens. Windows in the long back walls of the houses would light up like white squares of a giant luminous chessboard.

He released his grip slowly and then ran into the alley as the casement rattled and shuddered its relief. He walked around to the front of the house and sat and waited in the porch for twenty minutes. On the third night he waited until after ten o'clock, and on the fourth and fifth until well after midnight.

———*JC*———

Glenda did not return until the sixth day. She was home when Jim arrived there after work. He saw her figure in the lounge window, as he walked to the door. She suddenly darted out of sight into the hall and then there was silence. He knocked on the door but she did not answer. He tried several times and was soon frustrated into shouting. He fell to his knees and pushed his fingers through the letterbox and held the flap open. He called calmly at first, but his tone became increasingly angry when she did not answer. He shouted her name and begged her to come out. He was swearing at her inside his mind. He wanted to smash through the door and shake her and demand that she acknowledge him. He paused for breath and heard a voice yelling from above. He stepped back and looked up. There was anger in his eyes and this became fury when he saw the old lady from next door leaning out of her bedroom window.

'Why don't you leave her alone?' she shouted. 'I've had enough of you pestering her. I'm sure she's sick to the eye-teeth of it. Make yourself scarce or I'll call the police again. You'd think you'd get the message after all this time.' She shook her fist. 'Go on. Buzz off!'

It was a second before Jim caught on. His anger had suddenly turned to confusion as he insisted politely, 'I'm a friend of hers. I'm not who you think I am. She wants to see me. I know she does.'

The scowl remained on the old lady's face. She went on angrily, 'I'm not going to take any of your lip. Sitting in your car until all hours. You must have a screw loose. And now banging on her door like that. I've seen you in her garden.' She shook her fist again. 'I'm not scared of a villain like you. Either you go or I'll call the police.'

Jim was indignant. 'There's nothing they can do,' he suddenly heard himself sneering. He stepped boldly out on the pavement. 'I've got a perfect right to stand here and there's nothing either you or anyone else can do about it.' He waltzed around in front of her house and then looked up at her for a reaction.

'We'll see about that, sonny.' She disappeared into the house.

For a split second Jim felt an empathy for Bill. Had he really loved her as well? He snatched a nervous breath and walked away quickly. A minute later he was in the phone box around the corner dialling Glenda's number. He was trying to ignore the panic that had come over him. The ringing stopped and he held his breath as he waited for Glenda's voice.

'Glenda? Is that you? It's Jim!'

Still there was no answer. Only the soft, hollow breathing in his earpiece.

'Glenda! Answer me! It's me, Jim!' He banged the receiver on the glass and then put it to his ear again. 'Glenda!' he shouted. 'Glenda! Why won't you answer? Say something,' he begged. There was a long pause and then the line went dead. 'Well get fucked then!' he shouted, before smashing the receiver against the door. The glass did not break. He wanted it to and banged again, and then once more. The third time the small pane popped. He pulled the receiver out and smashed it repeatedly on the coin box until the earpiece was hanging limply by its innards.

A police car drove past with its light flashing but without a siren. Jim pulled the phone to his ear and pretended to be talking. The car turned into Glenda's road and the brake lights flashed on outside her house.

Jim slunk out of the phone box with his head down and walked to the pub.

The next morning he was already at the top end of Glenda's road when she left for work. The air was fresh and the sky was clear except for the faintest trace of night mist that the rising sun was rapidly burning off. The leafy trees stood in a sleepy trance, as yet undisturbed by the pushes and nudges of the usual sea breeze. It was going to be a hot day. He had a terrible hangover and his stomach felt like he had been drinking poison all night rather than beer. When he had awoken he had been certain he was going to be sick; he was still drunk and he had caught a bus and arrived at Glenda's road in a daze.

He leant against the lamp-post and held himself from falling. He was soaked with the sweat of panic and nausea. His heart beat loudly in his chest as if trying to alert his wandering attention that something did not feel right. He drew in a succession of deep breaths.

'You're probably dying,' the unruly voice whispered as his heart began to throb in his brain.

Jim tried to ignored the voice. Suddenly he was pressed hard against the lamp-post as Glenda rounded the corner and headed down the road. A surge of excitement drove the worry from his mind and, still half-asleep, he trotted onto her trail like a dopey bloodhound.

He pursued her; watching her intently. He studied the way she walked, the way her left arm swung while her right held her handbag in place. He looked harder, and with each step she took he began to see a marked difference in her. The vulnerable Glenda that he wanted her to be had evidently disappeared. He drew closer and studied more intently. Her steps were gentle and slow, as if she were walking without touching the pavement. She was wearing a short summer dress and sandals. Her hair had been cut, and brushed her shoulders gently as she walked. He saw her again as he had seen her that first day on the London Road. The grace in her movements reminded him of the unattainable object of desire he had been happy to follow that day. She was again a beautiful woman whom he had seen for the first time, except that now there would be no wonderful shyness in the dry cleaners, no new beginning.

Jim slowed as she looked around without seeming to look at anything. He could have mistaken this for preoccupation, but he knew she had lost her fear. It was confidence, and he *hated* it. He could have followed her all the way to work assessing these minutiae. He was happy just watching as long as she stayed close. But he knew they had to talk.

Glenda was waiting at her bus stop when Jim approached. He began casually, asking her if she would come out that night to discuss 'them'. She was direct. There was an uncompromising look in her eyes. The warmth in her face that he had treasured like a gift whenever she had looked at him had gone.

'It won't work,' she said, looking down the road for a bus. 'You always knew it was a fling, Jim, nothing more. I'm sorry if you're upset. I admit, much of the blame is mine. I needed someone and you were there to help. But I need to move on. I'm sorry, Jim, but it's over. I should have called you and didn't. That was wrong of me. But there's no going back. I've got to go. I can't argue any more.'

'But why do you have to leave? Bill's gone.' He knew it was the same old conversation.

Glenda looked down and did not speak.

'Glenda?'

She looked up. Her lips were pursed tight as though she were about to be sick in a public place. Her eyes glistened with spite. 'Ghost train,' she said. 'The one night I needed you, and you were busy. My worst fears could have come true that day and you were probably off down the pub. *That* day above all days. I thought my world was coming to an end. *He* was just playing his games but I was too scared to know that at the time. All I knew was how weak I was, and how strong *he* could be. I've never felt so low in my life. I was worthless and insignificant. It's such a shock to think that about yourself when you've spent so long convincing yourself that your life has some meaning despite the terrible things that happen to you. After telling yourself every morning that you can get by until things get better, which you think really will happen all of a sudden because you believe you deserve this. I called you and needed to be with you. I thought you could help me. But you weren't there. It was then that I *really* realised that I did not deserve what was happening to me. I knew I had to get away – and I mean really away, not just for a few days like Cornwall, although that trip probably saved my life. I was in such a state inside. I'm sorry, Jim, it's not because of that day. But if you come and ask me why? That was the turning-point. For the first time I had the courage to think about myself and how short my life is, and how much there is that I want to do. I've had enough and I'm determined to put it all behind me. *Him*, you, this fucking torture town. I don't need a man in my life. I'm sorry, Jim, but I just need to be alone. Very alone and very happy.' She paused and seemed to suddenly realise where she was; that she had been talking and was allowed to talk for as long as she liked without answering to anyone. 'It's all in the past now. Nobody can touch me. There's nothing more that can happen.'

Jim stared at her in astonishment. He felt as though his body had been drained of blood and his veins had been filled with lead. He thought he was going to fall over and die. Any moment now a hearse would come and take his stiff corpse away. The undertakers would talk about what they had seen on television the night before and which supermodels they would like to see naked, and Jim would hear this because they would think he was dead, when really he was still alive but without life. His sudden, profound sadness was too intense to simply disappear when his body ceased to function. It would infest his remains.

He opened his mouth to speak and was surprised when the words formed in his throat. 'I don't understand. What ghost train? When?' His face brightened innocently. 'It *can* work, Glenda. It will. I promise you it will.'

Glenda was not interested. 'What is it with you men? Why do you do this to yourselves? Why do you do this to me? You think after four years in the frying pan I'm going to jump straight back into the fire? You must be bloody mad. Both of you!'

The bus came and Glenda stepped on without saying anything, leaving Jim like a dog tied to a post, whimpering as its owner moves away. The bus drove off. Then it disappeared into the distance. A tear rolled down Jim's cheek. Nothing in his life could ever have prepared him for the devastation he experienced at that moment. The sadness would indeed be with him until his death. He was enraged yet impotent. He had the strength, but she had the power and control. He screamed at the top of his voice. No words came out, just pure frustration. He was so angry that he wanted to be run over by the next bus, or to start a fight so that he would be purged of the adrenalin that filled him. He scowled at a passing schoolboy on the other side of the road who had jumped at the sound of his outburst. Jim wanted the boy to say something so that he could react and vent more of his frustration. But the worried boy turned away and hurried on.

Jim telephoned Roger and told him that he would not be coming in to work that day. Then he wandered around aimlessly for a couple of hours, sitting on park benches because that is what he had seen people do in films when they needed to be by themselves. Finally he just sat on the pavement, put his head in his hands and began to cry. He cried as he had done the day he had realised as a child that life was not a repeatable game: that it did not last very long and would one day be ended, and he would never know that it had even begun. That ultimately, you could never keep *anything* you wanted.

————)/(————

It was past midnight when Jim got in from the pub. He was still numb from the shock, but not drunk. He had gone to an out-of-the-way pub near Hove and stared at his beer. He stripped to his underwear and headed straight to bed. The grey wedge of the half-moon glowed through the thin cloth of his curtains. There was a narrow gap where they were not fully closed and a slice of light found its way to the far wall where it cut a precise line into the blackness. The window was open and, every now and then, a soft breeze puffed the curtains.

His arms were crossed on his chest and his open palms lay on his shoulders. His legs were straight and together, and his feet formed a wide 'V' where they fell apart from his heels. He was, he realised, in the 'coffin position'. One day he would be stretched out in that very position for eternity. Glenda had left him and he was going to die alone. These thoughts mocked him and impelled him to bend his legs, uncross his arms and shuffle onto his side. At one moment he was telling himself to try and lie calmly and endure yet another night of this. The next he was sitting upright and trying to shake himself free of this worry.

This night was not as severe as others recently. It was not one of the overwhelming attacks of anguish he feared so much. The kind that pounced from nowhere and which could only be driven away by leaping out of bed and turning on the television in a desperate effort to come back to the assurance of the world around him. He would urge the television picture to come on; for the mist on the screen to fuse into the image of the late-night weatherman standing in a brightly lit studio pointing at black and white fluffy clouds. He would stare hard and listen to the man talking. This person was alive, and part of something greater. Surely Jim was included in this as well. His heart would slow from its hurry, yet he would still feel as if his body had suddenly been inflated with a gust of ice-cold blackness. In one terrifying moment he would believe that this time he really *was* going to die.

The scares of the recent weeks had not faded. Bill was

rotting and that should have been the answer to the questions that would not leave him. He wondered how long it would be before there was a knock on the door and the police would be there to take him away to the living hell that awaited him in prison.

He tried to sleep, but Glenda's words of rejection would not leave him. It was as if he had been blinded by a flashbulb: the moment was frozen in his eyes. He was trembling. He wanted to sleep. Everything would be different in the morning. He wanted to be waking up to the clink of bottles and the sound of children chatting on their way to school. He wanted to call her. To tell her that everything was all right and that they would soon resolve their difficulties. But it was no use, he knew. His time had run out.

The sound of a passing car filled the room. Its engine buzzed feebly as though a large insect were trapped inside the bonnet.

He was falling into a dream, and gasped as he pulled himself up from where he was dropping.

'The ungrateful bitch. You're worthless. You're a piece of shit to her,' the unruly voice told him.

'No!' he shouted aloud. 'I've had enough of you!' He bit his lip hard.

It was quiet outside and the only source of life in his world of red blackness was the movement of particles of dust under his eyelids. He drifted towards the deceptive goal of sleep like a parachutist descending slowly towards his target. He did not realise that he was already accelerating rapidly towards the uncontrollable free fall of his dreams. He was breathing deeply and slowly now. A train thundered over the viaduct behind the houses. When it had passed the scattered silences of the night began to regroup.

As he slept he began to dream about Glenda. She was kissing Bill and caressing him. They were naked and enjoying each other's bodies. They knew Jim was watching but it did not matter to them. They were happy and his presence was inconsequential.

The unruly voice whispered to him. 'Another failure. You cannot win. Follow her, but there's nowhere to go. You cannot win, you've lost. You cannot win!'

Blood dripped from Jim's lip onto his pillow.

Chapter Twenty-Four

Mrs Muurling was surprised to see Jim. He had not been to see her since they returned from Padstow. He smiled weakly as she answered the door and this prompted Mrs Muurling to ask, 'Are you all right? Is everything okay? You seem a bit down.'

'No, I'm fine. Really.' He did not understand his distraction, but his words were dismissive.

They went through to the back room and sat down. There was a long silence. Jim looked out of the patio doors.

After a while Mrs Muurling got to her feet, saying, 'A cup of tea?' She took his smile to be a 'yes'. 'How's Alan?' she called from the kitchen.

'Okay.'

'And Glenda? How's she? Is she at college yet?'

'I'm going to kill her,' Jim whispered. He poked his fingers into his eyes and began to push. His eyeballs yielded slightly to the pressure like unripe tomatoes, and quickly the pain told him he should stop. He clenched his teeth and pushed harder. A sudden thrust of agony dug into his brain and a blinding light flared behind his eyes. He jerked his fingers away and stuffed them into his mouth and began to bite hard. He blinked anxiously, half-hoping that he had blinded himself and half-hoping that he had not. The room was blurred for a moment before coming back into focus.

'I said, how's Glenda?' Mrs Muurling called again.

Jim pulled his fingers out of his mouth and looked at the deep indentations on his skin. He wanted them to bleed but the blood did not come.

'She's fine. She said to say hello. We might pop round together tomorrow.'

Mrs Muurling poked her head out of the kitchen. 'That'll be nice. You should have brought her round today. I like seeing her.'

Jim nodded again and smiled. He remembered Glenda's uneasy look when he had told her that Mr Muurling's letter had contained revelations of a murder. Even though she knew he was lying, it had pleased him that his irreverence had scared her.

'Has she made any plans yet?'

'She's gone off the college idea,' Jim said. 'She wants us to go abroad together to do a bit of travelling as soon as possible. I told her she should think about her education but she's convinced we should go away. We talked about it a bit – Europe, America, Asia – she's full of ideas. It's exciting, but I'm going to have a proper talk with her, maybe talk to her father man to man about getting her to stay here and get on with her studies.'

'That does sound exciting! You've *definitely* got to bring her over. I'd love to be a part of your plans. If you don't mind, that is.'

Suddenly Jim needed to leave. A distracting sensation told him that he did not have much time. He needed to hurry. He walked into the kitchen.

Mrs Muurling smiled. 'Won't be long.' She looked happy. She kissed Jim on the cheek and blushed. 'I'm sorry, but it really is nice to see you. It's been a couple of weeks. I was worried you'd forget about me. Both of you.'

'Have you thought any more about opening the letter?'

Jim asked.

'I need to prepare myself. I don't think I'm quite ready yet. It's funny: as long as it's unopened, I feel as though Tom is in the room with me. I haven't exposed my memory of him to the passing of the years and, I must admit, I'm beginning to think I never will.'

Jim looked down. Everything was now clear; he knew what he had to do. The necessary act that would complete the rest of his life was no longer hidden from him. It was no sudden flash of guidance, nor inspiration, merely an awareness of the knowledge. The quiet telling of insight.

'I'm sorry but I have to go,' he said abruptly as Mrs Muurling was about to speak. 'Something's come up. Something I've just remembered I've got to do.' He smiled apologetically. For once he was speaking the truth. 'Hopefully you'll open the letter soon. Maybe I'll read it someday.' He was calm and wanted to laugh at the melodrama of the situation.

Mrs Muurling lost her smile and she suddenly looked older. 'Yes, maybe you will,' she said after a pause.

Jim kissed her on the cheek. For a moment he wanted to stay with her a while longer. He liked her small, familiar world. Tea, cakes, the overgrown garden, the sound of children outside; her smile and her gratitude. All of these things represented their unlikely friendship. And that was one thing he had earned in his own right.

A minute later he had walked out of the door and all that security seemed never to have existed.

———*JT*———

Jim drove to Glenda's house and slowed to a crawl. The

curtains were drawn but the light was on. The subtle changes in light told him that the television was on. He was very nearly at a standstill when he noticed a car flashing its headlights in his rear-view mirror. He slammed his foot down on the accelerator and screeched around the corner.

The desire to touch her had gone. The unruly voice threw a picture of him strangling her into his mind but he was surprised that he could dismiss this so quickly. The satisfaction he had previously experienced did not come. She would never be his and it did not seem to matter.

With the decision came the panic. The ice-cold blackness was there again as Jim drove home. He was powerless and trapped. The imminent events were inescapable. He felt as if he were being sucked slowly into a space that was too small for his body. And the harder the force pulled, the smaller the space became. There was nowhere to go. It was coming to an end. He howled and stamped on the accelerator. He sped along the road towards the dead end ahead. There was a high brick wall in front of him. Glenda's face came to mind: big and smiling, protruding from the bricks of the wall. He pressed harder on the accelerator and hurtled towards it. The wall disappeared and all that remained was her incessant, contemptuous laughter. She knew, his friends knew, and above all *he* knew that he had failed. Again, the blame was his. He was paralysed by the childish fate he had created for himself. He had lost, and was happy to be thinking so cruelly. He deserved to die.

Jim's foot was flat to the floor. A head was still poking out of the wall ahead, but now it was his own. 'See how you fucking like this!' He grinned. 'I'll get you. Let's see how you like this then!'

The van's tyres screeched harshly on the road. For a

moment this noise filled Jim's ears. The sound was so loud and sudden that it seemed to have bored a hole into the front of his head. His muscles let go of his body and he slumped back into the seat. He was bleeding. He could taste blood on his lips. He opened his eyes and looked around. Blood was filling his mouth. He checked his body hurriedly for injury but there was none. It was quiet. The wall in front of him was full and silent. In the side mirrors the street looked normal. Everything seemed to be normal. His right leg was still pressed hard on the brake pedal. He put his face in his hands. He began to cry again. Sobbing at first in frustration, soon he was crying hard with fear.

If he could not kill himself he really *would* have to kill her.

Chapter Twenty-Five

The interest in Bill's whereabouts seemed to have died down within a few weeks of his disappearance. But Jim knew an anonymous note from him to Bill's parents could have interesting possibilities. The posters outside the police station had been removed and had been replaced by the portraits of more recent missing persons. The almost comical reminder of concern for Bill remained in the form of the posters stuck on the window of the chip shop by Bill's parents. They had also put advertisements in the local papers to try and entice him home. The story was that he had done this many times before, and even Mr and Mrs Chip-Shop did not seem to be too alarmed. They continued with their work, and all seemed well. But on closer inspection there was a depth of sadness in every movement of their bodies that translated into an undeniable aura of loss. It had dug deeply and irrevocably into each line and contour of their faces. The pain of their uncertainty was visibly consuming them.

Jim had continued to use the chip shop out of a macabre fascination with their grief. When he was sitting at one of *their* tables, eating *their* cod and chips, he was often overtaken by a compulsion to tell them where Bill was buried. 'Your bastard son Bill,' he would rehearse, 'I know where your bastard son is buried.' He would smile to himself. 'And I shovelled the earth onto his worthless head.' On one occasion he had been laughing when the father had looked over at him. Jim had caught his breath, and then continued to laugh, but nervously like a school bully who is not so sure of himself in the presence of a teacher. The father had allowed an unwelcome smile to barge its way onto his face and then had carried on with his work.

There had been no visit from the police. And even if there were in the future, Jim was now certain that there would be absolutely no way of linking him to the death. After all, they would catch Roger first; he was the murderer. Every angle of weakness had been covered. As far as he knew, Roger and Glenda had not seen each other, and so he was the only source of information.

Jim went to the pub that evening. He installed himself at the bar and chatted to Alan. They spoke about nothing in particular; the usual listless pub talk which gave Jim enough reason to stay out of the house for a few hours. However, at precisely ten thirty, Jim got up, leaving half of his sixth pint of Guinness and, to the amazement of the others, left.

He headed towards The Ocean Platter. He was hungry. He had not eaten properly for two days and knew that he might faint if he did not eat soon. His stomach began to rumble as he walked and the painful but welcome pangs of hunger quickened his step. The prospect of putting his new plan to work had enlivened his appetite. As he walked along the bright, empty streets, he was filled with an excitement that had been with him during the past few days, and which seemed to be increasing minute by minute.

The Ocean Platter closed at eleven o'clock. At ten forty, Jim was standing on the other side of the road rehearsing what he needed to say, checking his 'props' and then considering the logic and risk of this visit. But more than anything, as he saw the two figures moving behind the counter through the steamy window, he savoured the fact that at that moment, his future was in his precise control. It was about to move in the exact direction he had already chosen. He looked at his hands, moved his fingers like a pianist about to begin a difficult piece and smiled. It seemed so easy. He centre-parted his hair, put on a pair of clear-glass spectacles and crossed the road.

Bill's parents both looked up as Jim walked in, more out of reaction to the doorbell than interest in who had entered. They were both looking back down at their tasks within a split second. Jim looked through the alcove to the seated area at the back. This was the only part of the shop that was not visible from outside. He was prepared to walk out and return the next night if there had been anyone there. This was the only uncertainty to the plan. Clenching his fist in his pocket, he acknowledged the good luck he knew he was due when he saw that both tables were empty. His eyes immediately darted to Bill's face on the 'missing' poster.

He was about to smile when a man's voice said, 'What will it be, mate?'

Jim spun round and said with a pleasant smile, 'Cod's roe and large chips, a gherkin... and a can of orange, please.'

The owner put the order together and placed it in front of Jim.

'I noticed the poster on the window,' Jim said, placing his money on the counter. 'It's been there quite a while, hasn't it?'

The owner looked down into the till and counted Jim's change. Jim automatically put his hand out when the owner had collected the right money, but then, for a few seconds, neither of them moved. The owner seemed to be frozen still, maybe not even breathing, and Jim could not bring his hand back. Jim shifted his eyes across to the owner's wife. She was kneeling on the floor with her hand in a bucket of water. The surface of the water was still.

'He's our son,' the owner said, handing Jim his change. He looked down and then over to his wife. She was scrubbing the floor hard, gradually moving backwards on her hands and knees, magically producing rows of shining tiles from under her cloth.

'He's disappeared,' the owner continued, 'but we hope he'll be back anytime.' He had a strong Greek accent and Jim could see him as a young man, fresh over from Greece, starting a new life without the comfort of home and family. 'Is that all then?' the owner concluded.

Jim felt sorrow for the first time since Bill's murder. A fleeting, but unmistakable sensation of having wronged someone came over him. He wanted to leave and call his plan off.

He was about to turn and walk out when the unruly voice simply said, 'No.'

Jim immediately put his hand into his pocket and grasped the envelope.

'In fact,' Jim said, 'I'll have another can of drink, please. Same as before.' The fridge was to Jim's left and the front door to his right. The wife was still cleaning the floor. The moment the owner turned to get the drink, Jim was about to slip the envelope under the vinegar shaker and step quickly to the door when in a sudden change of plan he dropped it to the floor and stepped on it to make it dirty. The shop was about to shut and it could have been there for any length of time.

The unruly voice was pleased with this change it had suggested. 'Let the mother find it. More dramatic that way.'

Jim paid for the drink and walked out. He did not turn

but kept his head down and walked away slowly, holding the warm bag of food to his chest. When he rounded the corner he dumped it into the first bin he saw.

All of a sudden he had no appetite.

———— // ————

The man checks his watch. It is five to midnight. He is annoyed that he is now late and has to run. His mind keeps pace with his legs. He prepares himself for the two possible situations that may arise. If the girl is waiting for him, he will be happy. Things will not be a problem. He will accept whatever she says so that they will be able to begin a dialogue, and develop something constructive from there. That is what they have lacked in the past. When she became pregnant and had the abortion, he did not understand why he was not involved in the decision. They talked briefly but, as usual, they ended up arguing. He did not listen to what she had to say and he does not think she listened to him. He wanted a baby so much – but he has to forget it. He has wasted the past years with resentment; all it has brought him is loneliness. He has had enough of that. It is not living; it is like introducing a slow death into your life. Injecting your future with a numbing, lethal poison.

He darts across the road ahead of a speeding lorry. For a moment he is drenched in the whiteness of the oncoming beams. He disappears into the light, and hovers between existence and destruction. But his body responds to his mind's instructions in an instant. The lorry races past and he skips safely into the darkness of the pavement. He laughs and jogs into the outfield of the cricket pitch. It is a minute to midnight and he slows to a walk so that he can catch his breath.

He approaches the pavilion and stops. He looks around but

cannot see anyone. He tries to relax so that he can assess the situation. 'Allow her to be herself,' he says nervously to himself. Or if she's not there, let the coward face him and tell him what he really wants. He is prepared to listen. He needs this to finish. A part of him hopes that the girl is not here, that she has nothing to do with this. It will just be him and the coward left to settle their differences. He would not be surprised if the coward has come to punch him in the face for what he did to him outside the pub and outside the chip shop. He is nervous at the thought of allowing someone a free hit. It would be admitting that he has been wrong and allowing them to take their satisfaction knowing that he will not let himself respond. But that is what he has decided to do. This would be a good test. A broken nose (if the coward catches him a good one) and then a conversation.

His head spins at the novelty of such radical thoughts. It is like going to another planet and being forced to forget everything you have ever learnt, he thinks. Suddenly you have to cope with a new set of rules. They might all seem wrong, but you have to accept that they are right without question.

He thinks of his time in prison. He was only in for a few months, but that was long enough to make him never want to return. He considers being alone and knows that it is enough to make him accept these new rules. If only he had known this earlier. Why did he never listen to what people tried to tell him?

He shouts the girl's name but knows immediately that she will not be there. He shouts it again to make the coward happy and think that he has tricked him. He moves forward and waits. It is time to call the coward out and to force him to stand up for himself. He tries to put on a friendly voice but there is no response. He calls again, but still he does not appear. The man becomes frustrated. Someone is obviously making a fool of him when he is trying to resolve things. He calms himself with the thought that he was very nearly late. Whoever is supposed to meet him might be late as well.

Adrenalin and hope surge through his body when he hears a voice. He spins around to meet it and waits for the face to catch it up. It is a man's voice, confident and self-assured. He is now certain that the coward has found his courage and is coming for his revenge. He relaxes at this satisfying thought. He easily steels his body to receive the blows he deserves. He nods to himself and lets his open hands fall by his side.

Suddenly everything is wrong and he really has been shown to be a fool. It is not the coward, but the strong-looking one from the pub. He can see in his eyes that he wants to fight, even before this person's aggressive words have caused him to clench his fists and prepare himself for a battle. The world has faded quickly into the distance and the two of them occupy the inescapable black bubble that remains. The person is very close now and ready to pounce. The man stands firm. He is sad that things have worked out like this. He wishes he had not come, and that he had found something exciting to do that evening. He knows he can beat this person in a fight. There is not even a trace of doubt in his mind. This sadness makes him feel even stronger but he is desperate to be weak. He wants this person to be able to hurt him, but he knows if he loses his cool the person will not have a hope in hell.

This person is shouting, telling him that he is going to hurt him. This makes the man react inside but he manages to control his temper. He thinks of the girl and pretends she will be watching his defeat. It would please her that he was not so tough. She might even tend his wounds. He would have to remember to wince because they were supposed to be painful.

The person comes at him and instinctively the man jabs accurately and knocks him away. The person comes again and the man does the same. He tries to stop his fist from throwing punches but this person's snarling attacks have annoyed him. The person lands a blow to the side of the man's head. It is not a hard shot but the man is pleased that this person at least seems capable of hitting him if he stays still. The man has suddenly punched the person to the floor. He is angry with himself and about to walk away in disgust when the coward appears from behind a tree. The coward rants and raves about not hurting his friend and, for a minute, the man is tempted to punch him out as well for whining like a baby. But it is obvious the girl is not there and he cannot be bothered with this kind of play-fighting any more. He shakes his head and turns to leave. He is thinking how he has made a fool of himself by hurting the coward's friend, how sure he was that he would not get involved in that kind of thing any more when he has suddenly been thrown to the ground. The person he was fighting with is on top of him, shouting and angry, trying to strangle him. The man cannot help but laugh. The person is so weak and injured from the fight that the man shouts at him to squeeze harder. When that does not work the man jabs him lightly and repeatedly on the chin to try and enrage him.

He spreads his arms and lies back, begging himself not to fight.

Chapter Twenty-Six

Glenda pulled her front door shut and walked towards the bus stop. She tossed her hair back into the breeze and smiled. Her thoughts were elsewhere, like someone who has just won the lottery and is stunned by the wondrous possibilities of life that suddenly appear from nowhere.

When Jim saw the bus rounding the corner he turned his engine on. He was ready to pull out from his hiding place at the end of the road. He had bought a car a couple of days before from a run-down car yard on the outskirts of town. Three hundred pounds for a four-wheeled heap of rust, but at least it was legal. A car was now a necessity for Jim's plan to work. It was his lifeline to Glenda. He had tried the coincidental meeting on the bus: Glenda had ignored him. And he had come close to being spotted when he followed her on foot. It had been cold recently too, and standing at the end of the road in a howling wind at night was beginning to get to him.

He drove close behind the bus as it headed down the hill to the seafront. Glenda was sitting at the front of the bus, so Jim was able to tail it without any cars in front of him.

For the past three weekends he had seen Glenda leave her house at the same time in the morning, but had never been able to find out where she had gone. The previous weekend he had been waiting in a cab. The meter had already been running for twenty minutes when she appeared. They had followed the bus east along the coast, but by the time they reached Roedean school Jim was nearly out of money. He'd had to ask the cab driver to drop him off so that he could get a bus back.

As they now passed the school Jim looked down at the fuel gauge. It registered full. He knew that he had done the right thing when he had spent the best part of his savings on his seventh-hand Mini Clubman estate. Soon the bus was winding its way through the narrow streets of Rottingdean. Glenda got off just before the Conservative Club. Jim pulled over and jumped out of the car. He studied her as she walked along the High Street and then turned into a cul-de-sac. Halfway down, she turned into a path and walked into the waiting arms of a smiling couple. Jim was relieved and pleased with himself. It was not another boyfriend, unless this older couple who had just taken Glenda into their house had a particularly unusual way of spending their Sundays. It *had* to be her parents. Jim returned to his car and then drove past the house. Number twelve. He turned at the end of the close and drove back to town.

He did not go to work the following day. A quick phone call to Roger to cry off sick, a cup of tea, and then Jim was on his way to Rottingdean. He parked in the car park by the large pub on the front and walked the short distance to Glenda's parents' house. He entered their road and took a piece of paper out of his pocket. He held the paper in front of him and pretended to mouth some words as if he were reading an address.

There were no more than twenty houses in the quiet close. All of the homes were compact red-brick bungalows. Each had a well-trimmed, modest front lawn, and number twelve, Jim noticed as he approached, had a pink rose bush at its centre. The sky was grey and a stiff breeze whistled through the eaves of the low roofs. Jim was depressed by the scene. There was nobody to be seen, no life, not even birds on the telegraph lines or a cat sitting on a front wall. The wind seemed to have blown the atmosphere out to sea while the occupants sat without knowing in front of their televisions with a cup of tea. They were all waiting: for their next meal, their favourite programme, a good night's sleep, a nice day; for whatever. The entire road waited.

Jim broke the silence as he crunched along the gravel path of number twelve and rang the doorbell.

The door opened a little and a voice called through the gap: 'Yes? Can I help you?'

'I'm a friend of Glenda's.'

The door opened wider and an unsure face stared at Jim.

Jim stared back for a second, looking for a family resemblance. The man was tall and slim and was wearing a shirt and tie. He was probably in his mid-sixties, bald, but the hair he did have was short and neat.

'Er... hello. Are you Mr Brown?' Jim asked. 'Glenda Brown's father?'

'I am. What can I do for you?'

'You don't know me, but...' he paused for effect and said again, 'I'm a friend of Glenda's.'

Mr Brown screwed up his eyes. 'Are you indeed?'

'I'm Bill.' Tall, slim and dark hair. Jim knew he would fit the description. 'An old mate from the poly.' Jim gestured with his head towards Brighton.

'Oh yes?'

'Hard bloody work he is,' the unruly voice snapped. 'Glenda might have warned us.'

'I've been abroad,' Jim said hesitantly, 'and now I'm back I'm trying to catch up with some old friends. Glenda's one of them.' Jim held up the piece of paper he was holding with their address written on it. 'Most of us gave our parents' addresses to each other when we left college. We all knew we'd be on the move for a few years and not many of us owned houses then.' He forced a chuckle but Mr Brown kept his straight face. 'So here I am,' Jim said.

Mrs Brown came to the door. She peered over her husband's shoulder. 'Who is it, Eric?' She was also in her sixties but her skin was sunless and without a trace of wrinkles.

'This chap says he's a friend of Glenda's. From college. Bill, isn't it?'

'That's right,' Jim said with a brightness he had hoped to avoid. 'Me and Glenda took some classes together.'

'Which were those?' Mr Brown asked quickly.

'Mostly history classes,' Jim replied with equal speed. 'But some literature as well.'

Mr Brown nodded. He seemed satisfied. 'I suppose you'd better come in then. I can call Glenda at work, tell her you're back.'

Before Jim could protest, and against his better judgement, he gave in to the intrigue of this situation.

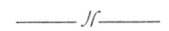

———— JF ————

'Thank you, Mrs Brown,' Jim said as she handed him a cup of tea. 'Sorry about this,' he said, rubbing his chin and running his fingers though his hair. 'I've been on the road for a couple of days and...' He was about to say that he had lost his shaver when he realised that as far as they were concerned, he *was* Bill. He paused and then said: 'I had my bag confiscated by the customs men at Newhaven. And that was on top of someone stealing my wallet on the trip over from Dieppe. I walked and hitched here. Took me two days. I'm afraid the more you need a lift, the less likely you are to get one. My clothes were soon sodden. I borrowed these from a truck driver. At least they were dry for a while.'

Mrs Brown voiced her sympathy. Mr Brown had sat down and was glancing occasionally at his newspaper. When he heard his wife's voice he instinctively looked up.

'Has Glenda mentioned me before?' Jim said.

Mr and Mrs Brown looked at each other and then Mr Brown said, 'No, I don't think so. It was a few years ago that she left college. I don't think she has kept in contact with many people.'

Jim took a deep breath before starting his rehearsed speech. Mr Brown was looking sceptically at him again, but Jim was determined to continue. 'I haven't seen Glenda for a while,' he said slowly. 'I had to go abroad on business. I'd been in France for a while out of necessity really. I was in the police force but left a while back. I realised I wasn't quite cut out for the monotony of shift work.' He chuckled and said, 'You might laugh at this but I decided to set up my own agency. A kind of lost and found bureau, like a private investigator I suppose.' He waited for a reaction but, as he had hoped, they were quiet with disbelief.

'That's why I had to leave the country. I was on a very sensitive case and my cover got blown. I couldn't go home so I thought it better to hop across the Channel and sit it out until it had all died down. I wanted to find Glenda to crash at her place for a few days until I could see how the land lay. But I only had her college address. We all gave our parents' as contact addresses. One good thing is this.' He tapped his head. 'Memory like an elephant.' Jim sat back. He smiled at the two puzzled faces.

There was complete and utter silence for a few moments. Then, Mr Brown stood up and walked to the phone. 'How about we give Glenda a call, Bill? Tell her about your predicament. See what *she* makes of this.'

Jim had been waiting for this. He nodded. 'Of course, I can't wait to hear her voice. And I'd love to see her face when she hears that I'm back. But I think there are a few things you should know before you ring. Especially as she's never mentioned me before.'

Mr Brown furrowed his brow and glanced at his wife. 'What's this all about then? Why *are* you here?'

'Right,' the unruly voice said. 'Sod you, that's it!' It had been bored while Jim had muddled through the preliminaries. Now came the good part. 'Let's see what we can do,' it urged.

Jim put a sad expression on his face and sighed. 'I knew I shouldn't have come here, it was bound to cause problems, but I was certain she would have said *something*.'

'What? Said something about what?'

'About us. About our engagement.'

'Stick that in your pipe and smoke it!' the unruly voice bellowed.

'You and Glenda, engaged?' Mrs Brown said quietly. 'When? Why didn't she tell us? Is it a surprise?' The two faces stared at Jim like a pair of children.

'By the look on your faces there's not much doubt that it's a bloody surprise!' The unruly voice went on gleefully: 'You're shitting yourselves.'

Jim tried to hide his satisfaction and put a look of confusion on his face. 'We were engaged when we were at college. It wasn't for long but I'm amazed she didn't tell you. Then I went off to police training at Hendon and we gradually drifted apart. When I came back to Brighton we started seeing each other but it wasn't really the same. And when I heard that she'd been seeing some bloke called Jim behind my back, well I'm afraid things suddenly ground to a halt. I punched this bloke out and then the matter was finished with. I spent a month in prison. That's why I left the police force. Still feel pretty bad about that, and beating this bloke up as well. All I really wanted was to see her and say that I'm sorry.'

Mr and Mrs Brown stared eagerly, taking in this information as someone who is starving might eat a bowl of gruel. They were fascinated, if disgusted, by these revelations.

'I'm sorry for breaking the news to you like this after you've been so nice to me. I just thought Glenda would have said something. How about calling her and telling her I'm back?'

Mr Brown jumped up. He marched across the lounge and planted himself in front of Jim. His eyes were wide, watery with sorrow as well as anxiety. 'What kind of person are you to come into our house and tell us stories like this about our daughter? If you think you're the kind we'd like Glenda to be involved with, then you're bloody well mistaken!'

'Eric!' Mrs Brown called anxiously.

Mr Brown did not turn but raised a pacifying hand. 'Okay, Susan. It's okay. Bill is just leaving.'

'Steady, old man,' the unruly voice cautioned.

Jim could feel its indignation spreading inside him. He drew himself to his feet and smiled cockily. 'Personally, I think it's a shame that my near-in-laws are treating me like this. I'm a little upset and I know that Glenda will be too when she hears about this visit.'

For an instant Jim considered pushing Mr Brown to the floor, but then the unruly voice was taunting him: 'Even you could hurt an old man. A coward like you. Go on then, do it!'

He turned and found himself walking out of the house with a sneer plastered across his face. 'Anyway, thanks for the hospitality. If you do speak to Glenda before I do, remember to tell her I'm back. Tell her Bill's back.'

Chapter Twenty-Seven

It was two days since Jim had visited Glenda's parents. He wanted her to worry and to have to find the answers to the flood of questions Eric and Susan would ask. And the tears... *they* would be worth all of his trepidation about the visit. He knew the hardest part was over and done with. And in the meantime, he could sit back and prepare diligently for the important days ahead.

During the morning of that second day, he made the first of his silent phone calls to the shop. And at the same time the following day, he made three more. Twice he cupped his hand over the mouthpiece when she answered and said nothing. She repeated 'hello' before putting the phone down. But the third time, after a long pause, Jim was about to hang up when Glenda said tentatively, 'Bill? Is that you?'

Jim gripped the receiver and smiled.

'Bill,' Glenda said angrily, 'I know you're back. My parents told me what you did and it makes me sick.'

Jim removed his hand so that Glenda could hear his breathing.

She continued, 'Why did you do that? Why do you want to use them to frighten me? Speak to me, you coward!'

Jim rasped his finger on the mouthpiece and hung up. Immediately after work he drove past the dry cleaners to check that Glenda was still there and, seeing that she was, went straight to her house. He left a sunflower and a note in an envelope on her doorstep. The note was made up of different sized letters cut from a newspaper and pasted across the breasts of a 'page three girl'. It read: 'Hi, slag. Guess who's back? I hope you're pleased. Eric and Sue seemed to be.'

A week later when Jim 'happened' to be walking past the dry cleaners, he was pleased with his look of surprise when Glenda rushed out of the shop to speak to him. But when she told him breathlessly about the phone call her parents had received from Bill's parents, after they had found a note in The Ocean Platter, the responses and facial expressions he had practised momentarily eluded him as he heard the word 'foster' between the words 'Bill's' and 'parents'. Suddenly he had no problem shaking his head in disbelief. For the second time, the feeling of having wronged someone returned.

He was relieved to be back in familiar territory when Glenda mentioned the silent phone calls she had had from Bill during the past couple of weeks. He responded accordingly. The look of fear in her eyes was reassuring. He was pleased things seemed to be back to normal.

'I don't see how he can be so cruel to his parents by visiting mine and not even calling his own,' Glenda said in tears.

Jim guided her into the shop and turned the sign to 'CLOSED'. He had always wanted to do that. He led her by the arm and sat her down. Her tears gave him strength. She had made him suffer so much, and now here she was feeling sorry for herself. She did not know that Jim's insides had died and were rotting as they spoke, creating a stench that only he could smell in his mind and that made him feel permanently ill. It repulsed him and he detested himself for having been so affected by the timid person who was now sitting in front of him.

'I find it hard to believe he's back,' Jim said. 'But then again, nothing that bastard does surprises me. I suppose I'll be next in line for the treatment. He's bound to get round to me sooner or later, even though we aren't still together.'

Glenda touched his arm. She looked as upset and scared as if Bill were in the room with her.

Jim took her hand and said, 'Is there anything I can do?'

She shook her head, seemingly remembering where she was. 'I really thought it was all over. You don't know how free I've felt recently. I was actually beginning to convince myself that I wasn't being punished for something awful I'd done in my past. I really was. I even felt good about myself, about my future.' She began to shout angrily. 'Why won't the fucking bastard leave me alone!'

Jim pulled her towards him. She pushed him away, and shouted, but he continued to pull her towards him.

'I'm so fucking angry!' she yelled. 'I want it to end!'

'I know you do,' Jim said calmly. 'I know you do.'

Chapter Twenty-Eight

Jim and Roger were sitting alone in the pub after work having a few pints. The last thing Jim remembered was a reference he had made to Glenda. He was very drunk and he knew it. Yet despite this he noticed Roger's sudden interest at the sound of *her* name.

'What about Glenda?' Roger asked. He seemed amazed and was silent for a few seconds. Then he began to laugh.

'Of course I could!' Jim was shouting. He had not meant to shout. Alan looked over at them. Jim leant forward and whispered, 'If she ever betrayed me I'd kill her. I know she suspects that something funny went on, but she knows that I would kill her. She knows I would. *I* know I would.' The veins in his neck pulsed and he clenched his fists.

Roger sat back to defuse the situation. 'She'd never believe anything like that anyway,' Roger said calmly. 'She might have done at first, but that would have been the shock of *his* disappearance. I mean I wasn't sure myself for a while. The coincidence was quite worrying. But he's back now anyway.' He took a sip of his beer and then continued. 'And anyway—' He began to laugh. 'I mean, you're not exactly the murdering type. *I* was worried that I could have killed him accidentally.' He lowered his voice. 'But I'm sorry mate, I had it all wrong. How could I have accused you of anything like that? We both know what you're like.'

He stopped laughing but was still smiling. His face was big and his eyes had narrowed into two contented slits. Some people in the world loved Roger. He could exist for many more years, being nice and feeling certain of himself and of the direction of his life. But only if he were allowed to. It would be so easy...

Jim broke this train of thought and gritted his teeth. He smiled. I'm not as fucking weak as you think I am, he thought loudly.

'Show them both what you did if they're laughing at you now,' the unruly voice said.

A few moments later Roger nodded. Jim was pleased. He finished his pint and downed another whisky chaser.

'You don't know me,' Jim said solemnly.

Roger stood up and walked to the bar.

Jim turned and nodded to Alan who was peering over Roger's shoulder.

'He knows as well,' the unruly voice told him. 'They all know that you don't have the balls. He's told them all. Now they think *he's* back, your plan has made you look like a wanker. I told you. Kill them all.'

Some more beer later and Roger had left and Jim was sitting on his own. His head was beginning to spin, and he concentrated hard to think straight. He recalled vaguely that Roger had laughed at him again. Jim had challenged him, and said that he could give him proof. 'Dead meat...' was that what he had said? Those words seemed right. They repeated themselves in his mind in an ominous hush, daring anyone close enough to hear. He was happy that he had finally managed to confess, even if this had been a lie. Nevertheless he had confessed with conviction. He was proud of himself. It was as if he had fulfilled a desire to swear in church within earshot of the vicar.

Finally Jim admitted that he was as drunk as he could get. Yet he was aware that his thoughts were more lucid than they had ever been before. He seemed to be standing at the bar, having another drink, but he could not be sure. It must have been Alan who spoke to him as he left, but he did not remember any words until he was a long way down the road on his way to the cemetery.

It was beginning to rain. Jim walked quickly into the sharp spray. It was everywhere and had soon coated his skin and clothes. He glistened as though he had been polished. It stuck to the carbon monoxide of the exhaust fumes and washed it into the gutters. It drummed on the pavement and scoured it clean. It was fresh and heartening. The light of the street lamps glowed and faded on his face as he moved from one to the next. His cheeks were red from the cold, and his eyes were bloodshot from the drink. He was angry, and the flickering orange light on his skin had life, like fire. All sounds were deadened by the drink and the noises had lost their edge as though they had been eroded by the rain. He ground his teeth together. They were made of rubber.

He was soaked through by the time he reached the cemetery. The twenty minute walk passed like a decade of life. It was over in an instant. The past now only existed as nothing more than a jumble of indistinct impressions that had flown by in a moment.

He walked through the gate and headed towards the grave. He moved off the path and stepped onto the grass. The ground was soft and he slipped and fell. He got up and patted at the mud on his backside. It seemed natural that he should lose his footing. He had staggered his way there, and the now soft earth was waiting, ready to cushion his fall. He stood still for a moment, reacquainting himself with his balance. Watery mud dripped inside his collar as the rain trickled down his hair. He knew he was not a coward. The others might laugh about him, but this would shock them all. Wait until they heard about the body he had unearthed. He would dig the body up. It would be *his* murder. Jim would confess to the killing and say it happened any way he chose. Even brave Roger would not have the guts to go to the police and say that he had done it. At last Jim would win; and better than that, everyone would realise that he had had their measure all along.

Mr Falmer's young grave had started to sprout a smattering of wispy grass; but the roots were shallow and the grass came away easily with a few rakes of his hand. Jim was on his knees, dragging soil behind him. The earth had packed down since he was last there and after ten minutes he realised that the deeper he went, the harder it was becoming to dig. He did not know how much time he had, but it seemed late and he needed to hurry. He ran over to the back fence and twisted feverishly at a slat that splintered free with a loud, satisfying snap. Then he was back on his knees stabbing the wood into the ground. He was still strong and his heavy blows were frantic, like the determined paddling of a canoeist who has lost sight of land.

He had been digging for no more than five minutes when his pace suddenly slowed. A few seconds later he was doing nothing more than prodding the earth with the wood. His face dripped with a brackish mixture of sweat and rain. He knew he was drunk, but it was not the same drunkenness as earlier. The alcoholic high had vanished. Only the desire to curl up and sleep remained. He concentrated, trying to command his limbs to obey him. His arms were weak, but he compelled them to continue.

He simply had no choice. However much he might try to convince himself in the future that he had had to stop because of fatigue, he knew his mind would not accept that excuse. The unruly voice would be unrelenting in its conviction: he had stopped because he was scared, not because he was tired. Because he was no longer drunk and brave.

He jabbed into the earth and screwed the wood down hard. He had found a fresh reserve of energy and within minutes he had found new rhythm. He continued like this for ten more minutes. Then he lay face down on the ground and stretched his arm into the hole. It was a foot across and about three feet deep. He dug like this for a couple more minutes but then stopped in frustration because earth was falling continually from the steep walls and he seemed to be getting nowhere. He rested his head on his shoulder and closed his eyes. His drowsiness made him forget his aching hands. He wanted to sleep but he knew he had to continue. His fingers were buried by a cascade of earth that seemed determined not to leave the hole. He grabbed at the dirt and flung it far past his shoulder. Then he tore an even larger handful and raised it up triumphantly. He squeezed it hard as though he were displaying the entrails he had just ripped out of the stomach of a kill. He stared at his hand, fascinated.

The splash of the rain had disappeared and there was no wind. Jim looked at the dark shapes of the trees in front of him. They were still and silent. He listened hard, but heard nothing. He was sure someone was nearby. He scanned the blackness in between the tree trunks but looked away quickly in case something appeared. Then there was a voice calling behind him.

'Jim,' it said quietly. 'Come away from there. Come

over here.'

The voice was familiar. He turned quickly. There was dark shape ten yards away. It seemed to be very big. The figure stretched out its arm and called again.

'Jim, come here. Come away from there.'

For a second Jim's thoughts were frozen on the image of Bill's decaying face smothered with earth and the black tarpaulin. But that could not be right; Bill was here, calling him now. The figure took a step towards him. This time it did not speak.

'Bill?' he said. 'Is it you? Have you come for me?' He was astonished by his own confidence. He was talking to a ghost and did not want to run.

The figure cleaved itself into two. A second shape appeared out of the first and stood motionless by its side.

'What do you want?' he shouted. 'Who are you?'

The first figure moved forward; it was only a few feet away from him when a weak smile came to Jim's lips.

'How? Why are you here?' he said.

Roger extended his arm. 'Get up, will you,' he said, still as calmly as before. 'Let's kick that earth back in and go. This is finished now. It has to be.'

Jim did not move. His mouth was open and his eyes stared without blinking. His explanation of what he was doing was trapped in his mind like a caged wild animal. 'I've got to. I have to do this.' He looked down at the grave. 'I have to tell everyone what I've done. I have to show you all the body. You wanted proof, well here it is!'

Roger moved closer and touched his shoulder. 'Listen, mate. Let's go and get a cup of tea and something to eat. Do you have any idea of what time it is?' Roger ignored the silence. 'It's after half two. We've got work in a few hours. You need some sleep.'

Jim raked at the hole and held a handful of dirt up to Roger. 'I've got to tell everyone what I've done. This! Look at this!' Roger took his arm and hauled him to his feet. Jim let the earth fall to the floor.

'Come on, mate. We'd better go. It's late. You've had too much to drink.'

Roger went to move off but Jim remained rooted to the spot. He stared at the twin shadow. Roger pulled him, but he would not move.

'Is that Bill?' he asked innocently.

'It's Glenda. I followed you here from the pub. You were drunk and ranting. You told me why you were coming here and what you were going to do. Do you remember? You told me to get Glenda to prove what you said was true. You were shouting. I followed you. When I saw what you were doing I went to get her. You need to hear what she has to say. I wanted to tell you but I didn't know how. It has to come from her.' Roger beckoned Glenda to them. 'It's all right,' he said to her. 'He's okay.'

Glenda walked forward, but kept her distance. 'Hello,' she said. Her face was obscured by shadow.

Jim peered at her, trying to fit a facial expression to the sombre tone of voice. He stepped forward inquisitively. Glenda leapt backwards. Roger tightened his grip on Jim's arm.

'It's all right,' Roger said. 'I've got him, he's okay.'

'So you both finally found me out,' Jim said sarcastically. 'You've come to see the evidence of my madness, is that it? Or my cowardice perhaps? I know what you're both thinking. You can't fool me. You're not going to come here and claim the murder yourself, Roger. The police will find me here. They won't believe you. I killed Bill, not you.' He turned to Glenda. 'Don't listen to what he says. He's lying.

I killed him. We had a fight, and I killed him. I did it for you, Glenda. You'd prefer it that way wouldn't you? You'd be free. Admit it.' He turned to Roger. 'You tell her, Roger, how it was me.' He threw his arms up in frustration. 'What am I talking about? You don't even know the half of it! Let me tell you, Glenda.' He stepped forward.

Glenda did not move. Her eyes were cold and her body was taut, ready to retreat if he came too close. 'You're drunk, Jim. Very drunk and confused.'

Jim smiled. 'I killed him for you,' he whispered. 'He's dead, buried down there. And you look at me in this way?' He wanted to be angry but his body was too tired to respond.

The unruly voice shouted. 'Walk away. Leave the two of them. You're stronger than them; fuck them both. You don't need them.'

Jim agreed with the unruly voice. 'I've had enough of this crap. I'm off.'

Roger still had hold of him. He looked at Glenda. She nodded.

'Look, Jim. We only want to help. I don't know what you expect to accomplish by this stunt, but I can tell you one thing for sure. You're certainly going to hurt the family of the person whose grave you're digging up.'

'Bill's grave, you mean?' Jim spat.

'I've had enough of this rubbish about a murder,' Roger said. 'Bill's done a runner. He disappeared. And now, unfortunately, it seems like he's back and up to his old tricks again. Nobody killed anybody,' Roger said firmly.

Jim laughed. 'But you were there, weren't you, Roger? We've got our little secret. Remember? The pavilion? The little fight? What? Do you think he just staggered to his feet and decided to leave town? The severe pounding of his head on the concrete persuaded him to start a new life in suburban Bracknell or something? He couldn't wait for his new adventures to begin and so disappeared immediately?' Jim was laughing. He had freed himself from Roger's grip and was back at the graveside. He kicked some of the earth back into the hole. 'I'm so sorry, Mr...' he checked the headstone, 'Mr Falmer. But the body I dumped on you a little while back does not actually exist. You were dreaming. Some people say death is like one long dream. Well you've had one hell of a dream already. I must admit that I was worried as to whether you and bastard Bill would get on in your somewhat restricted social afterlife. Or if he'd be too heavy and you'd be pissed off with having to bear the weight of someone you don't know for the rest of eternity. After all, you've only just begun to be dead; there's a long way to go yet.'

Roger pulled him away. Jim was nearly shouting. 'But I needn't have worried about all of that! My friend here didn't actually kill anyone, and I didn't bury him on top of you. Many apologies for disturbing you. It must be a weight off your mind, Mr Falmer, and your body.' Jim laughed. Suddenly there was pain in his right cheek. A stinging that felt like extreme heat or cold coming from inside his skin. He looked up and saw Glenda's arm moving away. Her open-palmed hand swept back to her side.

'Shut the fuck up will you!' she shouted. She paused as she allowed a delayed look of shock to race onto her face. She stared at her hand and then up to Jim. 'I've had enough,' she said slowly. 'I want it all to end. You've been so much help in the past. Why are you doing this? Why do you want to spoil things, Jim? You've seen him, you know he's not dead.'

'Have you told her the truth?' Jim said to Roger.

Roger paused. After a few moments he said, 'I told her about the fight. I went to see her a few times after that. I was worried about what I'd done. You were telling me everything was all right but I wasn't sure. She told me that you said you'd killed him, but still I wasn't sure.' There was a strange look on his face, something Jim had never seen before.

Roger continued: 'I knew I couldn't go to the police. That'd implicate us both. But I still wasn't certain. When Glenda told me that she'd heard that Bill was all right...' The strange expression became more prominent. His features seemed to have become separated and individualised from the whole. His eyes looked nervously and without the support of the rest of his face. 'I suppose I was relieved someone had seen him. I knew you couldn't kill anyone, Jim. You haven't got it in you.'

Jim gestured to the grave. 'Well, be my guest. The evidence is waiting. I threw his body in there. Roger killed him and I disposed of the body. Black tarpaulin, couldn't get a green one.' He waved a dismissive, confident hand and turned away.

'Jim, please, calm down. You're drunk,' Glenda said. 'Remember our conversation? We know he's alive. He's back.' She had lost her anger. 'I know you're scared. I'm scared too, but we can talk another time. We've got to leave here. We should go now.'

Jim was beginning to sober up. His head was spinning and he was not sure what was the truth and what was not. He believed his own lies, both versions; Bill being dead, and Bill returning to torment Glenda. Through his confusion he knew they were not about to dig up the grave, and if he continued to insist that they did, the contact he had with Glenda would be ended there and then.

'Look. This is getting silly,' Roger said. 'Everything will be different tomorrow.'

'And the grave?' Glenda said. 'What about the damage?'

Roger touched Glenda lightly on the arm. 'That's not a problem,' he said. 'We'll kick all this earth back. It'll look like animals did it. Let's just get on with it shall we?'

Jim looked at Roger and suddenly put a name to the uncomfortable expression on his face. It was fear. Roger looked away and walked to the grave. He flung the piece of wood into the hole and then began to kick the earth in after it.

Jim walked towards Glenda. 'Enjoy hitting me, did you?' He tried to smile. 'I know I bloody well deserve it though.' He raised his palms. 'I know, I know, I drink too much. You're right, though. I do feel a little jumpy now *he's* back.' He gestured to the grave. 'Don't ask me what the hell I'm doing this for. Maybe I thought wishing him dead could make it happen—'

Glenda interrupted. 'Let's not talk about it now. It's been a long night and I'm tired. I don't know why I came.'

'Maybe you couldn't bear the thought of owing me a debt?'

'If he really *was* down there, then surely my debt is to Roger?'

Roger turned at the sound of his name.

'It's okay, Roger,' Glenda said. 'No problem.'

'You would have owed us *both*,' Jim smiled. 'Just remember that. One day when it all gets too much, it would have been nice to come and dig up the fond memory of our relationship. See how wrong you were.'

'If you say so,' Glenda said, humouring him.

Jim's mind was beginning to work well now. He could ignore the distaste in his mouth and cause his lips and tongue to smile and talk as he willed. The plan could still work despite this episode. He smiled and said, 'I'd just like to finish things off amicably, rather than like this. I know I'm a bit drunk and we can't talk now, but a lot of things have upset me over the past months.'

Glenda nodded. 'I know,' she said. She paused for a while and looked deeply into Jim's eyes. 'I am sorry if you feel I used you. I didn't mean any harm. I needed a distraction from him—'

'And help,' Jim interrupted.

'Yes, and help, I know that. But I think things all got to be a bit too much. What with Bill, and me not used to seeing anyone...'

'This whole thing really was a mess, eh?' Jim said.

'Suppose so. But I didn't mean it like that, honestly.'

'Nor me,' Jim said to himself. 'I really didn't.'

Roger was kicking hard at the earth, dancing light-footedly around the grave as if he were performing a ceremonial dance. The drizzle had begun again and the strong wind warned of a storm in the distance.

Jim lowered his gaze and his voice. 'I wish we could come out of this a little better. A little friendlier. I mean we were friends once.' He laughed. 'We were even allies against a common enemy. I've got the scars to prove it.' He paused. 'I'd like to meet you for a drink or something. No big deal or anything. Just a quiet drink. To sort things out, maybe to understand. Kind of say goodbye and wish each other luck. No doubt now *he's* back you'll be disappearing as soon as possible, I know I would. This has been a bad business; it'd be nice to end it on a pleasant note.' He looked down for a count of three and then back up for the reply.

Glenda glanced over towards Roger. He was now on his

knees, shaping and patting the top of the grave. Her gaze came back to Jim. 'No, Jim. I don't think so.'

'It's no big deal if you don't want to,' Jim continued. 'I know I've been a stupid bastard. I just thought we could remain friends.' His mind cackled with derisive laughter at the cliché. He worried that she might hear this, and spoke to drown out the sound.

'Just a quick drink, one night this week?' Jim asked quietly. 'Go on. You can ask Roger to come if you like.'

'Why, will I need protection?'

'I think we both might if we go anywhere near The Northern,' Jim laughed. He looked away for a moment and then said, 'I just thought... I don't know.' He shook his head. 'I mean...' He took a deep breath. 'Look, what I'm trying to say is I know that things didn't exactly work out. They were far from perfect. But you have to admit that I did try hard for you. For a while you needed me more than I needed you. I was your freedom at first. Even though I'm no hero, I did help a little bit, didn't I? You did manage to forget about him for a little while, didn't you? And we had a few laughs along the way. It was even quite exciting, sometimes.'

Glenda looked down and nodded. 'Yes.'

'All I'm asking is for you to meet me once for a drink. Now I need some help and I'm asking you for it. The state of me recently, God knows I need it. And there's nobody else I can or want to turn to. Surely you can understand that?' Jim stood motionless for a few moments and then extended his hand. 'Please, Glenda. Please help me, just this once.'

Glenda shrugged her shoulders. 'I don't know what I can do, Jim. How can I help? I seem to be the problem.'

There was now a stern look on Jim's face. 'He was the

problem, and you know it. I'm not taking the blame, nor should you. I'm just saying that I don't want to be punished for something that was not my fault.'

'Put like that I can't say no, can I?' She held Jim's unsure gaze for a moment and then reached out to shake his hand. 'Yes, okay then. One drink.'

Jim took her hand. 'Only if you're sure.' He added, 'I really don't want to put any pressure on you.'

'No, it's okay, I'd like to. I suppose we *have* got a couple of things to talk about.'

For a moment Jim was drunk again and a dozen awkward seconds passed before he adopted the appropriate facial response. 'That'd be great,' he said as Roger came over.

'You two all done?' Roger asked. 'We'd better leave before we get ourselves into trouble.'

Chapter Twenty-Nine

The next morning Jim awoke with an alarming hangover. He was upside-down in his bed, fully dressed and lying on top of the covers. His head pounded and his mouth was dry. His whole body ached as though his bones were bruised. He dragged himself out of bed and ambled to the bathroom to get some water and paracetamol. He was shocked as he saw himself in the mirror of the bathroom cabinet: his sorrowful bloodshot eyes bulged out of his mud-caked face. He pushed and twisted the childproof cap and became aware of a pain in his hands. The soft flesh of the tips of his fingers was red and grazed, and his nails were lined with dirt. An image of him talking to Roger and Glenda charged into his thoughts from nowhere. Did he see Bill? What did he say to Roger? And was Glenda really there? Suddenly he was filled with panic as he remembered shouting the words 'my murder'. He could only think of the police. He paused, waiting for the unruly voice to speak, but it was silent. His thoughts turned to Mrs Muurling. Yes, he needed to see her, to apologise again, to explain why he had not been to visit her.

He called Roger to say that he would be late for work. It was half past eight. Roger seemed overjoyed to hear from him.

'Not a problem, mate,' Roger said chirpily. 'We all have the odd bad night. I'm just glad that it's all been dealt with and forgotten. Glenda's a nice girl. I'm glad you two have managed to sort things out.'

Jim hung up and called Mrs Muurling. He was excited and urged her to answer. 'Hello. It's Jim. Sorry it's been so long.'

Mrs Muurling did not sound at all surprised to hear from him. She began to ramble, as if they were already in the middle of a long conversation and she were drunk.

Jim was not sure if she was listening but spoke anyway. 'I want to come around if that's all right? The letter. I think you should open the letter.'

'I know, you said,' she answered matter-of-factly. 'You're a bit late, though. I was expecting you sooner.'

'What do you mean sooner?'

'You called last night to say you were coming over. I must admit you sounded a bit drunk. You woke me up. It was the middle of the night, but you were adamant you were coming over straight away. I waited for you this morning, but after a couple of hours I couldn't wait any longer. I don't know why, but I opened it.' She began to ramble again.

'I'm really sorry about that. I don't remember calling. What time was this? Hello? Are you listening?' Her voice had faded into the distance. She seemed to be talking to herself on the other side of the room. He shouted twice more and then hung up.

It was cool and fresh outside and the sun was veiled by a thin grey mist. Jim sniffed at the sharp air like a dazed boxer smelling some salts. He was still slightly drunk and his head ached. He decided to catch the bus a few stops down the route in the hope that the exercise could pump some vitality back into his leaden body. The bus came a few moments after he had reached the stop as though it had been waiting around the corner for him to arrive.

'Hove, please,' said Jim, stepping up to the driver's perspex guard. The clear plastic screen was holed like a Swiss cheese.

'That's seventy pence, please,' the driver said politely.

Jim slid the money under the screen and the driver punched out a ticket.

'Late night?' The driver winked.

A smile crept onto Jim's face and, for a little while, the pain of his hangover made sense. Everything made sense: no matter where the driver was from, they were both part of the same very exclusive club; that moment of that day in that history. It could only be shared by them, and would only ever be known to them. He felt good and was glad to be up. Those few seconds passed and Jim walked to a seat and put his ticket in his pocket. Then, as if the moment had never existed, he was standing outside Mrs Muurling's front door.

Jim marvelled at what he saw. He did not know what to say. His mouth was open wide, yawning like a Venus flytrap, as if his mind were trying to entice the words he needed into his throat in order to express himself.

'Come in!' Mrs Muurling said with a beaming smile.

Jim walked through to the back room in silence. What he then saw stunned him even further. Mrs Muurling came in singing. Jim realised she had been singing on the phone earlier when she had put it down without hanging up and had walked away. She looked great. Her eyes were sparkling and her smile was so wide that it looked as though it might hurt. She sat him down at the table and thrust the letter into his hand. She laughed at his surprise.

'Don't worry. I'm not drunk – well, maybe just a little bit – and don't worry about the top hat. Red rather suits me, don't you think?'

Jim nodded. He could not take his eyes off the red top hat she was wearing. And her medical chair. It had been painted red. He went to take a closer look but Mrs Muurling put her hand on his shoulder to stop him.

'Don't you want to read the letter?' she said excitedly.

Jim nodded and forced his gaze down to the paper in his hand. He immediately looked up again. Mrs Muurling was twirling in a gentle dance around the chair.

'Go on then,' she said. 'Read it to me, please. I'd like to hear it again.'

The paper felt heavy, like cloth. There was one sheet, handwritten in black ink. He looked down to the end, 'All my love, Tom'.

'Are you sure?' he asked. 'Am I disturbing you? I can go if you like. I've no right to be here. I shouldn't have called.'

'Nonsense!' she said. 'After all you've done for me. It was the urgency of your phone call last night that inspired me to open the letter. You have as much right to be here as anyone.' She sat down in the red chair and cocked the hat to one side. 'Begin, please.'

Jim read in a soft faltering voice, determined to take in every word:

Cornwall, 8th June, 1938

My dearest Edna,

What can I write?
A week might seem a long time to write a letter. A second is all the time you need to write a word; a minute for a sentence; an for hour a letter? This is the last day of our honeymoon and I have been trying to compose my thoughts. Work them out in my head so

that they will be as true to how I feel today, as I hope they will be in the future. I hope they will 'stand the test of time'.

And I suppose that is what this exercise is all about. Time and how it has a bearing on the way we pass our days. The way we experience the events in our lives, and how much we value the one continuing moment we have been given. It seems funny to think that one day, hopefully, both of us will be pulling these letters out to read them again. That will be in just over forty years. Towards the end of the century! What on earth will things be like? Will we still be using ships to travel from place to place? Will we still have as many wars? Or will the airships and aeroplanes have taken off into outer space to make friends with the men on Mars? How much more in love will we be? Can we be? What will have happened to our lives? Will we have children and grandchildren?

At the moment I am sitting at the table (by the front door in case we forget!) and you are sitting on the bed going through some of your things. You keep telling me we must pack soon. It is mid-afternoon and our train departs at seven tonight. Every now and then you look over and check my progress. I can see this out of the corner of my eye. When you do this I pretend to be hard at work on this letter. But, my darling, when you look away, and this is probably why we will be late for the train! I gaze in wonder and love at you. I am hopelessly distracted by you and want to come and join you on the bed. I don't want to leave this idyllic place. But my greatest consolation is that we will be leaving part of ourselves here. Some part of our love that will endure until the day we return.

Jim stopped reading and looked at Mrs Muurling for a reaction. She had taken the hat off and was rubbing her fingers around the brim. He waited a few moments and then continued to read.

Who knows if the philosophy of starting your old age with memories of your youth will increase our happiness in our final years together. The most I am wishing for is many years of youthful old age together. Time to reflect on our lives, time to appreciate the warmth of you by my side as we prepare for the quiet journey ahead.

Already I have spent the pleasure of one hundred years in one week being so close to you. I feel so strongly and passionately towards you, that at times I am worried that I don't deserve such happiness. I fear in some way it will be taken away from me as an act of punishment for being so contented. This will happen ultimately, yet I do not consider that thought too often. It is an unholy waste to taint the present with the future in such a way.

What shall I write? What indeed! The retrieval of this box will say it all. It is so much more than any buried treasure I could ever have dreamed of finding when I was a young boy eager to sail the world. The gold of pirates' plunder is nothing compared to what we will discover one day. This is our secret booty. It is safer and more valuable than any money in any bank. I have no doubt that the joy of these days will come rushing back as we reopen the box. It is our wealth.

But only when we recover it will we be able to cherish its riches. We must reclaim it!

I look forward to each of the moments along the way...

All my love,

Tom

XXX

PS As we seem to be having a little joke at time's expense, I have a little joke of my own! Watch out for my fiftieth birthday! I can tell you now, that whatever we do to celebrate, and for what will seem like no reason whatsoever, I will be wearing a red top hat if we go out anywhere! It's nothing symbolic, nor do I even know why I've suddenly decided to do this (you've just tapped your watch telling me to hurry – I'm smiling at the thought of this hat) – I'm just looking forward to seeing your face when that secret suddenly makes sense!

Jim placed the letter on the table. Mrs Muurling was trying to conceal her tears. He stepped over to the window and stared out at nothing. Mrs Muurling went to the bathroom and blew her nose. Jim turned as she came out. Her eyes were bloodshot and glazed, but she was smiling.

'Thank you for doing that,' she said.

'How are you?'

She sat down. 'Oh, I'm okay, thank you. A little shocked perhaps.'

'I can understand. The hat!'

Mrs Muurling smiled. 'I'm more shocked about that, it's

true. In a nice way, though. In the nicest way you can imagine.'

Jim stared at her for a few moments and then asked, 'Did he wear it?'

Mrs Muurling began to laugh. 'We went out to dinner. A very expensive restaurant. Tom was wearing a jacket and tie. He looked so dapper, he always did. But then, just as we were leaving the house he produced this ridiculous hat. Obviously it didn't match. It looked awful, but we couldn't stop laughing. He told me to trust him and that I'd understand one day.' She wiped a tear from her eye. She was still laughing. 'The head waiter gave us a funny look when we arrived at the restaurant. I'm sure he didn't want to let us in. But Tom always did have a way with people, and by the end of the evening the waiter even borrowed the hat to have a joke with the chef.' She put the hat back on. 'It really is like having him here, you know. He made me keep this hat. I always thought it was silly but that didn't matter. It was a good memory and I was quite happy to.'

'Is the letter what you expected?' Jim asked.

'It's better than that. It's a welcome release. As I said I didn't think there would be anything bad in it. In fact I was worried about the ordinariness of it. But I still could never be sure. I mean, look at what I left in the box.'

'How are you about that now? Do you still feel bad?'

Her tears had gone and her smile was contented. 'I suddenly feel rested. It might sound silly, but I'm at peace. It was beautiful to hear his voice again through his words, and I *know* he would not mind that I couldn't write anything. And the hat...' She burst out laughing again. 'It sounds so silly. But it's okay, Jim.' She was sobbing. 'It's all okay.'

Jim put his arms around her. After a minute or so she

stopped and blew her nose. 'And you?' she asked. 'Was it worth it? Is it what you expected? Have we inspired you?'

She walked over to the sideboard and picked the casket up. 'Here. Take it. It's yours.'

'But I couldn't.'

'Please, Jim. I'd like you to have it. I haven't got any children and you don't know how much good you've done me.'

'I don't know what to say.'

'Well, don't say anything. Just take it.'

'But I won't be able to do it justice, I won't know what to do with it.' Jim searched her eyes for any indication as to what had prompted this decision. There was none. She was happy, enjoying the satisfaction of giving a gift.

He accepted. 'And the chair?' He gestured with his head to change the subject. 'Any reason for the red paint?' He got up to inspect it, aware that his forehead was damp with sweat.

'No reason in particular. I read the letter this morning and the next thing I knew I had taken a taxi to the local hardware shop and was buying the paint. It didn't take long – it just seemed the right thing to do. I like it. I would never have chosen a black chair. I don't like darkness when you can have colour and light.'

Jim wiped his brow. 'Neither do I,' he agreed.

Chapter Thirty

The man is shouting but there is nobody there. He feels hot breath on his neck and is aware of a distant ache from what seems like a juddering blow on his head; his head that now feels as though it has been burst open like a smashed watermelon.

The man has been unconscious, asleep he thinks. His dreams have been bad but not scary. Upright oblongs of black shadow have been following him – not in pursuit though. That is why he is not scared. They are merely going the same direction as him. They are much taller than he is, and their number increases continually as they trail slowly behind. Their companions come from nowhere because once they are part of the group it is as if they have always been there. Then they are like the rest of them; waiting for those who will never come, because they too will always have been there. The man knows this. It is the truth. He must allow the oblongs to follow because that is what they do, just as the oblongs follow in order to enable him to move forward. He is faint, or maybe dizzy? The oblongs echo this by spinning while continuing their straight course. They do not diverge, but cut over the plain of the ground like a forest of ghostly tornadoes. They throb in a dusty, impenetrable clump. But of course they do not make any sound. He knows that this should be reassuring, but somehow, somewhere in one corner of his leaking mind, it is not.

Uncertainly, he approaches the surface of this dream. He is breathless, like a skin diver emerging from deep within the ocean. His senses return his consciousness to him and the startling realisation of being awake brings him that last little bit into reality. His eyelids flutter and jump. And then suddenly they are open at last. He wants to see the comfort of daylight, to feel the freshness of morning on his skin. But he cannot. His blanket is too cold. It is clammy like the hand of an untrustworthy stranger. ('But you know this hand,' his reason tells him, 'you held it for a long time before. The stranger left for a while, but now he is back.')

The man is barely alive. He is crammed underground beneath three hundred shovelfuls of damp earth. There is a space above his face where a pocket of air has been trapped. Six inches beyond this, the dark pink segments of a worm's body compress and extend through the ground as it pulses forward on its steady mission. The weight of the earth presses down on the man's body like a heavy book squeezing the wetness of life from a plant. His ribs want to expand with breath but they are being crushed under this force. His eyes are open and he is not sure where he is. He will never be sure. He will never know even this one small thing. He can taste the earth in his mouth and his tongue rubs at the inside of his cheeks and along his teeth. It dabs at the small grains of dirt that fall down his throat. They are as big as boulders. He takes a small gulp of air, not sucking greedily, but sipping with restraint and reverence, as one takes the offering from a cup at Communion. His lungs are burning. They are gripped by the flaming hands of suffocation and his mind is screaming at him to breathe.

The memory of the blows to his head has spread throughout his body so that he is now trembling involuntarily. This prompts a minuscule avalanche of earth to fall from the pocket of space above his face and tumble into his mouth. He would cough if he could, but the flaming hands hold his lungs flat and useless. The man's body convulses like a dying animal that is submerged in the jaws of a crocodile. The back of his head feels as though it is resting in a shallow pool of warm water. The level is gradually rising. As it does his legs begin to feel like two sticks of ice. The darkness and pressure force their way down harder and harder and harder. So hard that his body implodes slowly and his mind overflows with terror. He is now beginning to understand the horror of the remaining seconds of his life. The horror that is stuffed into his mouth and up his nose and raining and scratching at his unseeing eyes.

The worm is nearby, throbbing forward in its task. Another is drowning in the well of blood at the back of the man's head. More of their kind approach. There is even one far off that will eat his arsehole.

The air above is cool and abundant. A car drives past. The lady driving taps her cigarette into the ashtray. She wonders what she will watch on television when she gets home.

Chapter Thirty-One

Jim telephoned Glenda. Seeing Mrs Muurling so happy had turned his thoughts away from the past. As his hangover disappeared, so did the dangerous memory of the punishment he had nearly brought upon himself. Normality was now within him again. His surroundings were thankfully subdued. He had thought twice about calling Glenda. But when he looked at the casket he understood what he had to do. He would go through with the plan and that was that.

The conversation went well; they talked politely for a few minutes. Jim sensed nervousness and distrust in her voice and was concerned that she might have regretted saying that she would meet him. Neither of them mentioned the cemetery, although the knowledge of its presence in their thoughts sterilised each exchange as if neither could speak openly because they had a crossed line. Eventually she seemed to relax when he suggested going for a drink. He was relieved. The arrangements were made quickly and suddenly and the call was over. Jim put the phone down, somewhat stunned at how the proximity of her voice to his ear had been no more than a mechanical trick. The intimacy was illusory and misleading: it had never really existed. For a few seconds it had immersed him in its own reality as though in the space of a few breaths he had lived another life in a world he did not wish to leave.

Yet once his thoughts had returned to the present he was pleased that he still had the desire to end this matter once and for all. He tapped the casket and considered his plan.

Jim was already outside the shop when Glenda stepped off the bus. He was wearing his smart blue slacks and a badly ironed white shirt with a black bomber jacket over the top. He had shaved very closely and his jaw was speckled with pinhead-sized dots of dried blood. He had a sports bag with him on the pavement by his feet. As she turned to walk towards him he lit up a cigarette.

'Hello, Jim,' she said coolly, 'am I late? Have you been here long?'

He took a deep draw on his cigarette and paused before blowing the smoke over her shoulder. It was the first cigarette he had smoked in over two years; he did not know why he was smoking, beyond a vague notion that if Glenda were not surprised it would mean she was not observing properly and therefore not relaxed. The head-rush of the nicotine hit him. His feet felt as though they had dissolved into nothing and he was resting on a four inch cushion of air on the tingling stumps of his shins. He maintained his focus but was aware of a tremor in his voice. 'No. You're bang on time.' He pulled his jacket sleeve back and checked his watch. 'Eight thirty on the dot. I've only just got here myself.' He had promised himself that he would resist having a couple of pints before she arrived. His fluttering heart made him wish that he had given into that temptation. 'I thought we could walk down to the seafront and maybe go to a pub down there.'

They did not talk much on the way. Jim took one more puff of his cigarette and threw it into the road when Glenda was not looking. Glenda spoke and Jim replied with a smile; he did not know what either of them had said, but she smiled and continued to speak. Glenda spoke again and laughed. Her laughter was loud and Jim wanted to be sick when he heard the responding chuckle that came from his own mouth. Why was he laughing as well? Who was he laughing at? His legs shook. Surely he would fall over soon? But miraculously they carried him forwards. He did not want to go in that direction. The laughter was ahead of them. Everything was funny, everything about him, everything he had done was ridiculous. They spoke some more. She nodded at his words and lit up a cigarette. She offered him one. Jim caught his breath as his hand suddenly appeared in front of him. Its fingers were spread wide, and tendons showed through the vein-riddled skin. It was horrible. He nodded and said, 'Okay.' Thankfully that made the hand disappear. He was hot, and his stomach bubbled as though his insides were about to explode. His head was spinning and he knew he was imperceptibly speeding up and slowing down to try and stop it from falling off his shoulders.

The pub was bright and full of people. He thought Glenda's neck must ache from nodding. With each nod she had to lower her head down and then bring it up again; occasionally this happened a few times in under a second. He held his head still and tried not to look at his hand as the beer came towards his face. For some reason he allowed it to fill his mouth. Bitterness spread throughout his body. It was obvious Glenda could see what was happening and was quite happy. Hopefully there was no way she could know that he was inhaling invisible mouthfuls of air to keep him alive. Words and more words coloured the air in the space of the pub. They altered it with their presence, like ink in water, swirling and suffusing, until not only was the air full of words but the words were also full of air. The dilution was soon complete and the two were indistinguishable. She must be enjoying this – or at least it was part of her plan, or someone's plan. He knew someone had a plan. His nerves were like thin bells in his head and in his fingers and in his legs and everywhere. He moved and they rang a loud alarm for everyone to hear. It was an off-putting sound like the dull splash of someone wetting their bed in the middle of the night. The sound leaks into their mind and they cannot stop what they are doing, nor can they move away even if they want to. He was in the toilet staring at the six inch square ceramic tiles that were six inches from his face; he knew that his penis was too close to the porcelain and that spots of urine would sit on his shoes until they evaporated. He walked out of the toilet and stepped across the carpet. 'Let's go somewhere else,' he said.

Glenda was distracted. She nodded and said, 'Whatever.'

Jim picked up his bag. He heard himself speak in reply. 'I'd like to get some fresh air. Maybe take a walk.'

They made their way towards the sea. Jim's head cleared a little in the fresh air. He remembered that Glenda had asked him about his sports bag in the pub and he had not replied. He held it up as they walked and said, 'It's a surprise.'

Glenda was puzzled. 'What's a surprise? The bag?'

'Exactly,' Jim said.

They walked. He wondered why she was not scared. When he had said that he wanted to go for a walk, she had agreed immediately. Surely she should be apprehensive about being with him? His mind raced forward to the happy future they might have between them. The unruly voice quickly stopped this.

'Remember the plan,' it said.
The plan, Jim thought. She's here anyway. The plan.

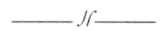

———*JC*———

Jim and Glenda passed the sweaty neon lights and piercing bulbs of the Palace Pier amusement arcade and walked down onto the beach. Fifty yards on, the sound of the screaming ghost train and the muffle of the concert hall had been consumed behind them by the pounding of the waves on the shore. They approached the West Pier. Despite the recent renovation work it was still deserted and broken, projecting defiantly out to sea on its mangled supports. The section between the land and the sea had been collapsed and then tenuously re-linked, so that it looked like a useless limb that had been cast out into the tide. Its presence commanded a sickening feeling of emptiness and finality. The abandonment was complete. The hundred year old amusement arcades were now home to spiders, birdshit and whistling sea winds. The rotting wood of its floorboards would crack if walked upon, dropping the walker into the iron-spiked sea. Jim was both fascinated and nauseated by the decay it signified. He had rarely been this close to it at night. They were beneath it by now, looking warily into its black spaces like children peering into the windows of a haunted house.

The pinnacle of his friends' bravery when they were younger had been to climb as high as they could on the limpet-encrusted iron ladder on its side. Reaching this meant swimming twenty yards out to sea, over the choppy surface of the cold water, not knowing if you were passing over a part of the pier that was already dead and rusting on the seabed, or if another piece were about to fall on you and engulf you for ever. And then when you reached the ladder you would have to bear the fear of not knowing where the steps began, or how deeply they were submerged. This was never mentioned. If it had been, they all knew it would immediately have become a challenge – one that they all wanted to avoid. So they ignored the subject and they could only imagine how black and lonely the pier must be at night when everyone was in bed, safe and dry.

He lit a cigarette to try and shake off its spell.

'Can I have one of those, please?' Glenda asked.

Jim passed her the cigarette he was smoking. 'You can have this one if you don't mind that I've had a couple of puffs. I only lit it because I don't like this place.'

Glenda took the cigarette. 'Then why do you come here?'

'Because it scares me. Because I have to.'

'What scares you? The sea? You don't like the sea?'

He gestured ahead of them. 'This scares me.'

'I must admit, it doesn't look particularly welcoming at night. It seems unsafe. But after all, it's only a broken-down pier. I'm not so keen on the sea myself.'

Jim put the bag down and turned to Glenda. 'No, you've got me wrong. I like the pier, I also like the sea.'

'But I thought you said they scare you.'

'They do,' Jim said wearily. 'The pier and the sea scare me.'

Glenda walked in front of him into his line of sight. She was shaking her head. There was anger in her voice. 'What on earth are you talking about? Did you bring me down here to play games and tell me riddles? What scares you, the pier or the sea?'

It now seemed irrelevant; he supposed it had always been irrelevant, and always would be because the answer was always known. What scared him? Dying or living? Neither did. Death was death and when you were dead it did not matter. And when you were alive, you were living and that was okay. But the two together scared him. Death dipping into life, or life dipping into death – whichever. It was the same thing.

He looked at Glenda and shook his head. 'I'm sorry, Glenda. I'm talking rubbish. This place always does it to me.' He bent down and opened the bag. A second later he was standing and smiling and Glenda had a look of horror on her face.

She screamed, 'Roger! Roger! Quick! Help!'

Jim froze in alarm; his body was tense, ready to be hit by whoever had scared her. She moved nervously away from him. Her scream had petered out. Roger was standing beside her, telling her that things were okay, telling her to relax. Jim was frightened, he did not know what was happening. Roger was talking calmly.

'Put it down,' he said. 'Just put it down.'

Jim looked at his hand. He did not understand.

'Put the knife down, Jim. Just relax,' Roger said.

Jim tossed it to the ground. 'Is there someone behind me?' he asked anxiously.

Suddenly Roger pounced and bundled him to the floor. He held his neck and shouted angrily, 'What the fuck do you think you're doing? The cemetery and now this!' He stood up and kicked Jim hard in the stomach.

Glenda moved in front of Roger. She leered down at Jim. Her face was screwed up with anger. 'You horrible bastard! You vicious little shit! I thought tonight you might possibly redeem yourself in some way. I really thought there was a chance. But after this I hope you rot in hell.'

Jim sat up and rubbed his stomach. He pointed to the bag. 'In there,' he said. 'There's your answer.'

Glenda went over to the bag.

Roger was holding the knife and still scowling.

Jim looked up and said, 'You can take that look off your face for a start. And what the fuck are *you* doing here?'

Roger did not change his expression. He lowered the knife but did not drop it. 'Glenda asked me to follow you both. After what happened at the cemetery she thought it might be a good idea.'

'This is getting to be quite a regular occurrence. We make a very cosy threesome. And what did you think I might get up to then, old friend?' Jim stood up and planted himself squarely in front of Roger. 'You thought I was going to do something nasty with the knife, did you?'

Glenda came over and emptied the contents of the bag onto the beach. 'I don't understand,' she said quietly, almost to herself.

Jim was still staring intently at Roger. 'Now *you* put that fucking knife down. Now!' Jim shouted.

Roger looked to Glenda. She nodded and he threw the knife beside the bag.

'There's an explanation for what I suppose might look a little strange.' Jim was still staring hard at Roger. 'But first I want an apology.'

'I was only trying to help Glenda. You must admit it all looked a bit...' Roger seemed lost. He looked to Glenda and then back to Jim. 'Glenda needed some help, and I saw you with the knife, she was screaming—'

'There's a good explanation,' Jim cut in, 'and I wasn't going to harm anyone. But I want an apology first.'

Roger looked at his feet and after a few moments said,

'Sorry.'

A moment later Jim was kneeling down beside the bag.

'And the knife?' Roger asked.

Jim picked it up and slid it blade-first into his back pocket. 'It has a use. I'll tell you in a minute.'

Jim put the empty bag to one side and rummaged through the contents. There were three folded plastic bags, a large roll of waterproof sticking tape, a ball of string, some screwed up pieces of paper, a towel and a pen. There was also the casket. He opened it in silence.

'Is that what I think it is?' Glenda asked.

Jim did not look up. 'What have you done with the letter that was in there?' he said firmly.

'Are you talking to me?' Glenda asked.

'Where's the letter?' he repeated.

'Look, what's going on?' Roger said. 'What letter? Why have you got all of this stuff?'

Jim stood up and faced Glenda. He glowered at her. She stretched an arm out to Roger.

Jim moved towards Glenda, all the time staring at Roger. Roger put a foot forward as if to intercept his path but then did not move. Jim pulled the knife out of his pocket and threw it at Roger's feet.

His eyes were cold and dismissive but he smiled and said, 'You can hang on to the knife, Roger. I don't need it for the moment. I just need the letter that Glenda took out of the bag while we were talking. Go on. Ask her. Ask her where it is, or if I'm lying yet again.'

Jim stopped. A small pebble rolled from the indentation his feet made on the stones. It slipped down the steep fall to the sea. Its dull clatter was smothered by the crash of a wave.

'There's no need,' Glenda said, 'I'm not hiding it from

you. I just thought you wouldn't show it to me.' She reached into her jacket pocket and pulled out a white envelope. It was not sealed and its small wing fluttered in the breeze like a fledgling kite.

'Did you read it?' Jim asked.

'No. There was hardly any time. You two didn't roll around on the stones long enough for that. I was scared. I've been wondering what was in the bag all night.'

'I was going to show you. You're part of it,' Jim said.

'I didn't exactly want to be part of anything when you brought out that knife.'

'I'm sorry,' Jim said. 'This feels like a dream, or maybe a nightmare. I never think clearly when I'm here.' He turned to Roger. 'Remember the ladder on the pier?'

'Sure, but—'

'I'm going down it.' He turned to Glenda. 'I need some hair.' He spoke calmly, but there was an assurance to his tone that could easily have been mistaken for aggression. He was relaxed, as though he had just woken up in the morning after a long peaceful night's sleep. 'Some of your hair, some of mine, to go in the box. And since you're here too, Roger, some of yours. You're involved as well.' He picked up the knife and sawed a lock from the side of his head. He bent down and wrapped it in a piece of tape and then put it in the casket. 'I haven't got any scissors, and I forgot to buy some. Hence the kitchen knife. Isn't that stupid?'

He stood up and handed Roger the knife and the tape. 'Will you indulge me? And end my obsession with Bill?'

Roger shook his head. 'I don't know what the hell you're on, but if you tell me what it's all about—'

'Yes or no?' Jim asked calmly.

Roger cut a small piece of hair and wrapped it in the

tape. 'In the box?' he asked.

Jim nodded. 'And give Glenda the knife. She knows what to do.'

'I'm going to read the letter first,' Glenda said.

'I want the hair first.'

Glenda did not argue. She cut her hair and handed it to Roger, who handed it to Jim. She immediately stepped back and pulled the letter from the envelope.

Roger eyed Jim keenly, watching for any move, but Jim turned away and sat down. 'This will end it all. It's going down the ladder with me. I'll finally finish it.'

Roger came and sat beside him. 'What's this ladder business all about? You're not thinking of doing anything stupid are you? You can't go out there safely.'

'Like I couldn't kill Bill?'

Roger was silent.

'Anyway,' Jim said, 'I didn't kill him. I wanted to but didn't.'

'You think you would have done if I hadn't arrived that night?' Roger said after a while.

'Probably not.'

Glenda came and dropped the envelope into Jim's lap. 'What's this then? Invisible ink? There's nothing on it. A blank bit of paper. What do you intend to do with that?'

'It's a very old and important blank piece of paper. I'm getting rid of it for a friend.' He moved away, wrapped the casket and its contents in the plastic bags, and sealed it with the tape.

Glenda and Roger were standing behind him. They were talking and asking questions. Jim could not hear their words. He had no desire to listen to them and his mind dwelled on the soothing sound of the sea. When the package was sealed, he bound it with string and threw a long loop over his shoulder. He got up and walked down the beach.

Glenda ran ahead and stood in front of him on the edge of the water. Her face was flushed. 'What are you going to do with that now? What's this? Some kind of great symbolic gesture? You throw the box and yourself away to the mercy of the tide, is that it? Does Mrs Muurling know you've got the box?'

Jim removed his shoes. 'She gave it to me by way of thanks. It's my box now. A gift for a favour. That's all over now, Glenda. I don't want to fight, but if you won't get out of my way I'll have to. You go if you want to. I didn't want to force you to come. You came of your own free will, although the evening didn't go quite as I'd planned.'

'And what had you planned? Would things have been different if Roger wasn't here?'

'Nice coincidence that he was, wasn't it though?' Jim said without looking at her. He tightened the loop of string on his shoulder. The casket hung down behind him.

Roger came and stood beside him. All three of them were up to their ankles in water. He shook his head and put his arm on Jim's shoulder. Jim felt his strong grip but did not try to move away.

'You and Glenda are leaving now, Roger. I'm going to the ladder. I have to see how deep it goes. Nobody is going to stop me.'

The moon shone high above the horizon. The sea's surface was empty. It appeared still and inviting in the distance. The ladder did not seem so dark and far away. The waves nudged Jim's calves and he nodded at the reminder. The other boys had stopped playing on the pier a long time ago. It was quiet and the skid-marks of their shoes in the green slime would have been washed away. He walked forward. When he was up to his waist, the water darted into his trousers like a new partner's over-eager hand. He was not prepared for this, not yet ready for the pleasurable shock. He caught his breath and sank to his knees. The water stuck his shirt to his skin like glue. He turned and nodded to Roger and Glenda. 'It's nice. It feels warm.' He pushed himself forward and began to swim. He glided through the water, and the casket trailed behind him.

The ladder was much nearer than he had expected. He was suddenly being washed into it. He gripped its rungs and looked up at the oppressive geometry of the ironwork above him. His feet fell forward and, magically, he was standing waist-deep in water, gently rising and falling with the swell. He looked to shore; Glenda and Roger were motionless, standing side by side like inanimate black blobs. He had wanted them to leave for fear that they might try to interfere. But their presence was comforting, even necessary. They were witnesses to his actions. He pulled his left leg away from the rung and sank slowly on his right. His left foot toed nervously for the step below as his torso slipped through the water. He slid his hands down the cold metal of the ladder, and in a moment the toes of his left foot were clinging like a bird's talons to the rung two feet below. He brought his right leg down and stood rigidly on tiptoes so that his chin just cleared the water. A boat floated across the horizon in the distance. It moved slowly and seemed to be hanging in the sky as though it might fall at any moment. He could no longer see Glenda and Roger's faces. Their bodies had disappeared behind an unending procession of small wave peaks that bobbed rhythmically towards the shore. They would still be looking, and this would be the point when they would have to decide whether to remain where they were or come in after him.

He waited; half-expecting, half-hoping to see Roger splashing towards him, shouting for him to stop, saving him yet again. But he knew this time he would not come.

The string tugged on his neck and the casket knocked lightly against something solid below. He sucked in a deep breath of air. It had a taste; like the thin tang of the future. He wrapped his arms around the ladder and swung the casket in front of him. Soon, he had hauled it to the surface and had unhooked the loop from his shoulders. He coiled up the wet string and held the box close to his knuckles. He took another deep breath and plunged under.

Suddenly he was straining to peer through the black salt that was stinging his open eyes. He fed himself down the ladder, allowing his legs to fall freely while grasping more confidently at the gaping space between each rung. He sank gently as though he were travelling through the buoyant void of space. Water rushed into his ears, trapping bubbles of air deep inside his head. Four rungs and then five, the pressure stabbed further into his ears. Six rungs then seven. He stopped and stared ahead. He thought he saw the waving tentacles of an octopus coming towards him. A long clump of black seaweed floated past. Its strands trailed through his hair. He shivered and thrust himself down to the next rung. His heart beat faster and suddenly his feet were thrashing for something solid to stand on, and his arms were flailing above him, trying to grab the bottom of the ladder. He swam frantically, not knowing if he was going up or down – or whether he was even moving at all. He shut his eyes tight and squeezed his lips together. A spiky ball of air was jammed in his chest, and for a moment a blinding flash of light that exploded from his mind lit up the sea. He dropped the casket. It was not important, nor was the futile thrashing of his body. His plan had not worked, nor did it now matter. He wanted to sink without effort to the seabed so that he could lay and rest and forget everything. He wanted the noise in his ears to cease and the cold blanket of the sea to tuck him in for ever. The roar in his ears had been quietened and there was now a blissful calm. His body responded quickly, and a moment later the sea had entered his nose and mouth and Jim was beginning to relax.

But something unknown to him made his legs kick. Something tiresome and unyielding forced his arms to stretch and fumble for the ladder. His head spun and he tried to force himself down, to go deeper where it was safe and warm, where his fatigue would be understood. However, as he tried to fall, he found that he was pulling himself up the scaly rungs, thinking about the small animals that lived in the shells he touched. He still wanted to be part of their fluid, dreamy world; they might understand and accept him. But the something would still not let him fall. He moved unhurriedly up the last few rungs of the ladder. His head very gently broke the surface of the water like a dark new moon rising unnoticed over the horizon. A second later he was shocked by the austere division between life and death and began to pant frenziedly. He pleaded with his body to fill his strained lungs and to give him life.

Chapter Thirty-Two

Jim was shivering when he walked out of the water. Glenda picked up his jacket but did not approach him. 'You look like you've seen a ghost – or you are a ghost more like,' she said.

Roger took the jacket from Glenda and walked to Jim. 'Take your shirt off and put this on,' he said. 'You'll freeze otherwise.'

Jim unbuttoned his shirt and let it drop to the floor. Roger threw the jacket around him.

'You're bloody mad, Jim. Absolutely bloody mad.' He looked out to the pier. 'Did you do it? Did you get down there?' he said after a pause.

Jim was just returning to his senses. He began to realise what he had just done. He shook his head in disbelief. 'I thought it'd never end.' He looked at Glenda. 'I didn't think I could do it. But I did. It's over, I think. Really over.'

Glenda stepped forward. She stretched out her hand. 'Well done.'

He did not know what to say. He was not scared. The thought of staying down there had not scared him. He shook her hand.

'It's as good a resting place as any for the casket, I suppose. It must have been difficult. What did you do? Tie it to the bottom or let it go?' she asked.

'I tied it there,' he said, not looking at her.

Their brief silence seemed to confirm the finality of something.

'I think it's about time we headed off,' Roger suggested after a few moments. 'You guys are welcome to crash at my place. I'm only round the corner.'

'Are you getting a cab?' Jim asked Glenda.

She looked at Roger and then nodded thoughtfully. 'Yes,' she said simply.

'Do you mind if I walk you to the taxi rank?' Jim said.

'It's okay, Roger,' Glenda said. 'You shoot off. We'll be all right.'

Jim smiled at him. 'We'll be fine. You bugger off now. I've caused you enough worries for a lifetime, let alone one night.'

'Bloody madman!' Roger laughed. He shook his head in appreciation. He waved and trudged off, still shaking his head.

Jim and Glenda walked off the beach and crossed the road towards West Street.

'Outside Hanningtons?' Jim asked. 'It that the nearest rank?'

'Yeah, we can walk along the front if you fancy.'

It was getting windy. The sky was clearing and the temperature had dropped noticeably. Glenda tugged at Jim's sleeve and began to jog. She gestured along the road with her head. 'C'mon, let's hurry. You'll catch your death like that.'

Jim did not respond. He continued his slow pace. 'I'm not cold,' he said. 'I'd rather walk. I need some fresh air. I must have swallowed a gallon of sea water.'

Glenda waited for him to catch her up.

'Besides,' he said, 'we need to talk. There are some things we have to say.'

Glenda's face lost its relaxed expression. Jim put his arm round her shoulders. She became rigid but did not move away. He squeezed her arm and pulled her towards him. The security he had known when he had lain in bed beside her those few times suddenly returned. Briefly he could see over the wall that obscured his view of the future. The years to come looked nice, inviting; his stomach tingled and he squeezed again. This time Glenda shrugged her shoulders and freed herself. She stuffed her hands into her pockets.

'Are you okay?' Jim asked, not waiting for an answer. 'It's nice out. I could stay here all night.'

Glenda spoke quietly. 'We'd better hurry, eh? You really will freeze.'

She stepped forward quickly but Jim matched her pace. 'Are you cold then?' he asked. 'You seem to be in a hurry.'

'It's gone one o'clock. I just think we should get on.'

Jim stopped and spun her around by her shoulders. 'Surely you can't want to get away from me *this* quickly? There's no reason for you to go back. You don't have to make any deadlines. There's no pressure for you to return. We could go out somewhere. There are places to go. Remember you can do what you like. We can go out and have a good time. You're free.' He smiled but he was nearly shouting.

Glenda stared contemptuously at him for a second and then said, 'Don't start with all that crap again. I thought you said all of that was over and done with? We're supposed to be friends, nothing more. You said it: "Let's be friends".' She freed herself from his grip and started walking.

Jim let her go. She marched ahead.

'Thanks a lot!' he shouted. 'Thanks a lot for nothing! After all I've done for you!'

A car raced by. It hooted at the spectacle Jim was making. He turned angrily and glared after it. The twin red lights shrunk rapidly into the distance. Soon the sound, the colour, the shape no longer existed. There was only his frustration. Glenda was twenty yards along the road. She could not escape him! Not again! Suddenly he was sprinting towards her. She continued to walk. Her shoulders were hunched when Jim reached her, cowering. He grabbed her by the throat and thrust her powerfully against the wall to their left. She gasped the beginning of a scream but he cut this short with a squeeze of her neck. He spoke slowly through his teeth.

'I was trying to be nice to you. I wanted to give you another chance. But look how you treat me.'

Glenda's body was suddenly lifeless. Her eyes were wide with fear. She tried to speak but could only shake her head. Jim released his grip a little. He looked anxiously up and down the street. There was someone coming towards them. He pulled Glenda along the wall and forced her into the dark recess of a restaurant frontage. He looked through the large window; there was no light but he could make out the grey shadows of the tables. They were cleared and laid, and the chairs were set neatly behind each place.

'If you shout I'll crush your neck,' Jim hissed. 'Then I'll smash your face to pulp. Just keep it shut and everything will be fine. Then we can talk. Nicely.'

The steps came closer. Glenda was shaking. He felt her larynx pump in his hand as she swallowed. He tried to stare into her eyes, to fix her to the spot. Glenda dug her hands deeper into her pockets and pulled them tightly around her waist. Jim felt them moving on his stomach and he pressed harder against her body. The steps were soon behind them and a few seconds later moving obviously along the road.

Jim increased the pressure on her throat. He pulled his head back and said, 'Right, you slag. Listen to me. I've had enough of your messing around. I want to tell you a few things. And you're going to listen.' He paused for a reply but continued when Glenda did not speak. 'For a start, Bill isn't back. He's dead.' He laughed and poked his tongue out at her. 'Your parents' house is quite nice, by the way. Your mum's not bad-looking either. Bill's dead and that's a fact. That's the only reason you're free. You won't recognise that, you bitch.' He lowered his voice. 'More to the point, your hero, Roger, killed him. You can shake your head all you like but it won't change that fact. I wanted to kill him for you, but Roger did it by accident. I just buried a lump of dead meat. I suppose I helped you and Roger at the same time without either of you knowing. Quite funny really.' His eyes blazed and he pushed the heel of his hand into her neck. She gasped. 'As for you, my darling, we're going to have to teach you a lesson. Some nice person like me tries to help you and all you do is kick me in the balls. Well? What do you say to that?' His fingers dug into her skin. He gripped her larynx. Anger had suddenly overcome him. He bit his cheek, willing the pain to come. Every muscle in his body was taut and strained to the point of snapping. He gripped harder. His hand was made of steel and he would soon be able to crush her skull like an egg. That would be the end. At last he knew this was the only way for him to be free. It was what he had to do. He felt good, finally alive. The plan was back on course; he no longer had to pretend. He was no longer scared – not of Roger, not of the sea nor of her. He would conquer them all.

Glenda slipped down the glass to the floor. Jim raised her slowly by her jaw. He wanted to pick her up by the head and swing her around and smash her into the wall. 'You are now going to die,' he announced in a whisper, pausing between each word. 'That's all there is to it. You are dying.'

A shocked smile came to Glenda's face. Her lips were dark and her face was nearly white. Without doubt she seemed happy.

Jim tried to stamp his foot in fury at this defiance, but it would not move. He tightened his grip on her throat in his mind but his hand did not respond. Glenda's smile had gone but so had her fear. Her eyes became narrow, like two deep black scars. Jim ground his teeth and pressed harder into her. Suddenly he was staggering backwards. A numbing current shot to his fingers and toes. Then it disappeared, along with his strength. He was by the restaurant again, slumped like an uncontained jelly against the door. Glenda had disappeared. He clutched at his chest and felt the handle of the knife. He pulled at the smooth wood and ran his finger around the hilt that was jammed against his ribs. He sank to the floor. His heart was being seared to the metal blade in the intense heat that burned in his chest. The smell of the charred flesh made him feel sick. He needed it to stop; he wanted the uncertainty to disappear. He looked across the road to the horizon. There was another flying ship, drifting aimlessly in the breeze. He looked down at his sticky black hands and began to understand why so much was happening in such a small space of time.

Epilogue

It is spring, and warm. The trees are full of leaves. Colourful flowers sway in the gentle breeze. The evenings are lengthening and people sit in their gardens with a drink and dream about happy days. You wonder how you managed to survive the winter. This year, every year, you believe that you will never have to come home from work in the dark again, nor shower in the morning in a frozen bathroom. You breathe in the grassy air and listen to the song of the birds in the trees. Life is good. It really is. You close your eyes and make plans. More plans for more happy days. The garden can wait. You like the grass long anyway. Scrunch your toes up and remember its feel: you are a child in the local park, shouting and playing; you are lying beside a loved one, idly stroking their thigh, spent and luxuriant under the pouring sun. Take another sip and remember; swallow and relax. Forget the lawn, let it grow under your feet, just for a little longer.

About 3 p.m. on a Sunday a lady carrying a small bunch of carnations walks through the large gates of Brighton and Preston cemetery. She wanted to bring yellow roses as usual. They were his favourite, their favourite, but she got in late last night and was up late this morning. She did not get to the florist in time and had to bring petrol station flowers. She reaches her husband's grave and kneels down to tend the earth. She plucks up weeds and removes a crushed beer can. All of these go into the plastic bag she has brought. Then she lays the flowers at the base of the headstone and sits down cross-legged. She puts her arms out behind her and, closing her eyes, offers her throbbing head to the sun.

It has been a good night; one of the better ones recently. Probably because she has finally managed to rid herself of her guilt that all of her 'new' friends are in their early twenties and she is in her mid-forties. What should she care? Life has to go on. It is none of her neighbours' business. They can peep through the curtains until the cows come home if they have nothing better to do. 'A woman of her age!' She lifts her head and laughs.

She looks at the arched tombstone and recites the carved words. She is embarrassed at what she is thinking. She looks to the right at the neighbouring grave. Obviously nobody visits Mr Falmer. The grass is being strangled by coarse weeds and there has never been any sign of attention except for that one time the sad-looking girl came with a bunch of daffodils. 'Bill. Bill Falmer.' The lady flushes as she remembers eavesdropping on the girl's conversation with Mr Falmer. The lady was almost tempted to strike up a conversation and ask what relation he had been to her. The lady had often talked to other mourners and found a comforting solidarity in their common loss. But this time she did not. The girl seemed troubled, talking in circles. One minute angry and the next sad. At times she even seemed strangely happy. Her boyfriend kept his hand on her shoulder trying to calm her. The lady felt sorry for the boyfriend who had to help her through her grief as the girl had sobbed for 'Roger' to make everything okay.

The lady looks back to her husband's tombstone and is again embarrassed by what she has to do today. She challenges her doubt. It is her decision and nobody else's. It has been long enough now and she knows she has to leave her Sunday routine behind. 'I'll only come once a month from now on,' she tells her husband. 'You have to allow me to start again.' She bows her head and is happy to cry. She loved him so much. Everyone knew they were the perfect couple. She had to fight so hard to convince herself that what he did was not because of her. She has never shown anyone the note he left under the bottle of pills on the bedside table. That would mean having to make sense of why she woke up and he was dead beside her. She could never explain that, nor would she ever understand what he wrote. Sometimes she wished she could talk to someone about it. Show them the note. Maybe they would make some sense of it? Perhaps it was written in some kind of code? She stands up. This is all nonsense. Nothing will bring him back. That was his fate, this is hers.

The sun is warm on her shoulders like a pair of relaxing hands, calming her and loosening her grip on her tightly held guilt.

'Don't bother waking me, I'm dead,' she says, dropping the screwed-up note onto the grass. Then it is over. She is about to leave when her memory throws a frozen scene from when they were young into her mind. Tears come again. Maybe not quite over. 'I miss you, you mad bastard.'

She looks to the left of her husband's grave. An elderly woman wearing a red top hat is on her knees trowelling the earth. The lady catches her eye. Smiles comes to their lips. The elderly woman nods slowly. She must have heard what she said to her husband, the lady thinks. She hopes she understands and does not think badly of her.

The lady ties the top of the carrier bag and dumps it in the bin near the front gates. She looks back. The sky and the trees seem to be glistening, wet, as if they have just been painted. Nice place on a nice day, she thinks.

The lady turns away and leaves the cemetery. She looks down at her feet, smiling as she walks slowly to her car.

First steps, she thinks. First steps of a new beginning.